70

282
WIL

RENDEZVOUS

RENDEZVOUS

STEVE FRAZEE

SAGEBRUSH
Large Print Westerns

First published in Great Britain by Isis Publishing Ltd
First published in the United States by Macmillan

Published in Large Print 2005 by ISIS Publishing Ltd,
7 Centremead, Osney Mead, Oxford OX2 0ES
United Kingdom
by arrangement with
Golden West Literary Agency

British Library Cataloguing in Publication Data
Frazee, Steve, 1909–
    Rendezvous. – Large print ed. –
    (Sagebrush western series)
    1. Western stories
    2. Large type books
    I. Title
    813.5'4 [F]

ISBN 0–7531–7294–1 (hb)

Printed and bound by Antony Rowe, Chippenham

CHAPTER
ONE

Upon the wreckage of a whisky barrel that lifted her somewhat above the mud and filth of Second Street in old St. Louis, Rhoda Marsh waited with her escort in front of the Beaver Palace, the riotous establishment of one Pierre Beauvais.

She was straight and trim, with the bright face of health and natural curiosity. Her hair was gleaming black; her eyes were dark brown — almost an Indian brown — and completely alive to all the lusty strangeness before her. Most soberly attired she was, in cape and unadorned bonnet and heavy skirts all of a somber gray. She was, in this booming year of the fur trade, just a few months short of being twenty-three. Quite obviously she did not belong even near the Beaver Palace.

Beside her the Reverend Jeremiah Shandy was standing with his shabby boots ankle deep in the mud. He was frail and old, with a dry grayness lying across his gentle, mobile features, but in his dark eyes was a strength that spoke of a power quite apart from the physical.

Trappers, Spanish muleteers, dapper merchants in well brushed beaver hats, dragoons, swaggering rivermen, keelboaters, sharp-eyed gamblers, roustabouts, and all the other assortment of frontier humanity slopped through the mud to and from the busy doors of the Beaver Palace. The tumult from within was enough to scald the ears of a man of the cloth, not to mention the more delicate senses of a young lady of refinement

St. Louis was roaring like the forge fires of hell from the profits of the great traffic in furs that was based on the dangerous work of a relatively few men far up the mysterious rivers that came down to the brown Mississippi. At the moment it seemed that most of the activity was centered on the Beaver Palace, which was far from being the Union House. And yet it was a place where all degrees of the citizenry often came.

They were an odd pair, the cleric and the dark-haired woman, but they seemed to draw together to make an island of their own against the rough tide around them.

Two burly Frenchmen, hairy-faced and cursing, kicked open the doors of the Beaver Palace and hurled an Indian into the street with such force that he skidded headlong into the mud near the wheels of a passing wagon. A squaw who had been waiting against the wall took one step toward the prostrate man and then settled back quietly where she had been. No token bauble of civilization showed on her buckskin dress or around her neck. Darkly, patiently she watched her man trying to rise from the street. There was only darkness in her expression, too, when she saw Rhoda Marsh watching the Indian with sympathy.

The Reverend Jeremiah Shandy spoke as if pained and embarrassed, not for himself, but for the sins of others. "I fear I shouldn't have allowed you to come here with me. Perhaps it would be better if I took you back to the hotel and returned alone to see my brother."

Rhoda shook her head. "I don't mind waiting here." She glanced at the doors. "Maybe your brother is already in there. Why don't you —"

"I think not. We'll wait a few minutes longer." Shandy watched two drunken rivermen lurching up the street arm in arm, and it was obvious why he didn't want to leave his charge alone. Last night his brother, James Shandy, of the Rocky Mountain Fur Company, most flatly and profanely had refused to aid Rhoda Marsh to cross the prairies. Jeremiah sighed. Even as a boy James had been wayward and profane, more given to rough exploits than to meditating upon the glories and rewards of righteousness.

But Jeremiah was not cast down yet. It was the future that counted, and he was still firm in the conviction that he could make James understand that it would be a jewel in his crown to aid those devoted to bringing the light of religion to the Indians. James had not seen Rhoda last night. He did not know her purity and dedication. It was one thing to refuse a brother's request, but quite another to refuse a noble spirit like Rhoda once you had seen her in person. Jeremiah believed that the depth and strength of her devotion would stir even James, and that was why Jeremiah had brought her along this morning, even unto the doors of

3

the lair of sin. But the Beaver Palace was nothing compared to the place where the Reverend Jeremiah Shandy had found his brother last night. Madame Carpentier's house was . . . He refused to think more about it.

Perhaps his brother was inside already, as Rhoda had suggested. Jeremiah still hesitated to leave his charge, hoping to catch James either entering the Palace or coming from it. They might have a long wait. He observed that Rhoda was getting the devil's share of attention from the two drunken rivermen, who had paused at the door of the Beaver Palace.

"Pay them no mind," Jeremiah advised. He himself feared no man.

Rhoda ignored the profane stares and stood serenely, if somewhat precariously, upon the barrel. The quality in her that made the rivermen stare also made them hold their tongues. Presently they staggered into the Beaver Palace.

The Indian who had been thrown into the street was standing now, clutching a mud-smeared red blanket in one hand and swaying back and forth, but not quite falling.

"I should take you back to the hotel," Jeremiah murmured.

"No, we'll wait." Rhoda turned to call to a tall frontiersman striding toward the doors of the Beaver Palace. "Sir!"

The man took two more steps before he decided that such a word as "sir" could apply to him, and then in one smooth movement changed course abruptly and

4

came toward Rhoda, his moccasins squishing mud as he walked. "You talking at me?" he asked.

"I am, sir. We are waiting for Mr. James Shandy, of the Rocky Mountain Fur Company. If he is inside, would you be kind enough to inform him that we are out here?"

"Jim Shandy, huh?" The frontiersman studied Rhoda with blunt interest. He was a young man, dark as the Indian who was now tottering across the street. Clean shaven, with white, flashing teeth and deep-set blue eyes, he tipped his head slightly in an odd gesture as he looked at Rhoda. "Shandy, huh?"

"Mr. Shandy, yes," Rhoda said. "If he's inside —"

"He ain't. I seen him at the wharf a few minutes back."

"Thank you, sir," the Reverend Jeremiah Shandy said.

"Sir, hell," the man said, but his mild oath was inoffensive. "Name's Ree Semple." He scarcely glanced at Shandy.

The frankness with which men looked at women out here had been, at first, alarming to Rhoda Marsh. Their stares were explicit, and Semple's was no exception, although she could not say that he was being unduly forward. After all, it was she who had called him over.

Semple was dressed in quill-worked buckskins. His long, sandy hair appeared to have been chopped with a sharp knife. Hanging from his shoulder or suspended from the belt around his lean waist were various beaded cases, and the stained handle of a broad knife protruded from one of them. She had heard that some

5

of the prairie men even carried such heathen things as fetishes in those cases.

"Thank you, Mr. Semple," Rhoda said.

But Semple was not so easily dismissed. He continued to stare at her. He was not more than a few years older than she, Rhoda guessed, but there was something wild and raw and untamed in him that was not common to the men she had known at home in Massachusetts.

"Allus glad to help a woman, else why was beaver made?" Semple said, grinning. Then he turned away quickly and went into the Beaver Palace.

"Mountain Man," Jeremiah explained. "They don't see white women often, and they —" He felt that he was getting into something beyond his scope, so he cleared his throat and looked at the Indian, who was now walking away close to the buildings with the solemnity of drunkenness.

The Indian's wife paced after him. Though her eyes gazed straight ahead, she saw everything about her, and hated everything she saw.

"With the Lord's help, that is the kind of debauchery you will aid Elisha Slocum in conquering, Rhoda."

Rhoda looked doubtfully at the Indian. He swayed suddenly and fell sidewise into the filth of a narrow alleyway. His squaw picked up his blanket and waited.

"Can't you help him?" Rhoda asked.

" 'Twould be useless, in his state," Shandy muttered. "They have no souls when they are in that condition." He had cleared his throat to enlarge upon this somewhat unorthodox point, when he saw his brother approaching. "James!"

Jim Shandy was walking with a tall, cadaverous-looking old man who was wearing a heavy black cape in spite of the fact that the sun was shining strongly now and the drying pools of water were filling the air with sticky heat. Shandy's tall beaver was sensibly set. His dark cravat lay neatly against his white ruffled shirt, and the tops of his boots showed a fine gloss. Indeed, he looked the part of the St. Louis businessman that he was, Rhoda thought, although only a few years ago, according to his brother, James had been a trapper for the Rocky Mountain Fur Company.

"James, we've been waiting for you," Jeremiah called as he started forward through the mud.

Irritation settled hard on Jim Shandy's face. "Excuse me, please," he said to the old man beside him. "I'll be only a few minutes."

The old man in the cape raised one hand slightly to acknowledge the apology. His eyes, bright with a hard amusement, passed over Rhoda and her companion. He smiled faintly as he observed the broken barrel, and then went on to the Beaver Palace.

Habit made Jim Shandy start to remove his hat as he came toward Rhoda and his brother; then he dismissed the gesture as unnecessary and dropped his hand quickly. His roughness was not even thinly disguised by his fine attire. Beside his brother, James was a giant, flat-cheeked and hard hewn. Rhoda thought at once that he was far more suited to the buckskin he had forsaken than to the dress of a gentleman. There was about him the same air of restless wildness she had observed in Ree Semple. He spoke curtly to his brother. "I told you last night I can't do nothing about helping a woman get to Fort Cass." He stared at Rhoda. "This is her, huh?"

"Miss Rhoda Marsh, yes," Jeremiah said. "She must be there by mid-July. You will help her, James." He spoke softly, but with an assurance that further irritated his brother.

"Have you any idea where the hell Fort Cass is?" James asked.

"Only vaguely," the minister said, "but I do know that our missionaries and their wives have gone far beyond it to the Oregon country."

"Yeah." Jim Shandy looked Rhoda up and down boldly. She felt the heat rising in her face. "Why do you want to go 'way out there just to marry a damn' missionary? You could do a heap better right here in St. Louis, I'm thinking."

Rhoda met the bold stare without flinching, although it annoyed her to know that she was blushing. "I doubt that, Mr. Shandy."

"She will meet her betrothed at Fort Cass," the minister said. "They will be married immediately and start back to his mission. All we ask of you —"

"You already asked it and I can't help you. My pack train left a week ago. I wouldn't even have let her go then, if she'd been here." Jim Shandy began to turn away.

8

"You must help us," his brother insisted quietly. "This is the Lord's work, James. It will be a jewel in your crown."

"Jewel, hell! I don't give a damn whose work it is, and I wouldn't take the blame for sending a white woman across the prairie even if it was possible." James turned suddenly to Rhoda. "Now, if there's something I can do for you here, Miss Marsh, feel free —"

"No, thank you," Rhoda said.

"There is no risk," Jeremiah answered. "The Lord will make her journey secure, and the party she travels with will be under His protection too."

Jim Shandy grunted. "So far the Lord ain't protected nobody I know of that went out there. The trappers —"

"He would," the minister said, "if they renounced the ways of the heathen and delivered their hearts —"

"Jesus Christ! Let's not start that again." James turned away. "I can't help you, Miss Marsh, and that's final."

"You *will* help her, James," his brother said.

Puzzled and angered by Jeremiah's quiet, sturdy faith, James swung toward him again. "Stubborn as ever, ain't you?" He frowned, as if thinking. "Come back in the middle of the summer. Maybe I can do something then."

"No, James. We will not be dismissed like that. Rhoda must be with her betrothed by midsummer. If Elisha Slocum doesn't find her at Fort Cass when she is supposed to be there, he may be lost to the cause. He has written of the hardships and loneliness of the

9

mission. Some of those around him have wives, while he —"

"Let him woman with an Indian, then! Any fool that goes skyugling off to preach to savages ought to take what he can find." Jim Shandy turned away once more, and this time he kept going toward the Beaver Palace.

"Wait!" his brother cried.

"I've got business."

"Come back! You must help. Elisha Slocum has business too, the Lord's business!"

"To hell with Elisha Slocum!" Jim Shandy went on into the Beaver Palace.

Rhoda and her companion looked bleakly at each other. The minister was grayer than usual, and one hand was pressed against the pain in his chest, but his unbreakable fighting spirit still burned in his eyes. "Be of good cheer; we shall still find a way."

Rhoda looked at the mud around her, at the brown roll of the Mississippi showing in the gaps between buildings. Fort Cass was far, far up the great river, and then up the Missouri, and then far beyond that, on a stream whose name she couldn't remember. "Perhaps it *is* impossible for me to fulfill my promise to Elisha this summer."

One of the broken barrel staves turned under her foot, and she shifted quickly to keep from falling. A red-faced dragoon, plowing unsteadily toward the Beaver Palace, shouted, "I'd put my coat down there, girlie, but it's the only one I got!"

"To fulfill the will of God is never impossible!" Jeremiah said.

10

The dragoon said, "You're on the wrong street for preaching, old man!"

Jeremiah ignored the soldier. "I know my brother, Rhoda. He curses goodness because there is a fear of goodness within him, but I saw him weaken as we talked to him. We'll wait, and when he comes out I will speak to him again. Right will prevail!"

There was little doubt about the minister's faith, but his optimism concerning his brother left Rhoda unconvinced. Yet she knew that she must not doubt, for that was the first sign of sin and error. Such a feeling had attacked her when she was ready to leave Massachusetts on the first part of her long journey to a wild country to marry a man she hadn't seen for three years. She had fought the feeling and gone ahead, but again, in Cincinnati, doubt had assailed her when she met the Reverend Jeremiah Shandy, who had been entrusted by the Missionary Society to make all arrangements for the last part of her journey. He had seemed too frail, too unworldly to cope with the rigors of the frontier, even though she soon learned that his zeal was unbounded. Once more she had fought away doubts, and now she must do it again. But who could believe that Jim Shandy was going to change his mind?

She said, "Is there anyone else in St. Louis who might help us?"

"None whom I know. Have faith. My brother will help us. It is the will of God."

"I hope so," she said. She stared coolly above the head of a leering riverman who made an obscene gesture at her.

"Begone, you beast of Satan!" the minister cried, and waved his arm as if to brush the riverman away. The man scowled, muttered, then went into the Beaver Palace. A moment later the tumult in the place increased to a bedlam of shouts and curses. The doors flew open with a crash, and Ree Semple, grinning like a white-toothed demon, walked out with a struggling muleteer in his grip.

Semple spun the man around until he held him by both wrists from behind; then he jammed one moccasin against the muleteer's rear and drew the bow. When he let go, and straightened his leg, the man went flying into the mud. Semple then threw Rhoda and the minister a companionable salute before plunging back into the fray inside.

After a time the uproar subsided a little.

"Patience," Jeremiah said. "All things pass. My brother will be coming out soon, and then . . ." He went on talking, but Rhoda did not hear him.

She was thinking that he was truly a good man. There was a reward waiting for him, but it was not of this world; and she knew that spirit alone sustained him until he saw her safely on the last step of her journey and carried out what was to him the will of God — although the order had come from Ezra Hastings, president of the Board of Commissioners of the Missionary Society.

There it was, the doubt again.

But if she had faltered, she had also rallied, and if she had rebelled secretly against the fact that the Missionary Society, more than her own desire, had betrothed her to Elisha Slocum, she was determined now to rebel no more. With the help of God, she was going to sustain Elisha in his lonely and discouraging mission of spreading light among the heathen.

A group of voyageurs in bright woolen shirts burst from the Beaver Palace, singing with their arms around each other as they stumbled into the street. Though Rhoda's French was the formal, precise kind she had learned in Mrs. Upjohn's Seminary, she caught enough of the sense of the song to make her ears burn. And yet, there was a ringing, jolly lilt to the tune.

Such things she must get used to, she told herself. She had already learned that foul language shocked her but did not outrage her, that the bold, suggestive stares of men disturbed her but did not terrify her, and that coarseness was not, of itself, evil. In fact, much of what she had learned, and was learning, might well be excellent training for the wife of a missionary.

A faint sense of betrayal rose within her as she realized that she had a growing desire to see what was going on inside the Beaver Palace. Not that she had any intention of entering, but since she was already exposed to the sight and sound of evil pouring from the lair of sin she could scarcely be ruined by having a better view of the source.

The Reverend Jeremiah Shandy would be horrified to know her thoughts.

CHAPTER
TWO

Across one end of the Beaver Palace ran a balcony guarded by curving ironwork. It was on this elevation so simply but effectively removed from the rougher classes of humanity that gentlemen were wont to sit and drink and discuss business affairs while viewing from a safe vantage the frequent disturbances that swept across the main floor below.

There were, to be sure, more elegant places in the city to drink whisky and talk business, but perhaps shadiness begets shadiness; at any rate, deals which greatly affected hundreds of men in the distant Rocky Mountains, men who would never be allowed up the stairs to Pierre Beauvais's balcony, were often consummated around the iron tables.

The men affected could curse or applaud as they pleased, on the Popo Agie or the Wind River or deep in the Bayou Salade, when they got news of the transactions, six months or a year later.

Shandy started up the steps, annoyed because he had had to leave Sherman Randall to talk to a dominie in the street. Such an action might be taken by Randall as an indication of weakness. Randall was one of the old he-bears of the American Fur Company. Weakness of any kind didn't go down with that outfit.

Part way up the steps, Shandy paused to look at Ree Semple, talking in a corner with two mule traders from Santa Fe. Ree was around at the wrong season. A trapper belonged in the mountains. Who was he working for now? All the fur companies spied on one another. Was he working for Rocky Mountain, sent here by Milton Sublette or Jim Bridger or old Tom Fitzpatrick to spy on Shandy? That didn't make sense. But he could have been hired by Bob Campbell or Bill Sublette, whose pack trains carried goods to the Rocky Mountain rendezvous. Bill Sublette was in the East now, and Campbell had gone early to the mountains. They'd left Shandy in charge of sending the pack train out. Maybe they didn't trust him.

Shandy guessed he had a right to feel a little fitchery, for he'd been in the business end of the fur trade just long enough to learn how cut-throat it was, and long enough to plot his own treachery. It was a sure thing. Right now he was about to pull a deal that would stun the whole fur trade, something that had never been thought of before. It would make him rich. To hell with Ree Semple and imaginary worries!

At the top of the stairs Gabriel, the vicious little knifeman who passed upon the social fitness of those aspiring to set foot on the balcony, bowed with mock civility and murmured, "M'sieu' Shandee". Jim Shandy might be an agent of the Rocky Mountain Fur Company, but in Gabriel's opinion he had been too lately an uncouth trapper to have a gentleman's standing. His mockery stung; it always did. Shandy wished he could take the smirking Frenchy beyond the Upper Missouri and watch the oily bastard come apart when Blackfeet erupted from the willows. More immediately, Shandy was inclined to take the heavy pistol from under his coat and use it to smash the sneer from Gabriel's small black eyes. Being a gentleman of business, however, and knowing that Sherman Randall's cold eyes were on him, Shandy passed on to the conference table.

Joseph Bogard poured him punch from a silver pitcher. "I understand you were talking to a pretty woman, Shandy. I never knew you to leave one so quick."

"A damn' bothersome woman," Shandy said, but he was really thinking of his brother. The fool would still be waiting in the street, waiting to plead and argue. Shandy gulped at his drink. Hell in a handbasket! It was sweet, sickening punch without a drop of alcohol in it. That was Randall's doin's. He never drank whisky.

The thin and bloodless old man observed with delicate amusement Shandy's reaction to the punch. "It will help keep your head clear, Mr. Shandy. I'm assuming that you have some kind of business offer to make."

It wasn't like dealing with Indians, when you could go on for hours and come out ahead by beating them at their own waiting game. Randall had a reputation for doing business quickly, and to his own advantage. Bogard didn't matter here. He was slow and sleepy looking, with a face that was starting to bulge with

16

creeping fat. He did only what Randall said, but he did it well.

Randall was the big knife. He looked as if he should have been dead ten years ago, but his eyes were sharply alive and piercing. A faint smile was always ready at the corner of his thin lips. It was said that no man understood the fur trade as he did, including Kenneth Mackenzie and yet Randall had never been above Chouteau's Landing near the mouth of the Kaw.

Shandy tried to shrug away a fear of Randall. He was only a man, after all, and greed was the key that unlocked all of them. Randall would deal.

"Yeah, I've got a proposition," Shandy said. "It involves a lot of money."

Randall sipped at his punch. "That's always interesting. Whose money?" he asked gently.

"It ain't stealing, if that's what you're hinting at," Shandy answered.

Randall nodded. "Splendid. Let's hear this honest proposal." He lifted a heavy chain that lay across his black waistcoat and snapped open the ornately engraved lid of a small watch. It was, obviously, a woman's watch. Before he closed it he looked briefly at a picture on the underside of the lid.

"You in a hurry to go someplace?" Shandy asked.

Randall looked surprised. "I'm sure I have enough time to hear you out, Mr. Shandy."

Bogard drank his punch noisily. He looked down at the main floor, as if he found more of interest there than at the table.

Shandy played his own bluff. "If you don't want to hear what I've got to say . . ."

"We're waiting to hear it," Randall said.

"Your outfit, the American Company, don't operate from pack trains. Your trappers and the Indians bring their furs into your posts to trade, places like Fort Union and Fort Cass," Shandy said.

The fact was so elementary that neither Randall nor Bogard deigned to comment. They looked bored.

"On the other hand, the Rocky Mountain Company sends pack trains with goods to trade for furs wherever we hold our summer rendezvous. I sent the train out last week. You know all about it." Without thinking, Shandy took a drink of punch. He almost spat it out.

"Do you know where the Rocky Mountain's rendezvous is this summer?" he asked Randall. Of course the man knew. Although he had never been across the prairies, he had a remarkable knowledge of the workings of his rivals. Every trapper for the Rocky Mountain, every free trapper, and every Indian who had been at last year's rendezvous had been told that this year's meeting would be at Big Meadows on Wind River. Randall would be lying in his teeth if he said that word of the rendezvous had not come to him from the field.

"Of course we know where your rendezvous is," Randall said. Once more he glanced at his tiny watch.

Shandy shook his head. "It's not on Wind River. We changed it secretly before the rendezvous broke up last season." That was a lie and a bluff, but it might be worth something later on. Shandy needed every advantage he could manufacture before he reached the actual point of his deal.

"So it's somewhere else," Randall said. "You've been wasting our time so far. I suppose you realize that." He glanced at the noisy scene below. A group of voyageurs were dancing, their faces shining with good nature and drunkenness, the tassels of their woolen caps aswing.

Shandy came to the point. "Suppose that pack trains from the American Company got to our rendezvous before our own pack train?"

The change in Bogard's expression was remarkable. He had been emulating his superior's attitude by looking bored, but now his fleshy features came alive and you could almost see the dollar signs sparkling in his eyes.

Randall's face became a gray mask. The faint smile at the corners of his mouth disappeared, and his eyes grew as still and bright as those of a captive bird.

Ah! That had hit them where they lived. By God, they weren't looking now at Jim Shandy like he was dirt beneath their feet!

They knew; they were thinking. Profits on goods exchanged at the rendezvous for furs often went as high as 2,000 per cent. Bitter as the rivalry was among all the fur companies, no one had ever attempted to snatch a competitor's furs by getting to rendezvous first with a pack train of trade goods.

They were making their leisurely way toward Wind River now, trappers of the Rocky Mountain Company, free trappers who never went near the posts of the

American Company or any other company, and with them was a wealth of beaver.

Randall knew. What didn't he know about the fur trade?

Company loyalty, especially in the Rocky Mountain, was a great thing. Men like Milt Sublette and Bridger and Mordecai Price would hair out like mad beavers at the very thought of selling plews to American. They might even keep a few company trappers from doing it, but only a few.

Take a man who had waded icy streams on the fall and spring hunts — what was he going to do when he saw spread before him all the stuff he'd craved during the winter: whisky, coffee, sugar, not to mention the necessities like blankets and powder and shot? Foofaraw for his Injun wife was no small item either. After a few drinks, little loyalty to anything would be left. Whoever got the goods to rendezvous first was sure of a fortune in beaver plews. It was that simple.

Shandy watched Randall's face, afraid of the old man's tremendous knowledge of what went on everywhere in the fur trade. During the winter Shandy had made the same proposal to a minor official of the Hudson's Bay Company, and had been turned down flat. It might be fatal if Randall knew he was second choice.

"Your pack train has already started," Randall said at last.

Shandy nodded. There was plenty of time later to tell what he cared to about the train.

20

Randall made a thin sucking sound with his lips. He poured himself another glass of punch. "All this assumes that we can beat the Rocky Mountain pack train to the rendezvous by a sufficient margin to get the trading done ahead of all competition."

"Yeah. When we come to an agreement, I'll tell you how that can be done," Shandy said. This early in the bargaining there was no need to tell them about the miserable quality of horses and mules in the Rocky Mountain's pack train, a deficiency Shandy had carefully arranged in advance.

He had greatly underestimated Randall's shrewdness and Bogard's efficiency. Randall asked, "Didn't you tell me, Bogard, that the Rocky Mountain train had about the poorest collection of animals you'd ever seen?"

Bogard grinned. "The clerk, Big Nose Yenzer, had a fight with Shandy about that. Shandy tried to convince him it was the best he could do."

Randall watched Shandy with gentle amusement. "So it would seem that we can beat your pack train to the rendezvous on Wind River without any great difficulty, thanks to your selection of the pack animals."

Shandy felt a cold uneasiness settling inside him. He was out of his depth with this pair, but he presented a wooden expression and stuck with his bluff. "You might not find that the rendezvous is on Wind River."

"I think we will," Randall said. "I think I would have heard about any change, no matter how secret you claim it was."

"You'll have a lot of goods sitting out on the prairie, with no buyers," Shandy said.

"We could, in that extremity, take everything on to Fort Cass." Randall smiled as he drew his heavy cape a little closer around his shoulders. "I'm beginning to wonder if you have any proposition to offer, Mr. Shandy."

Shandy was sweating now. They were trying to steal his idea right out from under him. He was betraying his own company, and if Randall had his way the betrayal wouldn't return Shandy one cent. But the toughness that had carried him through ten years as a trapper asserted itself. Scarcely realizing it, he dropped all the false airs he had tried to assume since being elevated to high position in St. Louis.

"Think you're smart, you coons, huh? You figure I didn't know you were Blackfeet at heart. I got a hundred big California mules ready to leave here in two hours' time. I'm thinking they'll be three days gone afore you can gather goods and load one pack horse. They'll overtake the Rocky Mountain train, and then who's going to beat who anywhere?"

Randall and Bogard studied Shandy carefully. "The gentleman has a point, perhaps," Randall murmured.

"You're damn' right I have!" Shandy whacked the table with his fist. "Now, do we get down to business or not?"

Randall's lynx-sharp eyes peered at Shandy with a hard, unreadable expression. "You do better when you revert to your former ways, Mr. Shandy. Yes, let's get down to business, but first — just one guarantee."

"Yeah?" Shandy asked suspiciously.

22

"Your personal guarantee that our train will beat the Rocky Mountain's to the rendezvous, whatever it may be."

"I'll give you every chance to do that, but I ain't taking your train through, if that's what you mean."

Randall looked down on the barroom floor. He spoke to Bogard. "What's Ree Semple doing in St. Louis at this time of year?"

"I hear he deserted the Hudson's Bay Company." Bogard looked uneasily at his employer. "I don't know just what he is doing."

"You should know a little more about Semple's business here, Bogard, don't you think?"

"I'll find out," Bogard said hastily.

Randall turned back to Shandy. "No, we don't expect you to take our pack train through, but I insist on your personal guarantee of success."

"I'd be a fool to make a promise like that!" Shandy protested. "I've given you the idea. I'll help you, but I ain't guaranteeing nothing."

"I'm afraid you must," Randall said quietly.

The unease that Shandy had thrown off for a time returned in doubled strength. What Randall wanted was a guarantee secured by Shandy's life. The American Fur Company had a bloody, ruthless record. Its own employees hated and feared the company. Sometimes engagees who had served their contract period with American started downriver from Fort Union with a letter of credit for their wages — and disappeared mysteriously. Killed by "Indians".

Give an iron-clad promise of performance to an outfit like that? And yet Shandy knew he had to. There was a fortune in this deal. "All right, I'll give you your damn guarantee!"

"Splendid, Mr. Shandy." Randall's voice was toneless. "Now, what's your price?"

Based on the number of packs of beaver plews traded at rendezvous in previous years, $100,000 in furs was about right for this year, Shandy figured. The furs came pretty cheap, considering the ballooned prices of trade goods. Forty per cent of the gross profit was the figure Shandy had in mind.

He looked at the cold, lifeless face of Sherman Randall and knew he'd never make the figure stick. It was this year or never; Shandy guessed he could come down a little. "Twenty-five per cent of the gross profit."

"So?" Randall tried the punch again. "Though I've never been up the river, I understand it's sometimes worth a man's life to transfer from one fur company to another."

Bogard smiled. "Not to mention an agent selling out his own outfit in an underhand deal."

"You two don't scare me one bit!" Shandy said angrily. "Take it or leave it!"

"Let's not even speak of withdrawing," Randall said. "You especially, since you've already given your guarantee in the matter." Though he spoke mildly, there was a point in his voice as deadly as that of the poniard of little Gabriel over by the stairs. "Ten per cent of the net, Mr. Shandy, a month after our train returns from the rendezvous."

"God a'mighty!" Shandy cried. "That's robbery!"

"Take it or leave it," Randall said. "Our pack train is going out day after tomorrow. Your share will be 10 per cent of the net." He smiled. "I'm sure it will be quite enough to get you a long distance from St. Louis."

"What if I don't want to take your miserable figure?"

The bitter old eyes watched Shandy with cynical humor. The history of the American Fur Company was in that look. Far-reaching power. Violence. Ruthlessness.

Shandy was in the American's hands now. He'd put himself there. If he tried to back out, the least they would do would be to expose him. The most they could do . . . Shandy remembered the swollen body of an American Company engagee that had bumped against a keelboat on the way up the Big Muddy. A hundred and fifty dollars the company had owed the man. No one had ever accused Randall of ordering such murders. No one would ever say it outright either.

Randall kept watching Shandy.

Ten per cent was robbery; still, it was a lot of money, and a man would be alive to spend it. If he didn't take it, American would send a train out anyway.

"You agree?" Randall said.

Shandy couldn't speak for anger. He nodded. They'd handled him like Ree Indians tormenting a scared voyageur.

"Bogard will talk to you hereafter concerning any minor details of the agreement," Randall said.

Shandy watched the two of them leave, past the bowing Gabriel, across the crowded floor below, where Randall, walking in front of Bogard, opened the way before him as surely as a white wolf stalking through a pack of coyotes. Ah, yes, Shandy thought with bitter envy, every man-dog of them down there knew who Sherman Randall was and what he represented.

Shandy watched them go out; then he picked up the silver pitcher and hurled it to the floor. "Whisky, damn it! Bring me something fit to drink!"

A waiter came out of the shadows behind him and picked up the dented utensil. His calm look conveyed a maximum of insult with a minimum of expression. "Yes, Mr. Shandy?"

After the third drink Shandy felt better. Ten per cent was considerable money, and from now on he wouldn't have to raise a finger to earn it. Once he had it in hand, he could light out for the East and be a gentleman.

He was having another drink when doubts began to stir like a great worm in his mind. Just what did Randall expect of him now? How far did that guarantee go? That thirty-day wait for his money after the American pack train came back with the furs was a bad thing. By God, it was worse than that; it was trickery!

While the average trapper at the rendezvous, ripping the earth up with his spree, would hardly remember who he had sold his beaver to, men like Milton Sublette and Bridger, with financial interests in the Rocky Mountain Company, would be red-eyed and roaring like Old Caleb. And there would be a few trappers like Mordecai Price who were so fiercely loyal to the Rocky Mountain and the outfit that packed goods to them that they would be ready to kill if they even suspicioned treachery.

26

Mordecai had been an Ashley man, and helped Ashley get rich; and he was such a friend of the five Sublette brothers and Bridger and the rest, that what hurt them hurt him too. If he ever got wind that Shandy had sold the rendezvous out to American, he'd scorch the prairie coming to St. Louis.

Damn Sherman Randall and his thirty days! He was sneakier nor any Piegan that ever lived. He was taking what Shandy had tossed in his lap, and figuring to let the Rocky Mountain Company tear him apart. That was the reason for the thirty-day stall.

Maybe Rocky Mountain wouldn't find out, though. It would be hard doin's for Jim Shandy if they did. The full realization of his own stupidity so enraged Shandy that he could feel blood hammering against his temples. He tried to crush the whisky glass in his hand. Everything had seemed so simple — and profitable — until he'd got down to dealing with Randall.

Bad as things were, they went even further to hell a moment later.

Tall as a Cheyenne chief, Mordecai Price stalked into the barroom below.

Shandy started like a man with the guilty horrors. His medicine had gone bad. His treachery had been smelled out in advance. Before he realized what he was doing, Shandy had moved back to a table farther away from the balcony ironwork. They'd sent Mordecai, that's what they'd done! Somebody in Rocky Mountain had got wind of Shandy's talk with the Hudson's Bay man last winter.

Kill him!

Then Shandy began to get hold of himself. It could be chance that had brought Mordecai here, when he should be in the mountains. He saw Ree Semple starting from the corner. They were old *compañeros*, them two. Either one of them would take a heap of killing. The two of them together made a bad fix of things.

Even if Mordecai suspected nothing now, let him get a hint that American was sending a pack train overland and he'd go streaking out like a Pawnee with an arrow in his butt. There wouldn't be a rendezvous at the meeting of the Popo Agie and Wind River when the American train got there. It would be somewhere else. And Shandy had pledged his life that American would get there first.

Mordecai got in at the bar. Ree was working toward him, grinning as he came. Shandy observed how dark and hard-worn Mordecai's buckskins were. Like as not, he'd just got in.

It had better be a short stay for him, or the knife the American Company was holding at Shandy's throat would move the wrong way.

CHAPTER
THREE

Mordecai Price had been in St. Louis one hour, and already the odors and sounds and the press of civilization were stifling him. He felt edgy. During his years in the mountains he'd sloughed off a part of his life that he could never regain. He didn't want it back, and the feeling of not belonging had grown keener every time he returned to St. Louis.

He was about ready to light out again. A thousand miles away, they were coming down from the high, clear streams, slouching along on their shaggy ponies, heading for the Big Meadows and the rendezvous. He could see the whole scene, smell the air, look across the blue distance. And here he was like a lone Sioux in a Crow village. Hanged if he warn't a stranger among men of his own color! They just didn't shine, these strangers.

Two voyageurs moved quickly to make room for him at the bar. They knew a Mountain Man when they saw one, and he was a big one, with sharp gray eyes that peered hard at strange faces, as if evaluating them for treachery. His hair was long and dark, his heavy-boned face hard-angled. The buckskin coat folded around his lean middle reached almost to his hips and was so hard worn that much of the decorative beadwork was gone. There was a heavy Navy pistol in his belt and a thick-backed knife in a Sioux case hung handy where he could reach it. Six feet four he stood in his moccasins.

When the bartender poured the first drink, Mordecai laid Old Belcher, his rifle, on the floor close against the bar. The voyageurs took care not to put their feet close to the buckskin case.

Mordecai looked curiously at the glass of whisky, and then reached to pick it up.

The knife came down like a hammer from the air. The point of it smashed the glass and whipped the contents in a stream across the front of Mordecai's coat. Hard gripped in a brown hand, the point of the blade skidded off the thick bottom of the glass and drove into the wood. A big voice roared in Mordecai's ear, "Welcome to St. Louie, hoss!"

The wide-eyed voyageurs bumped against each other in falling back from Mordecai as he made a half-turn. His knife streaked from its case and his wrist made a quick down jerk as he threw the weapon.

Ree Semple yelled, "Wagh!" but he had no time to move his feet before Mordecai's heavy knife plunged into the floor so close to Ree's right foot that the blade was resting against the moccasin. "Same to you!" Mordecai yelled.

The two Mountain Men grinned at each other, and then embraced like Indians, except that no Indian would have appreciated the pounding they gave each other. Grinning, the voyageurs moved back to the bar.

"Whar you been all robe season, old coon?" Ree shouted.

"Some around Santy Fee." Mord picked his knife from the floor. He used the back of it to knock Ree's Green River loose from the bar, and then he tossed Semple's knife high and spinning.

With only half an eye on it, Ree caught the weapon by the handle as it came down. The voyageurs looked at each other and shrugged, both in admiration and horror.

"You look scrawny and thin-haired, Mord. Can't stand wintering in the mountains no more, huh?"

"Was there, looking. When did Hudson's Bay find you was a pork eater and throw you out?"

Semple grinned. "Quit 'em, I did. They was so honest I got plumb lonesome for being robbed every year at rendezvous." He tossed off his drink. "Rendezvous on the Green this summer?"

"Wind River. You know it."

"Guess I heard, sure enough," Ree said. "You going to work all your life for Rocky Mountain — for nothing?"

"What other outfit is there?" Mordecai grinned.

"Beaver is six dollars a plew, but whar does the trapper come off when it's all over?" Ree complained.

Mordecai shrugged. "You've always had the gripes about that, Ree, since the first time I took you up the Big Muddy and showed you the difference between goats and elk."

That was a sore point with Ree. He didn't like to be reminded that Mordecai had five more years' experience in the mountains, and that he had taught Ree how to place his first trap. Ree glanced around the noisy room, as if to challenge any man who had overheard Mordecai's remark.

"So you was the mother bear the first year I was in the mountains," Ree admitted. He threw his whisky glass over his shoulder and called for another one. "You still ain't larned how to make any money out of furs."

"Have you?" Mordecai was enjoying himself. The whisky was mellowing his feeling of isolation, and he always liked to jaw with Ree. Like as not, before things was over, they'd have a good, friendly fight over that canoe they'd lost years before on the Yellowstone.

"I got an idea or two —" Ree sized up Mordecai and decided to let it go. "You going out to rendezvous?"

"I might could." Mordecai looked at the balcony. "When I came in I saw Jim Shandy sitting there, but now he's gone." He didn't care much for Shandy, but Bill Sublette and Campbell seemed to like him. There was no hurry about seeing him. Mordecai could find him at the warehouse later and get an outfit from him when it was time to strike out for rendezvous.

"He's still there," Ree said. "Moved about the time you come in." He paused. "He was having a powwow with Bogard and old Sherman Randall. He seemed to be trying to make something big of the fact."

It wasn't unusual for officials from different fur companies to get together and drink themselves blind and talk big and friendly, while all the time planning how to cut one another's throats. Mordecai had done it himself. Competition was really getting terrible, though. The American was stirring up trouble with the Crows against the Rocky Mountain, and doing their best to get the Blackfeet on the warpath too. Of course, that didn't take much doing at any time, against anybody.

Mordecai forgot about Shandy. He wondered if Ree had learned any new fighting tricks since the last time they'd tangled in Pierre's Hole. That had been a real good fight.

"Might wander out to rendezvous myself," Ree said. "What'd you do all robe season, Mord?"

"Went south with the bufflers, looking for new trapping country. My stick floated me clean into Santy Fee afore I was done. Come back here with Blas Wimarr, him and his two hundred mules stole from Californy. Broke most of 'em to packing on the way, he did. I helped considerable."

Ree threw another whisky glass over his shoulder. The bartender glared at him but replaced the glass. "Find any likely beaver country?"

"Some," Mordecai said. "Who you working for, Ree?"

"Done told you — nobody." Once more Ree studied Mordecai thoughtfully, as if Ree had something important on his mind but was unsure of the reaction if he stated it. "Your new trapping country will make money for the Rocky Mountain, huh?"

"I reckon."

"You always was a damn' fool in some things, Mord."

Mordecai grinned. "I never dumped a canoe over and lost a whole winter's catch."

Ree's white grin was easy but his eyes tightened. So old Mord was itching for a fight. Well, he could have it. "That Sherman Randall, when he went out of here he looked like something that fell out of a hearse on a steep hill. Him with all that money, and still wanting more."

"You got Sherman Randall on the brain, or something?" Mordecai asked.

Ree had another drink.

From the shadowy balcony Jim Shandy watched the two Mountain Men with growing unease. Maybe Ree had quit Hudson's Bay, and maybe he hadn't. What if he knew about the offer Shandy had made the British last winter? He wouldn't, though; he was just a trapper, but he was shrewder than the usual run. He never got drunk at rendezvous until he'd done all his trading. But he'd been all over the riverfront and around the fur warehouses for ten days. He'd been there when Shandy sent Big Nose Yenzer out with the pack train to meet the Rocky Mountain's keelboat, which had gone upriver earlier with rendezvous supplies to be shifted to the mules and horses at the mouth of the Platte. Semple had seen what kind of animals Big Nose had. In the middle of the night Shandy had started that pack train off, but Ree had been there. Now he was talking to Mordecai Price. What were they saying?

Another thing: Ree had seen Shandy meeting with Bogard and Randall. Shandy knew that a greenhorn in the mountains saw Indians behind every bush, and maybe that was his trouble now, but by Old Ephraim those two below were enough to worry a man! He beckoned to a waiter behind him, and at the same time reached into his pocket.

A little later one of Pierre Beauvais's kin casually joined the voyageurs near Ree and Mordecai.

The two Mountain Men had gone through a bottle. They got a second one. It would wind up in a fight, Shandy knew; it always did when Ree and Mordecai got together over whisky. They'd rip up the prairie, and afterward they'd be thick as thieves again.

The second bottle was almost gone when Shandy saw the spy the waiter had sent leave the voyageurs. A few minutes later the waiter came to report. "They are making a quarrel now about who upset a canoe in the Yellowstone River once —"

"Hell with that!" Shandy said. "What else?"

"Raoul says that one told the other, the big one told the young one, that he did not know dog of the prairie from beaver. Then the young one —"

"What are they saying about the fur business?"

"Ah, yes. There is something. Raoul said that the young one told the big one that the Hudson's Bay Company treated its men better than your company."

Shandy cursed. "Is that all they're talking about?"

"There was something about a Flathead woman who had been captured by the Sioux, and then the big one captured her from the savages and they —"

"Tell that idiot of a Raoul to get back there and keep his ears open."

"Yes, Mr. Shandy." The waiter hesitated.

"Yeah, yeah," Shandy said, and gave him another coin.

Down on the floor Ree and Mordecai were getting nowhere in a discussion of the relative charms of Indian women and white women. Mordecai held that white women were too scrawny, too scared, and too talkative.

"I seen one outside a minute ago —" Ree began.

"I seen her too, such as she was. White women just don't shine. Now, you take a Snake squaw —"

"You didn't let me finish about that woman outside." Because the bartender had long quit supplying Ree with glasses, Ree drank from the bottle.

"What about the one outside?" Mordecai asked.

"I forget now. I keep thinking about that canoe."

"Why'd you upset it?"

"Maybe you're right," Ree said, and his sudden acquiescence so stunned Mordecai for an instant that Ree was able to get in the first blow, a walloping, powerful clop that knocked Mordecai reeling into the startled voyageurs. They held him up instinctively, and Mordecai regained enough balance to kick Ree in the belly.

Ree grunted like an enraged grizzly, then came at Mordecai with his arms flailing. As fist fighters they were fit to lick Indians only, who never used such a method of combat. After a few thumping blows they went to wrestling, a mixture of the backwoodsman's butting tactics, the riverman's gouging and biting, and the Indian's snaky use of legs.

They went to the floor in a rolling crash that swept two dragoons off their feet. One of the soldiers took

36

affront. He leaped up and kicked Mordecai in the ribs. Ree promptly pulled the man's feet from under him, and Mordecai dived into the dragoon's belly with his knees doubled up.

That ended the first phase of outside participation.

Summoned from an early dinner, Pierre Beauvais, fat and stubby and thoroughly dangerous, surveyed the combat from the kitchen doorway with a practiced eye. The heavy benches along the wall were solidly fixed, and there was no other furniture in front of the high bar.

Pierre shook his head at his burly watchdogs: it did not look like the kind of affair that would end in a killing and give the place an evil name. Pierre went back to his excellent dinner. Let the barbarians work off their great energy.

As wrestlers Ree and Mordecai covered a heap of territory. When they were on the floor they managed to make sudden twists and rolls that knocked the feet from under unwary spectators who crowded too close to them. When they were struggling on their feet, they were dangerous also, for Ree had learned a new trick.

He threw Mordecai over his shoulder with a jolt that was enough to wrench the arm from the shoulder socket of an ordinary man. As Mordecai flew into the densely packed crowd, his hard body bowled over several spectators. Shock and concussion did not improve the combative natures of two onlookers who slammed their heads together trying to spring clear. Outraged, they began to pummel each other. Their friends joined in.

A Spaniard who had received the impact of Mordecai's flying feet leaped on Mordecai's back as the Mountain Man was rising. The Spaniard was an excellent rider, but he had boarded a bad steed. Mordecai hunched his shoulders and reached back to get his hands around the man's neck. When Mordecai twisted and threw his arms forward, he sent the luckless Spaniard sailing into a group of rivermen who promptly began to pound him, and then one another after certain blows went astray.

A muleteer then declared for the honor of Spain and leaped into the fray against an American dragoon. Some of the voyageurs began to fight each other, for whatever honor was in that. The small fires quickly spread into a general conflagration.

Bemused by the activity, Mordecai turned his head to watch a man flying past him. He watched too long. Ree charged with his head down and butted him in the belly. It chanced to be near the doors. Mordecai went backward through them to land on his thighs against the staves of a broken barrel in the street.

A hand touched his shoulder, and he glanced up to see a brown-eyed woman steadying herself to keep from falling. He'd come within a hair of knocking her clean across the street, but she didn't seem overexcited or scared. She caught her balance again and withdrew her hand. For an instant Mordecai would have sworn that she was looking at him with more curiosity than disgust.

He blinked and said gravely, "How'd do?"

She didn't answer, but he was almost sure there was a faint smile on her lips as she looked back toward the Beaver Palace, whence came the sounds of the dangedest whingding Mord had heard in a long time. It sounded like eighty-nine Walla Walla Indians trying to kill a bear with clubs.

Danged if it wasn't almost like rendezvous. "Just a friendly doin's," Mord explained, and went back inside.

Ree, grinning happily, was fending off occasional elements of spinning humanity that came whirling out of the general brawl, and bellering for more action. He whacked Mord on the shoulder. "Looks like they all swallered grizzly hair, it does. I wonder what started it?"

"No way of telling — now," Mord said.

They beat their way back to the bar. One of the voyageurs had been watching Mordecai's rifle. He indicated it with his foot. Mordecai shoved the half full bottle at him and called for a new one.

The canoe business settled — until the next time — Ree and Mordecai began to discuss gambling. Pierre came from his interrupted dinner a second time, angry now, and set his burly crew to work. The combats around the room began to diminish. The last pair to be separated consisted of two keelboat men who were struggling in a corner, each trying to bite the other's nose off.

"Rendezvous, I swear!" Ree said, and he and Mordecai laughed.

Pierre gave them a dark look, then shrugged and returned to his dinner.

It was then that Jim Shandy walked over from the foot of the stairs, ignoring Ree. He said, "I'm tickled to see you, Mord, old hoss."

Shandy had been a trapper, and he could still talk the language. But he didn't smell like no trapper any more, not in them fancy duds. It just didn't make sense to Mordecai that a man who had been out there and made 'em come could feel right about staying in St. Louis the year around. Still, Shandy was a Rocky Mountain man, and always had been, and he was one of the big ones here at this end of the business. Mordecai shook hands with him.

It might have been a mite hasty, the way Shandy asked, "What are you doing here, Mord?"

Mordecai explained where he'd been.

"I see!" Shandy said heartily. "Then you're aching to get to rendezvous real fast, huh?"

"Got time." The whisky and the fight had loosened Mordecai up considerably. Him and Ree could do a heap of things before St. Louis wore thin.

"Yeah, I reckon you have." Shandy acted like something was sticking in his craw, but he was easy enough about ordering up another bottle of whisky. "I'll tell the watchman to let you into the warehouse when you want to sleep." He walked off real sudden.

Ree padded across the floor and peered from the doorway. When he came back, he said: "He went up the street with that woman and the old preacher. Who are they, Mord?"

40

"No idea. Let's get some doin's started. This here place don't shine no more, Ree. Let's head for the Rivermen's House."

Carrying the bottles, they went out. "I figure I'll gamble some," Mordecai said. "Got me some big Mexican silver from Wimarr, and I feel real lucky."

"Wimarr got a buyer for them mules?"

"Hell, I don't know." Mordecai flipped one of the heavy coins.

"Rendezvous is sure enough on the Wind?" Ree asked. "They ain't changed things?"

"You had Randall on the brain, and now you got rendezvous. Sure it's on the Wind. What for would anybody want to change it after it was once said?"

"No reason, I guess," Ree said. "What for did Shandy want to send out no-good mules and horses in the pack train when he could've got about eighty good mules at the time?"

"Shandy knows his business. You always got the gripes about everything any fur company does, Ree."

"Guess so."

They walked through the drying mud, lean, solid men in dirty buckskins. They were a breed apart and they knew it, and those who gave way before them knew it too. They finished one of the partly filled bottles. Ree threw it up and broke it with a pistol shot.

"Poor shooting," Mordecai said. "I always shoot down the neck of the bottle when it's spinning. Then, when it spins on around, the bullet drops out without busting the bottle. When you can do that —"

"First liar ain't got no chance." Ree let out a war whoop. "I can lick any five men in the Rivermen's House, if you can handle just one of them!"

"We'll see."

Neither of them paid any attention to Raoul, the Creole spy and hanger-on, who was following them at a discreet distance. Inoffensive and quite efficient, Raoul Gervais picked up information for any fur company that cared to hire him.

CHAPTER
FOUR

Sprawled on a pile of tanned buffalo robes in the Rocky Mountain warehouse in the black of early morning, Mordecai didn't hear the fellow coming until he was almost beside him. He grabbed for Old Belcher, his rifle. It should have been beside him in its beaded case, but it wasn't there. He felt for his pistol. It was gone and his knife was gone too.

The man said, "Mord! Mord, you asleep?"

By then Mordecai had rolled over against a stack of baled goods and was on his knees. He kept feeling for his rifle, trying to remember something about it, even after it came to him foggily that it was Shandy standing there in the darkness calling to him.

"Mord, wake up!"

Mordecai grunted. He was as much awake as he was likely to be for a long time. It must have been the worst spree he'd ever been on. His head felt like it was falling off his shoulders, and the stupor that had kept him from waking when Shandy came toward him was still as thick in his brain as morning fog on the Missouri. His head kept jerking lower. He was going to die if he didn't get on his back or side.

He got on his back only after he pitched on his face and then rolled over. Shandy was talking, but Mordecai didn't understand him and didn't want to. "Go away," Mordecai groaned. It was blacker than a wolf's mouth in the warehouse, but ordinarily that would not have disturbed his sense of time.

Something had made him all fuzzy. It was night and that was all he knew, but somewhere in the previous afternoon and evening there ought to be a few clear spots.

Mordecai remembered one of them. Old Sledge. Yeah. It was in a game of Old Sledge that he'd lost his horses to a sad-looking Spaniard. They must have been his horses. Wasn't it Blas Wimarr who had said something about giving them to him? How had Blas got into the warehouse anyway? No, it wasn't Blas; it was Shandy.

Mordecai kept pawing the robes, feeling for his rifle; it was impossible that he'd lose Old Belcher. Why, a man would liefer lose his squaw any old day than the best rifle gun that ever went west of the Mississippi!

"Whar at is my rifle?" he shouted.

"You lost it gambling."

"That's a dirty lie!" Mord tried to get up to drive the lie down Shandy's throat, but he fell over something and went flat on his face. Gamble Old Belcher away? He'd never do that.

Mordecai lay on the robes and tried to remember, and some of it came back. They'd gone to the Rivermen's House, him and Ree. They'd had some fun there because Mordecai could remember throwing a man over the bar three times before the fellow quit climbing back. Somewhere they'd run into Blas Wimarr, who was having a celebration because he'd sold all his mules to the American Fur Company. What did the American want with so many mules? Well, it didn't matter. Where was Old Belcher?

"What'd you do with my rifle?" Mord yelled at Shandy, because Shandy was close at hand.

"You gambled it away, I told you."

It must be a lie, but as Mord kept pawing around a terrible truth began to dawn. Somewhere last night there'd been a bright-eyed little Creole playing hand with a bunch of Sioux. It was a game just made for Mord. Why, nobody could get ahead of him playing hand. His eyes were too sharp.

But the awful feeling began to grow. That Creole had worked his hands faster than a white-faced hornet. Some of the time he maybe didn't even have the button in his cupped palms when he was shaking them. That could be.

Mordecai groaned. He'd come all the way to St. Louis to get beat at his own game. He seemed to remember something about losing some money too, but that didn't count. The government made money as easy as pouring lead into a bullet mold, but nobody made rifles like Old Belcher.

Old Belcher was no Hawken; it was special made by a gunsmith in Pennsylvania. Milt Sublette himself had brought it back as a gift for Mordecai.

Wagh! What a night for bad medicine it must have been! Mordecai tried to pull a robe over him. When his senses returned in the morning, he'd find some way of getting Old Belcher back.

"Get up," Shandy said. "You've got to do something."

Mord grunted. All he wanted to do was sleep.

Shandy jerked the robe off him. Shandy was a son of a bitch that Mord would throw clean out of the warehouse — if he had the strength to get up.

"This is company business," Shandy said.

"Hell with the company."

"She's going upriver on that steamboat, and you're taking her, Mord. It's important."

"Hell with her." It must have been right after Ree cached off someplace all of a sudden that Mord had lost Old Belcher. Ree had got sort of excited when he found out that Blas had sold his mules to the American Fur Company. Hell with who? "Who's *her*?"

"I've been talking about her for ten minutes," Shandy said. "What's the matter, Mord? Can't you hold a few drinks?"

"I can drink more whisky, kill more Blackfeet, wrassle more grizzlies, catch more women —" It wasn't worth it. Mord tried to pull the robe over his head. There was one place where the whisky hadn't tasted so good. That damn' little Creole who had been everywhere — What was his name?

"Get up!" Shandy yelled. "There ain't much time left. You going to rendezvous this summer, or lay there like a drunken riverman?"

"Ain't going nowhere," Mordecai mumbled. Rendezvous. That was the first thing Shandy had said that made sense. Out at rendezvous whisky never stunned you like this. You could have your doin's and then sleep in the shade all day, with a squaw to watch over you so nobody could pull any jokes, like setting your clothes afire or tying your leg to a wild pony.

"Get up!" Shandy shouted. "I want to talk to you about Old Belcher."

Mordecai got up then. He reeled and fell against a stack of robes higher than his head. He kept trying to find his rifle. By Old Ephraim, he'd never felt so robbed or naked since Ree turned that canoe over in the Yellowstone!

"Come on," Shandy said.

Mordecai bumped against bales and stacks of goods as he followed Shandy to the front of the warehouse, where a candle was burning in a tiny office. Mordecai leaned against the wall. He was sicker than a dog. He felt like he'd been poisoned.

"She's got to get to Fort Cass by the middle of July," Shandy said. "She's going to marry a missionary who's coming down there to meet her."

"Let her marry him."

"Wake up, Mord! You're the one that's taking her there."

"I ain't taking no white woman nowhere." By God, he had been poisoned! They'd doped his whisky. Suddenly Mordecai rushed from the office and was sick against the warehouse doors. Poisoned and then robbed in a crooked gambling game! Somebody was going to pay for it.

His head was a little clearer when he went back to the office.

"This is company policy, Mord. The government is always howling because of whisky and corruptin' Indians. We'll have something on our side when we can say the Rocky Mountain took a missionary across."

Mord was unimpressed. It wouldn't be the company taking a female missionary; it'd be Mordecai Price. He turned to go back to his bed.

"You've got to do it!" Shandy said. "It's a big thing for the company. I've got orders to see that she gets there."

"You take her then." Mordecai went on to the door.

"Afraid you can't do the job, huh? Ree Semple says he can."

"Good. Let him do it."

"He's a Hudson's Bay man!" Shandy shouted. "Or maybe he's even working for American." He was all upset. "You're going to take her, Mord. Last night you lost everything you own but your clothes. I even gave you a hundred dollars of company money, and you lost that too."

"They'll get it back," Mordecai said sourly.

"Unless you listen to me, there's one thing you won't see again — and that's your rifle."

Mordecai lurched away from the door and went toward Shandy. "You got Old Belcher?"

"I got everything you lost. Followed you around like a brother. Wasn't for me, you'd be over the levee with your belly knifed open. You was drugged, Mord."

"You really got Old Belcher, Shandy?"

48

"Everything but your hosses. I'll give you the money to pick up another outfit somewhere up the river. The boat is going to Fort Union, but —"

"Union!" Mordecai growled. "I ain't riding no stinking steamboat to Union."

"You don't have to. You can get off somewhere near Bad River, say, cut south of the Sioux Hills and go straight to the rendezvous at Big Meadows. After three or four days there, if you like, you can take her on down the Big Horn to Cass."

The first part of the route wasn't Mordecai's idea of a quick way to rendezvous, but he had bigger details than that bothering him. "That woman part — that don't shine with me at all, Shandy."

"You ain't marrying her. All you're doing is taking her to Fort Cass. She won't be the first white woman to cross the prairies, and she'll get there faster than if she was traveling with a big party. Besides, there ain't no parties going out right now."

Mordecai scowled, trying to sort out details from last night. "Wimarr and Ree was talking something about a pack train going out right away. Why couldn't she —"

"Drunken rumor, that's all," Shandy said. It was hanging by a thin hair. Ree had caught on fast when he found out about the American's deal with Wimarr for the mules. That was when he'd slipped away to see what was going on at the American warehouse.

Mordecai would have caught on too, if he hadn't been so drunk, and if Shandy hadn't hired a man to dope his whisky. It still might come through to him. Ree — there were ways to handle him, because he didn't care a whoop about the Rocky Mountain Fur Company; but if Mordecai stayed in town long enough to get his senses back he'd ruin everything.

Mordecai wagged his head. "Ain't taking no female missionary with me nowhere."

"You got to! Company order."

"I didn't get it from Milt Sublette or —"

"You won't get another Old Belcher from him neither!"

Mordecai's head was full of rocks knocking together, and his belly felt like there were two wolverines fighting inside him; but it was still the idea of losing Old Belcher that hurt the worst. "Let's see my rifle."

"You'll get it along with the rest of your plunder when you're at the wharf and ready to get on the *Rosebud*. Your debt to the company will be wiped out too."

The way things had gone, Mordecai was ready to leave St. Louis anyway. But a woman missionary, wagh!

Shandy was all confidence now. "I can get somebody else that ain't so dead set against taking a long trip with a pretty woman."

Pretty woman? A white woman pretty? They started to come apart when you touched 'em, or else they was like the ones him and Ree had been with some last night, dirtier than fish-eating squaws and a heap more foul-mouthed. "I'm going back to bed. Get somebody else."

Shandy blew up a fury. He almost made the mistake of grabbing Mordecai. "Your damn' rifle will wind up with some engagee that'll use it to break wood! It'll lay

50

out in the rain. Maybe once a year the barrel will get washed out. The stock —"

"Shut up!" Mordecai braced against the wall and tried to think. He had to have Old Belcher back. The rifle was like one of his arms or legs. The price was high, but he had to have the rifle.

"It's time to start right now,". Shandy said.

River fog was heavy outside, with a dampness that made Mordecai wonder why he'd ever left the mountains. He slouched along with a bubbly feeling in his belly and his mind still fuzzy from yesterday's doin's. It seemed like Shandy was going out of his way to reach the wharf. Farther along the bench where the big gray and yellow stone warehouse of the American Company sat, blobby lights shone and Mordecai heard men's voices.

Shandy said, "I see the American is rushing to get some goods on the *Rosebud* at the last minute." Almost without pause he added, "I hope you understand how important it is to get this woman safe to Fort Cass."

"Yeah. Where's my rifle?"

"All your plunder will be at the wharf."

They slipped down through mud to greasy planks. Lanterns were moving jerkily on the wharf. An orange light was coming from the stack of the boat. The bitter odor of wood smoke came to Mordecai. His stomach tried to rebel but there was nothing left in it.

"Over here," Shandy said, and led Mordecai toward two cloaked figures at one end of the landing. "Here he is, Miss Marsh — Mordecai Price. He's one of the company's most trusted men. He'll get you there."

Mordecai heard the woman sniff. She said, somewhat doubtfully, that she was glad to know him. Mordecai refrained from answering.

The second shadowy figure said, "Get us a lantern, James. I should like to look closely at this man before —"

"Ain't no time for that," Shandy said.

"Where's Old Belcher?" Mordecai demanded.

"There will be two of them with me?" the woman asked Shandy. "This Mr. Price and Mr. Belcher?"

"Yeah," Shandy said absently. He yelled a name, and a man came through the fog to him. "Here's your stuff, Mord."

Mordecai felt a little better when he got his hands on the cold weight of Old Belcher. He complained that the case was gone, and Shandy said it couldn't be helped. The man had everything else, pistol, shot pouch, powder horn, possibles sack, and knife. He even had Mordecai's pipe and tobacco.

Only after the fellow was gone did it occur to Mordecai that there had been something about him vaguely remindful of the little Creole who had worked such a blinding game of hand.

They were yelling on the *Rosebud* for everyone to get aboard.

The man with Miss Marsh began to pray, asking the Lord to aid her in crossing the prairies, asking that she might be given strength to do some almighty fine work helping her husband bring the Gospel to the Indians.

Mordecai lurched away. His moccasins were wet and they almost betrayed him crossing the springy landing planks. For an instant he came within a hair of falling between the boat and the wharf. Shandy yelled for him to wait up and help the woman with her plunder, but Mordecai had all he could do to get himself aboard.

Miss Marsh carried some of her own stuff, and Shandy brought the rest. They piled it against Mordecai's legs.

"Take good care of her now," Shandy said. "Remember how important this is to the company." He went back to the wharf.

Mordecai sniffed the strange odors of the woman. She smelled about like most missionaries, he guessed.

From the wharf the woman's companion called, "Goodbye and God speed you, child!"

Somewhere on the boat a heavy voice replied, "Same to you, child!"

Rivermen hauled the planks in. The boat began to drift gently as stumbling, cursing men pushed her away from the wharf with long poles. Not trusting the dampness and whoever had been handling his rifle, Mordecai raised Old Belcher and pulled the trigger. It had been charged, sure enough, and too heavy at that. It made a hell of a roar and flame.

The woman jumped and let out a startled gasp.

Midships on the boat someone mistook Mordecai's shot for send-off noise, and fired a pistol. Several others joined in. Mordecai reloaded his rifle properly.

Somewhere over there against the hill St. Louis was quiet and sleeping, except for the dim lights at the American Company warehouse. Sparks gushed from the stack. The *Rosebud* shuddered as the wheel began to fight the Mississippi.

Miss Marsh asked, "Where can I find quarters, Mr. Price?"

"Anywhere there's room to flop." Mordecai walked away from her, feeling his way forward through a disorder of bales and boxes. He stepped on a prostrate man, and the fellow cursed him. Mordecai growled like a bear and stepped hard on the fellow with the other foot.

Forward of the boilerhouse on the main deck he found a place to lie down on the fog-damp planks, cradling his rifle against him to keep it dry. He went to sleep quickly.

CHAPTER
FIVE

When Mordecai woke up, the smell of the river was in his nostrils and he knew without opening his eyes that the morning fog was gone, and just how the brown bluffs on the west bank would look. He felt considerably better. He was headed toward rendezvous, and as soon as he got a little something in his meat bag — And then he remembered the missionary woman.

He opened his eyes cautiously. She was about ten feet away, sitting on a box, looking upriver. Her bonnet was in her lap. With her black hair shining in the sun she was some different from the way he'd pictured her. Why, hell, it was the female that he'd almost knocked off the busted barrel in front of the Beaver Palace!

She lacked the heft of an Indian woman, he judged, but she wasn't skinny. Take white women, though, they just didn't shine. He saw two boatmen watching her from the corner of the boilerhouse. They thought she was something, all right.

When Mordecai started to rise, he found his feet and legs hedged in by the woman's plunder. Come time to leave the boat, he'd have a few words with Miss Marsh about that pile of foofaraw. He wasn't running no pack train to Fort Cass.

Right now it was time to eat.

"Mr. Price," Rhoda called.

Going around the boilerhouse, Mordecai stopped to look back. If she thought he was going to wait on her, she had another think coming.

She hesitated and then said, "Good morning."

Mordecai grunted. He went in search of food.

Standing high in the muddy water, with a shallow draft, the *Rosebud* was little more than a steam-powered keelboat, without cabins and with nothing but storage space below the main deck. Right now boatmen were still busy stowing the cargo that had come aboard last night.

She was an American Company boat. If you didn't know, you could tell by the number of open-mouthed greenhorns just abeaming at the prospect of going upriver to work for the company. Wasn't two in the bunch that wouldn't wish they'd stayed home once they reached Fort Union and discovered that the American was all work and damn' little pay.

Mordecai found the engine crew's coffee bucket slung on an iron hook under the slow drip of a leaky steam line. It was strong and muddy and hot enough to dehide a buffalo. He tipped the bucket up and drank. One of the stokers glowered at him and started to protest, and then sized him up again and was silent.

He must have been plumb bedazzled last night when Shandy got after him. Suddenly he remembered that Shandy hadn't given him money to buy an outfit. Well, that didn't cut much difference; there were all kinds of ways to skin a cat.

He began to explore the crowded deck. Sticking out from behind a pile of mooring line were a pair of leggins and huge moccasined feet. By Old Ephraim, there just might be one man aboard with something in his possibles sack besides cheese and stale bread.

It was Ree Semple lying there on a buffalo robe, with his hands resting on his belly. He grinned at Mordecai. "How'd you get Old Belcher back?"

"Shandy." Mordecai scowled darkly. "Do I remember straight, you didn't lose nothing gambling last night?"

"You can't remember that straight, Mord — but I didn't." Ree sat up and hauled his possibles sack around. "Got some dried buffler."

"This child has got a place for it." Mordecai sat down cross-legged. He was chewing his first big mouthful when he heard loud laughter and Rhoda saying, "I'll thank you to mind your own business, sir!"

Ree grinned. "There's your squaw, Mord."

"Maybe she can convert whoever's pestering her."

"She ain't no missionary. She's going to Cass to marry one, is all."

"Same difference." Mordecai crammed more meat in his mouth. "How do you know so much about her?"

"Got acquainted while you was laying there like a drunk Omaha. I rustled her some breakfast too. I seen her yesterday and talked to her in front of the Beaver Palace."

Just the man to take her to Fort Cass. It might take some doin's, but if Ree didn't think she was being shoved off on him — he was a hardheaded coon — it might be arranged.

From around the boilerhouse Rhoda said, "You keep your filthy hands off me!"

"She didn't say 'sir' that time." Still chewing, Mord got up to see what was going on. He stopped at the corner of the boiler-house.

A black-whiskered boatman was holding Rhoda by the arms, gripping her bear-tight, grinning at her. "Hell, it's only a kiss I'm after, woman. I ain't asking you to go ashore in the brush with me."

A bellow of laughter came from the other boatmen watching the scene as Rhoda twisted her head away from the man's hairy face as he tried to kiss her. She saw Mordecai standing with his rifle across his hips.

He thought she was going to yell for help, but she didn't. Once more she twisted away from the boatman's face. He rubbed his whiskers against her neck and laughed.

"You'd better hold her down with a forked stick, Bill!" one of his friends said.

Mordecai guessed it had gone far enough. "You want to kiss him, Miss Marsh?" he asked.

Rhoda gave Mordecai a look of pure fury. "You drunken idiot! Do something!"

"Bite his nose," Mordecai advised. He rolled a hard piece of gristle around in his mouth and spat it out as he stepped forward unhurriedly. "Get your paws off her."

The boatman acted quicker than Mordecai expected. He let Rhoda go and stepped back, drawing a heavy knife from his belt. "You mind your own business, trapper." He was drunk, Mordecai observed. From the corner of his eye Mordecai saw that Ree was standing behind him.

Mordecai walked slowly toward the boatman. Ree raised his rifle carelessly and pretended to blow dust from the lock, while the heavy barrel swung slowly across the bellies of the boatman's friends.

"Put the knife away or fight, you bastard!" Mordecai said.

The boatman backed around a winch and then stopped. He held onto the winch with one hand and made a sweeping stroke with the knife as Mordecai came closer. "Stay back! I'm warning you!"

Mordecai shifted Old Belcher to one hand as the man started another stroke. The knife clanged on the barrel. Mordecai drove the rifle like a lance. The muzzle struck the boatman's chest and knocked him away from the winch. As he staggered back, Mordecai followed and drove the rifle into him again.

The boatman went against the rail, over it, and into the river. He howled bloody murder just before he struck the water. Other boatmen grabbed up poles and lines and rushed to the side. They fished their floundering companion out just short of the wheel.

Ree grunted his disappointment. "I always wondered what them blades would do to a man."

Rhoda watched in horror the man's close escape from the churning wheel. She turned on Mordecai. "You almost killed him! He couldn't even swim!"

"Mostly they can't." Mordecai looked at a nick in his rifle barrel. "You said do something, didn't you?"

"I didn't mean for you to kill him!"

"He ain't dead."

"You tried hard enough."

"Hell," Mordecai said. He walked away. Yup, the thing to do was to sluff this job off on Ree.

The boss boatman came stomping forward. When he got the story he cursed and said to Rhoda, "I'll fix him, lady."

The boss boatman was a brawny lad with a flattened nose and one down-turned eye. He ordered a pole thrown overboard, and as soon as that was done he himself tossed the offending Bill after it. Bill went under, and for a while it was a close thing whether he would get the pole or not.

He made it. Spectators began to make bets on where he would land, or whether he would get ashore at all. Rhoda came over to where Mordecai and Ree were standing. "I've never seen such brutality in all my life!"

Ree said nothing. He squinted at the boatman, slowly kicking toward the bank behind the pole.

"You tried to drown that man, Mr. Price, and all the time you had your mouth full of something." The last part seemed to outrage Rhoda more than the first.

"Buffler meat," Mordecai said. "I generally always chew when I eat."

They watched the boatman drag himself out of the brown water far downstream. He shook his fist at the *Rosebud*. A few men laughed. A few cheered. To Mordecai it was a trifling thing to be forgotten five minutes later, except that Rhoda Marsh was still indignant toward him, like as if he had caused the whole thing.

60

"Should've let him kiss you," Mordecai growled. He walked away to finish his breakfast.

He could hear Ree trying to soothe the woman. That Ree, he was a great hand with women of all kinds. Let him go his best. When all at once he found himself the man who was going to take Rhoda Marsh to Cass, it would serve him right.

Mordecai stayed plumb away from them both. He munched from Ree's well stocked possibles sack. He napped in the shade and plotted like a Blackfoot. Ree took care of the woman, and brought her food from the company mess. He had the boatmen rig her a canvas shelter against the boilerhouse. One of the greenhorns, blushing to the tips of his ears, rustled a wooden bucket and put it in the shelter.

Late in the afternoon Mordecai saw the first boil of Missouri water bursting darkly on the lighter surface of the Mississippi. He went forward to watch, putting one foot on a capstan. There she was, the Big Muddy. Her powerful under-running currents laden with the silt of a wild, far country surged deep below the tamer waters of the Mississippi, and then came exploding upward.

It was the Missouri's last violent complaint against merging with a stream that flowed sluggishly through tamed and conquered lands.

To Mordecai it was like meeting a loved, savage companion. He was staring happily at the brown churn of Old Muddy when Rhoda came up beside him. She watched the river for a time with a strange expression.

"How far do we go up that?" she asked.

"A right far piece," Mordecai said. She was going all the way to Fort Union, whether she knew it or not. Mordecai was leaving just as soon as he got a few things worked out in his head.

"Mr. Shandy said we'd get horses somewhere near the Bad River."

"Yeah." Her face was already considerable darker from the sun, Mordecai noticed. She wasn't the kind that turned Turkey red, like some when their noses got an inch beyond the shade of their bonnets. This woman acted like she didn't give a darn about facing a little weather.

She couldn't have any idea of what it was 'way out there: no house to step into when it started to blow up a rain, no store to trot over to when you wanted a piece of cloth or something to put in your belly, and no other white women to gabble with. Yet she didn't appear to be put out.

Maybe not, so far. The *Rosebud* was one thing; the lonesome land was another. Wait until Mordecai put up his bluff about wanting her to leave the boat suddenly.

Right there was where Ree was going to get stuck.

"I didn't mean to be ungrateful, Mr. Price. It was just that I was shocked by the roughness of everything. Mr. Semple has been telling me something about the life out here, and while I still deplore the brutality I do understand that some things are different from Massachusetts."

"A heap," Mordecai said. She could sure spout words. It took him clean back to the days when his ma had tried to make him speak like Uncle Mordecai

Fletcher, who'd been the dangedest stump-shouting lawyer in all Kentucky.

"We'll travel with your pack train, once we overtake it, I suppose," Rhoda said.

"Who said that? Jim Shandy?"

"No. Mr. Semple said that was what you'd do."

"Might do that." So Ree was feeding her ideas, trying to find out what plans Mordecai had in mind. What was Ree up to, anyway? A whole heap of things that had happened in St. Louis had begun to trouble Mordecai some, now that his head was clear and he'd had time to do some thinking.

What was Shandy's idea in telling him to go clean up to Bad River before starting across the prairies, when the Platte trail was the best way? Not that Mordecai had given a second thought to following the advice; he'd pick his own route going anywhere.

Shandy sure had been in a sweating hurry to get Mordecai started toward rendezvous. "You really a missionary?" he asked the woman.

"No. I'm going to Fort Cass to marry a missionary and help him."

"How come Jim Shandy was helping you?"

"Mr. Shandy's brother is a member of our Missionary Society. He met me in Cincinnati and accompanied me to St. Louis. At first his brother didn't seem inclined to help us, but then, as soon as he came out of the Beaver Palace that day you were fighting in there, he changed his mind. The Reverend Jeremiah Shandy was confident that the Lord would prevail upon his brother, and He did."

Mordecai blinked. He said, "Yeah. The Lord changed his mind, huh?"

Rhoda hesitated, and then said, "What else would you suggest?"

Some of the thoughts growing in Mordecai's mind were too black to suggest to anyone. The first thing that he had to do was shift the responsibility for this woman to Ree Semple. "You trust Ree pretty much, don't you?"

"Why, yes. He seems to be a gentleman."

A gentleman! Jesus Christ. "He sure is," Mordecai agreed. "Not only that, but he's one of the best men on the prairie you'll ever meet. He can sneak through a Pawnee camp at night and not even stir up a dog. He can pick out a fat cow running through dust at two hundred yards and shoot plumb center. He can —"

"I'm sure he's an accomplished plainsman, Mr. Price. What's your point?"

Mordecai shook his head. "I might have to leave the boat a little sooner than I thought." He took a deep breath and met Rhoda's eyes squarely. "I'm thinking Ree could take you all the way to Fort Union on the boat. That's safe traveling. Then it ain't hardly no trip at all from Union to Cass." What was a couple of hundred miles, especially if Ree, not Mordecai, was dragging a white woman with him?

"That's odd."

"What's odd?" Mordecai asked.

"Your having such great confidence in Mr. Semple. He told me you were the one who taught him everything he knows about the plains and the mountains."

The dirty bastard! That was the first time he had ever admitted that to anyone. Mordecai would have sworn that Rhoda was holding laughter behind her eyes, like a tickled Indian.

"Mr. Semple also said that he might have to leave the boat unexpectedly," Rhoda said. "You see, it did occur to me, after observing your conduct and condition last night, that I might be better off with another escort, so I asked Mr. Semple, but he declined to accept the task."

Mordecai grunted like a gut-shot bear. He went aft to find Mr. Semple, the gentleman who declined tasks.

Ree was dealing Mexican monte on a blanket. There was loot gathered around his legs, so it was evident that several greenhorns and boatmen had learned something of the game the hard way.

"What do you know about the Rocky Mountain pack train, Ree?" Mordecai demanded.

Ree turned over a card. He hauled a handful of Spanish dollars and a knife into the pile of loot around his legs. "No more'n you, I reckon. It left to meet the keelboat at the mouth of the Platte last week. Why?"

"Where'd you go last night after we met Blas Wimarr?"

"Huntin' better whisky." Ree grinned as he riffled the cards. "Blas said he'd keep an eye on you until I got back." He waved a big paw over the blanket. "Freeze into it, boys! Bets on the table and borry from your mother-in-law after she's done!"

There wasn't nothing to be learned from Ree when he didn't want to say it. Mordecai went back to Rhoda.

"You're still my guide?" she asked.

"Yeah." Mordecai gave her a sour look. He'd promised to take her to Cass, no matter if he had been poisoned-sick at the time. He wasn't the kind to go back on his word. Of course, if she deserted him, that would be different. Then Ree would have to take care of her. Fact was, Mordecai couldn't travel fast with a white woman along, while it didn't matter whether Ree traveled fast or not; at least it didn't matter to Mordecai.

"You've already received your money, haven't you?" Rhoda asked.

"What money?"

"The two hundred dollars the minister gave to his brother, your fee for taking me to Fort Cass."

"Hm-m," Mordecai said, and that was all the answer he gave. Talk about a man getting drunk and losing his beaver . . . That Shandy. It got darker the more Mordecai thought about it.

Rhoda gave up getting an answer out of him. She quit studying him and looked upstream again. Her dark hair made a heavy mass on her neck. She lifted it a little and said, "I suppose it gets cooler the farther up we go?"

"No," Mordecai said. "This trip I figure it'll get a heap hotter."

66

CHAPTER
SIX

When Joseph Bogard sent word for Jim Shandy to come to the office of the American Fur Company, it was insulting proof that the American now regarded Shandy as a hireling; and when Shandy went, even though in a rage, it was an admission that the view was correct.

He had to wait a half-hour while Bogard finished some business with a representative of an Eastern manufacturer.

A rawness was coming from the river, and Bogard had a fire in the small stove in his office. He warmed his coat-tails while he talked to Shandy. "Mr. Randall requires one more step to ensure your guarantee to American."

"To hell with his step. I've done my part."

In spite of fatness, there was a certain strength in Bogard's face. "Not quite, Mr. Shandy. You're to leave at once to make sure that the Rocky Mountain train doesn't travel too fast."

"It won't. I gave you my word on that."

Bogard puffed out round cheeks. "Yenzer is a competent man. Then, too, it's likely that he'll be joined by Price."

"Mordecai has got his hands full. I fixed it so he won't ever catch that train."

Bogard shifted to warm his front at the stove. "Yes, you saddled him with that young woman, after you had him drugged and cheated out of all of his possessions." He didn't even trouble to look around to gloat over Shandy's anger.

"You and your miserable spies!" Shandy growled.

"Price is still dangerous. Semple went upriver with him. You should have done something about Semple, Mr. Shandy." Bogard spoke to Shandy as Randall often spoke to Bogard, in a tone both superior and threatening.

That Ree was gone was news to Shandy. He should have had them both killed right here in St. Louis, Mordecai and Ree too. He'd considered it, too, but the odds had been bad: Ree had stayed sober and watchful, and Blas Wimarr, in spite of being drunk, had been a fly in the ointment.

"We have reason to think that Semple is still with Hudson's Bay," Bogard said. He turned to look at Shandy. "They've been crowding farther east all the time. Suppose they, too, have been considering the idea of beating everyone to rendezvous?"

Shandy watched the fat-faced man with a cold fear. What had he found out? "They won't come that far east."

"Why not? We've been wondering for a long time why the British haven't tried it. If they're ready to move from an advance base somewhere east of Fort Boise, Semple has time to get word to them and bring them to rendezvous before either Rocky Mountain or American can reach the place."

"What for do they need him?" Shandy asked. "Anybody can find the way to Wind River."

"If they're making the move this year, all they're waiting for is news that American is sending a train to beat the Rocky Mountain. That will wipe out any last scruples Hudson's Bay may have about open competition east of the mountains." Bogard shrugged. "We're going to wipe out the Rocky Mountain Company anyway, whether you know it or not, but we don't want Hudson's Bay beating us to the first course of the feast."

"I didn't guarantee anything about the British."

"Perhaps not, but if they should win you're going to lose out." Bogard smiled. "I'm afraid you're much too simple for this end of the fur trade. That's why Mr. Randall says you may be of more use to us out there where you properly belong."

Shandy fought back a desire to slam Bogard against the wall and choke him.

"You're to leave at once," Bogard said. "Whatever you do to ensure that the Rocky Mountain pack train is delayed is your own business. All we demand is results."

"I ain't going nowhere, damn you!"

"You're not with trappers and Indians now," Bogard said quietly. "We want you to leave within two hours. I assure you that it's your only course."

Shandy knew that he could take three steps across the room and tear the fat, insulting bastard to pieces with his bare hands. He wanted to, and it was not

69

Bogard that stopped him. It was the power and the reach of the company that the man represented which kept Shandy standing rigid and savage.

"I suggest that you start moving," Bogard said.

Shandy was hooked. He knew it. "I want some money in advance on our agreement."

Bogard smiled and shook his head.

Rage carried Shandy through the next point. "I'm not waiting thirty days for my money after the pack train comes back. It's cash the day after the furs reach St. Louis, or the deal's off!"

"No one cancels an agreement with American." Bogard warmed his hands over the stove. "However, I'll see that you get your 10 per cent two days after our train returns."

"I'd rather have that promise from Randall."

"I can speak for him in this matter," Bogard said. "You will be paid."

Shandy guessed it was the best he could do.

From the window Bogard watched him leaving. Trappers were all the same, stupid but necessary. Shandy's chances of coming back to St. Louis to collect his money were very slim. If his own company didn't find out what he had done, and take care of him, the leader of the American pack train would drop a few hints at rendezvous that would start the ball rolling.

Bogard turned back to the stove. Randall was unduly concerned about Hudson's Bay. True, Ree Semple had acted like a spy for somebody, but again, he was only an ignorant trapper. He undoubtedly was working for the

70

Rocky Mountain Company, not Hudson's Bay. Let Shandy take care of him as he saw fit.

On his way back to the Rocky Mountain warehouse, Shandy observed that he was being trailed by two men who looked like hungry swamp runners. He could take care of them, he didn't doubt, but American would have no trouble hiring another pair to keep check on him. It occurred to him that he would never be safe in St. Louis again.

A Negro messenger was waiting for him at the warehouse. "Mistuh Shandy, dere's a man wants to see you real bad ovah at the River House."

Shandy brushed the messenger aside and went into his office. Parson Bill Kerr and Mike Nesmith, they would do. One-time trappers of sorts, they had lately worked as ferrymen and boatmen when the spirit moved. He'd take them along with him, if they were sober enough to ride.

The Negro came hesitantly to the doorway. "Mistuh Shandy, dis man he say he your brother. He —"

"Boy, you get down to the Rivermen's House as fast as you can. Find Bill Kerr and Mike Nesmith. Tell them I want to see them right away. Right away, understand?"

"Yassuh. But it's de River House I'm talking 'bout. Dis man he say he your brother, Mistuh Shandy. He's dying away fast."

Jerry? Shandy had forgot that he was still around. "What's the matter with him?"

"He sick here." The Negro held his chest and rolled his eyes. "Maybe he gone while I been waitin' here."

"Get down to the Rivermen's House and find those two men, damn you!" Shandy shouted.

"Yassuh, but dis sick man —"

"Never mind the sick man! I haven't got any brother. Now git!" Shandy tossed the Negro a coin.

The messenger left. Shandy began to figure what he needed for the trip. Most of the equipment was right here in the warehouse. Kerr and Nesmith might cost him more than they were worth, but they were fairly reliable cut-throats with more than passing knowledge of prairie life, and they certainly were thickheaded enough to carry out his orders without questioning the reasons behind them.

They showed up fifteen minutes later, both miraculously sober. Within the two hours set by Bogard, Shandy was on his way.

Mordecai felt that he had been on the *Rosebud* long enough to be halfway to Union. All a boat did was eat wood, belch smoke, cramp a man's legs — and get nowhere.

The *Rosebud* was tied for the night to a small island two hundred yards from the west bank. Late that afternoon they'd passed an Ottoe camp. Some of the Indians had raced their ponies along the bank, waving and yelling. The greenhorns had got all excited.

Mordecai stood on deck, staring at the dark water. Rhoda was asleep in her shelter. Three stokers who got up now and then to keep the boiler fired, and some pork eaters sound asleep on the stern, were the only people left aboard besides him. All the others were on the island, sprawled around a fire, listening to Ree tell stories. It was a wonder Rhoda wasn't over there too, the way she and Ree had been making up to each other lately.

Tonight was the time.

She wouldn't go, Mordecai was sure. Then it wouldn't be his fault. Pretty damn' sneaky, he thought, but that was the way it had to be. She'd be safer on the boat anyway.

It wasn't her fault that Shandy had used her. She was a real fine woman . . . But that had nothing to do with the whole business. Shandy, damn his black thieving heart, had dumped her on Mordecai to keep him from getting near the Rocky Mountain train.

It smelled like a fish eater's camp: Shandy meeting there in the Beaver Palace with them American Company thieves, after he'd sent out a Rocky Mountain train that was crippled, according to Ree, by having poor animals; Mordecai losing everything but his pants and getting rushed out of St. Louie when his brains was all numb. Just before that the American Company had been buying mules by the acre, and then working all night at their warehouse. Sure, they were hustling out a pack train. There was only one place where it was going, too.

Ree wasn't working with them. He hated their guts and they had no use for him. Who was he working for, spying around like he'd been doing? For Shandy?

Someone on shore began to play a mandolin. Voyageurs on their way to Union struck up a lively song. Let them sing. They wouldn't have much to sing about after they went to work for American. The boatmen tending the boiler rose and threw on more wood. "That'll hold her for a spell," one of them said. "Let's sneak over and have a listen on the island. Might get a drink too."

The boatmen went ashore. They would have howled like fiends if they had seen how free Mordecai made with their lines a few moments later. He cut rope to bind together firewood for a raft. He lowered the raft over the side and secured it, and then went forward and scratched on the canvas where Rhoda was sleeping.

"Ree?" she asked.

"Not him, it's me." Not everything in the world was Ree, Mordecai thought disgustedly. "Not so loud." He glanced at the island. "Get up real quiet. We're leaving the boat."

"What?" Rhoda stuck her head out of the shelter.

"We're leaving."

"When?"

"Right now. Can you swim?"

Rhoda was silent for a time. "Yes, but —"

"Good. Get ready. And you can't take all that pile of foofaraw you brought along."

Mordecai knew she was staring hard at him through the darkness. "You're actually saying we're going to leave the *Rosebud* tonight?"

"Yup! Right now." That ought to do it, Mordecai figured. No white woman that ever was born would crawl out of a warm bed and swim the Big Muddy at night. He grinned to himself. It was sneaky but it would work, and it would leave Ree stuck with Rhoda.

74

"Why can't I take my baggage?" Rhoda asked.

"I got only a small raft to float stuff on." Just about big enough for Old Belcher, it was.

"Make it bigger then. I'll be ready in ten minutes, but I'm taking all my baggage."

"You mean you're going?" Mordecai's satisfied grin slid into a heap.

"If this is the way it has to be done, I'm going. You're supposed to know your business, so I won't argue. Make the raft big enough to carry my things."

Mordecai rose and walked away. She wasn't bluffing. Now what the hell was he going to do?

He made the raft bigger.

Shortly afterward Rhoda began to carry her heap of plunder over to him. The boat was lifting gently, as if it lay on peaceful water. Rhoda paused to peer into the blackness toward the west bank.

"It ain't going to be easy," Mordecai said.

"Yes, I can see you're making it as difficult as possible."

"You can stay with the boat."

"And be forever getting to Fort Cass, certainly so late that I would miss Elisha? You've tried every way you could to discourage me, Mr. Price, and I know you were sure I wouldn't leave this boat tonight. Ree warned me that you'd probably suggest something like this."

"He did, huh?" Mordecai muttered.

"If this is the way it must be, I'm going — unless *you* decide to back out."

Hell was afloat and no pitch hot. Mordecai damned Ree and the stubbornness of the woman in the same thought. Now she had him over a log, and his pride wouldn't let him squeal for mercy. He slipped over the side, down into the water to his chest as he held to the mooring line. "Let your plunder down. Give me the rifle last thing."

She lowered her luggage. Mordecai lashed it on the raft. On the very top of the pile he tied Old Belcher and his own meager traveling equipment. "Let's go," he said.

She was scared then, and her voice showed it. "I — I can't see the raft."

Mordecai climbed back to the deck. "You going or not?" Looked like he was going to win after all.

He heard the rustling of garments. Rhoda thrust a pile of skirts at him. In the dim starlight he saw the whiteness of her legs. By Old Caleb! She had stripped to the breechclout! "What are you doing, woman?"

"I can't swim in skirts." Rhoda went to the rail. She hesitated. With an armful of skirts and his mouth hanging open, Mordecai stared at the pale nakedness of her legs. "I can't see the raft," she said.

The voices of men that had broken away from the crowd on the island made Mordecai look over his shoulder. The stokers were coming back. "Git!" he said.

"I can't see down there."

Mordecai picked her up. She gasped and tried to fight away from him when his wet buckskins touched the flesh of her legs. He dropped her over the side. She gasped again when she struck the water. Mordecai slid down the rope. She had found the raft and was clinging to it.

"Don't put no great weight on that," Mordecai warned.

Her voice trembled as she said, "My skirts! What did you do with my skirts?"

Mordecai had dropped them on deck when he picked her up. He hauled himself back up the line until his head was above the planks. The stokers were coming aboard. With one hand he raked the pile of garments to him and dropped them toward the raft. He let himself back down once more into the icy water.

He could hear the stokers talking as he cut the mooring line. In his free hand he held the float that he'd tied to the end of a tow rope. The raft began to move. It bumped lightly against the hull of the *Rosebud* until Mordecai, swimming deep and strong, pulled it clear.

There was a brief stretch of quiet inshore water and then they were caught up in the swift, powerful current. The seething sound of the Big Muddy all around them was like some terror from an unknown time. The darkness made the river seem limitless. The sound of the mandolin grew faint.

Mordecai had cut himself an awful big hunk off the plug and he knew it. He shared some of the Indians' mystic dislike for action after darkness; but after a brief feeling of having made a bad mistake, his white man's mind steadied down to the hard, logical facts of his position.

All they had to do was swim across the river.

"Is Old Belcher riding good?" he asked.

For a moment, when Rhoda didn't answer, he had a terrible fear that she had gone under. Then she spoke up, all shaky and mad. "To hell with your Old Belcher!"

She was scared and sore at the same time, and that was good. By Old Ephraim, he had to allow she was a heap different than any white woman he had ever known. And maybe in some things she had more guts than any squaw he'd ever conswansummated with, too.

Slowly, steadily, he pulled for the far shore.

Mordecai had studied the river before dark. It wasn't so bad. All you had to do was stay afloat and angle across, and after a half-mile, maybe, you'd come in. That is, if a log or rolling tree didn't sweep you under for good.

Twice he spied the bulk of huge trees heaving their sluggish way downstream. It took a heap of hard swimming to clear one of them.

After her one outburst he heard no more from Rhoda until they came ashore. Her teeth were chattering then. She and Mordecai fought their way up the bank, slipping and falling in the mud. Once in the trees Rhoda dropped flat on the ground.

"No time for resting," Mordecai said. "We got to get to that Ottoe camp and trade for some hosses."

"You son of a bitch!"

Mordecai was getting the plunder off the raft. The woman's outraged cry startled him, and then he grinned. "Fine talk for a missionary."

78

"God forgive me, but that's what you are for getting me into that river!"

"You're out now. Quit bellyaching, woman." Mordecai carried her stuff into the trees. Damned if she didn't have more baggage than an English brigade leader. "Let's go."

"You're not going to hurry me!"

"That's where you're wrong. I got reason to be in a hurry."

Rhoda didn't rise. Mordecai heard her stirring the contents in one of her bags. "Come on," he said impatiently.

"I lost my shoes in the river. Shut your mouth."

Mordecai felt in his possibles sack. "You can tie on a pair of my moccasins until you —"

"No, thank you! I've not become a savage — yet."

Mordecai fretted at the slow progress they made during the night. Near dawn he located the Ottoe camp by the barking of a dog, but it was well after daylight when they came in sight of it, a small group of lodges standing against trees near a stream.

Rhoda stopped instantly, lifting one foot as if to rest it. "Are they friendly?"

"Friendlier than white people. Come on."

It was her first contact with Indians in their native state. She stayed close to Mordecai all the time. They came pouring from their lodges, tall men, wide, shapeless women, naked children. An old man who had nothing to distinguish him but gray hair and the biggest pocked nose Rhoda had ever seen rode out with several younger men to meet them.

They all looked grim as fate, but after Mordecai made signs and talked, the Indians fell off their ponies and began a hugging match.

Rhoda found herself ignored. From that time Mordecai, too, seemed to forget all about her.

She found herself in a lodge of women. They poked at her and poked at her possessions, jabbering and grunting their alien tongue. These of course were not mission Indians; there must be a great difference. They placed food before her and she ate, thinking of dog. It wasn't dog, she kept telling herself, but still she kept thinking of dog all the time. An old hag pulled her shoes off and stared at them, laughing as she showed the other women the strange footgear.

And where was Mordecai? She heard him talking, heard his laughter. He came briefly to the lodge and took away one of her bags, waving aside her protests by saying there was no time to explain at the moment.

She knew a few words of Flathead talk, things that Elisha had written her, but they were no good here. The only English the Ottoe women knew was either blasphemous or obscene, but they used those few words over and over, delighted to display their knowledge of white men's talk.

They goggled at the comb she took from her personal pack to rake the Missouri mud from her hair. When she started to put her hair up again, the women raised an unearthly grunting. They braided it for her, and her protests availed nothing.

From the stock of goods she was taking to Elisha she gave them presents, combs and beads and small mirrors. Every woman in camp appeared instantly, it seemed. She didn't know whether she was giving too much or too little. Later she would have to talk to Mordecai about such things.

Later . . . All at once the strangeness and newness of her position assailed her. That terrifying swim across the river was something she would never forget. And then the dawn on the big, empty land. She had been dead-tired then, ready to drop, but Mordecai had kept striding on.

At this moment, if she could return to the safety of the boat, she would go gladly. Why, the trip was hardly started, and her only protector was a surly brute of a Mountain Man. True, he had not been forward. In fact, he hardly seemed to know that she was a woman.

But from now on how would he be?

She was tired and frightened. She thought of her aunt in Massachusetts, far, far away. The heavy odor of the lodge oppressed her, and the dark, barbaric look of the Ottoe women added to her feelings of lostness.

Two old hags spread robes for her, waving the other women from the lodge. They gave her toothless, wrinkled grins and patted the robes. These people were friendly, God forgive all other thoughts about them! Maybe they could take her back to the *Rosebud* later. Surely, with their help, she could catch it again when it stopped for wood someplace.

She stretched out on the robes to sleep, placing her bags and packs close to her. But before she went to sleep she asked forgiveness for calling Mordecai Price an evil name. But she had been so relieved to get ashore, and then so furious about the ordeal he had put her through, that she couldn't help it.

Thinking of it made her mad again. That was exactly what he was for forcing her to swim!

Though he tried to hurry his trading with Fast Runner's band, Mordecai spent until midmorning getting the outfit he needed. Somebody had given Rhoda good advice about trade goods, and that was a fact. She had plenty of beads, good flints, and a heap of vermilion in paper twists, as well as some foofaraw like tiny hawking bells.

From Fast Runner he learned that the Rocky Mountain train, with Big Nose Yenzer in charge, had gone upriver ten days ago. Considering that they were traveling light with the pack critters to pick up goods from the keelboat at the mouth of the Platte, they weren't making very good time. Of course, it took a little time to beat a pack outfit into shape. Big Nose was the man to do it, too.

During the trading Mordecai sensed that something was being withheld, some fact that was tickling the Ottoes. Fast Runner asked him where he had got his squaw, and if she rode as badly as she walked, since Rhoda had been limping when the Ottoes first saw her. One young buck offered to trade two poor ponies for her; but all that still wasn't touching the real reason for their amusement, Mordecai was sure.

He was about ready to get Rhoda and leave, when Ree stepped out of a lodge, grinning and yawning at the same time. "You could have saved us all the swim, Mord. They had a skiff."

The Ottoes laughed. They didn't understand the words, but the surprise on Mordecai's face was enough. It was very funny, one white man trying to outrun another, only to discover the second man 'way ahead.

Mordecai didn't think it was funny. "What are you up to, Ree?"

"Just going to rendezvous, is all, like you."

"You working for Shandy, damn you?"

The look of disgust Ree showed was an honest answer. "I think the same as you do about Shandy." Ree showed his temper. "Who says I can't come here, do some trading for horses, and have me a nap?"

"You got that right," Mordecai said darkly. He went to get Rhoda.

It stunned him to see the way she looked when the Indian women woke her. Her hair was braided. Put the right clothes on her and she could danged nigh pass as a Cheyenne woman. That hadn't been Mordecai's idea when he did some trading with one of the women, but it sure struck him now.

"I got some clothes for you." He pointed to a woman holding a sack-like Indian dress and several pairs of moccasins.

"Thank you, but I'm quite comfortable in my own —" Rhoda saw Ree. She gave a happy cry of surprise and went to him. "Where in the world did you come from?"

Mordecai watched them grumpily. It was a sight, the way Ree smirked. Mordecai took the clothes from the squaw and tied them on one of the pack horses. "Let's go!"

Rhoda came over to him. "Since Ree has joined us, and is going on with us, I've decided to continue by land."

"Who said he was going with us?" Mordecai growled.

"Why should you object, Mr. Price?"

Mr. Price! Mordecai was getting sick of the politeness. Well, since Ree was here it wouldn't hurt to have him along, especially since Mordecai could watch him and maybe find out what he was up to. "Let's go, then," he said.

He leaned against his pony while Ree helped the woman with her plunder. Took a whole damn' pack horse to carry just her stuff, it did. Some of her trade goods were now in Mordecai's possibles sack. He'd straighten that out with her later.

Look at that Ree! Acting like a Memphis gentleman, the way he was bustling around to help her. Even helped her into the saddle. The Injun women tittered and covered their mouths. Couldn't blame 'em, seeing something like that. Old Caleb and his seven brothers! She was going to ride sidewise. In a Sioux saddle, high in front and harder than the devil's heart. It wasn't made for doin's like that, but let her find out for herself.

Mordecai took out with his two pack horses. Ree had a pack horse of his own, but that was his lookout. For a while Ree stayed behind with Rhoda, and then rode up to join Mordecai.

"Had her about convinced on going back, and then you showed up," Mordecai said.

"Promised to take her, didn't you? Been paid, ain't you?"

Mordecai looked at Ree darkly. "You going all the way to rendezvous?"

"Going toward it, but I ain't sure just when I'll get there," Ree answered.

They kept looking back. Both of them could see how miserable and uncomfortable the woman was in her unnatural position in the saddle. Ree started to turn back toward her.

"Leave her be," Mordecai growled. "We got a thousand miles to go, and I ain't starting to hand-teach her things she can learn herself — if she's got a lick of sense."

"Wal, the pore little thing she —"

"Leave her be!"

Rhoda stopped in a grove of trees. Fretting, Mordecai and Ree waited for her to come out. They waited fifteen minutes.

When she came out she was riding astride. Ree gawped like a stranded fish when he saw her long ruffled pantaloons that reached almost to her ankles. Her skirts were pulled high and bunched around the saddle. Ree opened and closed his mouth without speaking, and then said: "Wagh! So that's what they're wearing under all them skirts these days. She looks like a Mandan dancer getting ready to cut a whingding!"

After a while Mordecai noticed that she had unbraided her hair and put it up.

CHAPTER
SEVEN

They had been two days above Chouteau's Landing when they left the *Rosebud*. The way Mordecai sized things, the best way was to cut over to the West Fork of the Soldier, go north to the Big Blue, and then angle west toward the Platte.

Even counting on the miserable quality of the mules and horses in the Rocky Mountain pack train — if Ree was telling the truth, Mordecai was about ten days behind the pack train and would do well to overtake it this side of Chimney Rock, considering how Rhoda was dragging along.

The first night she hadn't even eaten when she fell out of the saddle. She just flopped onto the robes Ree spread for her and went to sleep. The next day Ree had to lift her into the saddle, and a fine picture that made, with those ruffled pantaloons whisking past his face.

In spite of his determination to make her travel fast, Mordecai hadn't been able to do it. She sure wasn't no squaw when it come time to pick up and move. It would take the gristle off a painter's tail, the way Ree was lavishing attention on her. Every day he rode beside her, swinging his arms around and talking. You'd think he was the man who discovered the Rocky Mountains, to hear his stories. He was back there now.

Mordecai signaled for him to come on ahead, and after a time Ree came trotting up. "What's up, old hoss?"

"You working for the American Company, Ree?"

Ree haired up instantly. "Easy with that kind of talk. I ain't took up outright with thieves yet."

Mordecai laid it down flat and hard. "I'm thinking Jim Shandy made a crooked deal with the American. I'm thinking they got a pack train coming behind us, figuring to beat the Rocky Mountain train to rendezvous."

"So?"

"You been hinting at it, Ree. Why?"

"Maybe to help you out, seeing as how you set such great store by the Sublettes and old Bridger."

Mordecai glanced back toward Rhoda. "Where do you figure to make beaver out of it?"

Ree grinned. "Where could I, if I ain't working for neither outfit?"

"I'll kill you if you lied about that, Ree."

Ree still grinned, but his eyes were as hard as Mordecai's. "You might try to, Mord."

They stared at each other. Ree wasn't the clumsy, overeager brat Mordecai had taken up the river long ago. He'd walked the high country and wolfed out the winters with the toughest of them. He'd swallowed grizzly hair. The wilderness was in his blood now, and nobody was going to scare him down.

Mordecai remembered how he'd got his name that time on the prairie three days above the Ree villages, when he was still so green that he'd blundered into a Ree war party and got himself unhorsed. When the rest had caught up to him, there he was sitting on the packs of furs beside a dead pony, with his rifle in one hand and a pistol in the other, challenging the six Indians in front of him.

He'd scrooched around so much on the packs of furs, turning to try to cover all the Rees, that his pants was plumb polished on the seat. There he was, white and defiant, with a frozen grin. When Mordecai had asked him why he hadn't stood up face to face with the Indians, Ree had said, "Couldn't. Got a busted leg."

It was a long time ago. Beaver were everywhere then. Mordecai looked at Ree with mixed feelings, thinking how the years were spinning away, the years that had made a shock-headed, big-footed kid into a man who could grin at Mordecai Price and say without bluff what Ree had just said.

"I'll kill you, if I ever start to," Mordecai said.

They were friends and they understood each other, so they didn't carry it any further.

Ree said, "I'll be glad to get to buffler country. I swear them Ottoes made this dried meat we got from carcasses they found floating down the Big Muddy."

"Likely," Mordecai said.

Rhoda called plaintively, "Don't we stop for nooning?"

"Up there by the little crick ahead," Mordecai said. "Tell her, Ree. You tell her everything else."

"A man would think you are jealous. If you was a missionary, Mord, you might have a chance with her." Ree grinned and swung back toward the woman.

She wasn't stiff, Mordecai observed, when she dismounted and walked into the bushes beside the small stream. She was hell for tidying up when there was water around. He and Ree sat cross-legged on the ground and munched dried buffalo.

When she came back from the stream, Ree put a buffalo robe down for her to sit on. She chewed dried meat and drank from a small bottle encased in a weave of rushes. Her face was really brown now, Mordecai observed. She looked as healthy as a young Teton girl.

"How far is it to the Platte now?" she asked.

"I can still smell the Missouri," Mordecai said. "If you listen hard, you can hear the dogs barking in Fast Runner's camp." He rolled on his side and closed his eyes.

As if to cover up for the rebuff, Ree asked, "What kind of coon is this feller you're marrying, Rhoda?"

"A fine man. His life is devoted to bringing Christianity to the Indians."

"No offense, but they don't hardly need it. About everything they get from us gives 'em a bellyache or makes 'em madder than a bee-stung bear. Seems to me like your feller Elisha Slocum could've stayed to home and done something useful like making rifle guns or —"

"You have your views, of course, being a trapper," Rhoda said. "You may not know that the Nez Percés sent a delegation all the way to St. Louis, pleading for someone to come and teach them Christianity."

Mordecai opened one eye slightly. When Rhoda got all het up about something, her face was bright and alive and she looked you square in the eye. She was doing that now to Ree.

"I know about them Nez Percés," Ree said, "but they wasn't looking for quite what some folks said."

"What do you mean?"

"Oh, they said they wanted to learn about the white man's God, sure enough, but what they meant was they wanted to get some of his medicine so they could hunt better and kill their enemies better and —"

"Are you a Christian, Ree?" the woman asked.

There, let Ree get his tail in a crack. He'd started this thing. Mordecai watched through his slitted eye.

"Wal," Ree said, "look at it this way, I don't do no killing except when it's necessary, or robbing or stealing, except from Indians, and they treat me the same way, so there ain't no bad feelings about that. When I marry up with an Indian woman, I treat her pretty good, usually."

That ought to sweep her back some, Mordecai thought, but danged if she didn't stare at Ree and then start to grin. Then she sobered up, like she thought she wasn't acting proper.

"Doesn't any Mountain Man ever go back and settle down?" she asked.

"Ain't nothing left for most where they come from."

Rhoda glanced toward Mordecai. "Nothing for him either?"

"Naw!" Ree said. "He'd just as well been born in a grizzly den up in the Big Horns. He'll be out here till he goes under."

It riled Mordecai to have his fate decided so freely by Ree. He rose and said, "Let's go."

"You're always in a hurry," Rhoda protested.

"Got to save them Nez Percés and Flatheads."

Mordecai saw the hot temper in Rhoda's eyes. She could get haired up, sure enough, like when she'd cussed him after that swim from the boat. She was some like a Snake squaw he'd once had . . . Them Snakes was the prettiest of all, and a heap more steady than a Crow woman, to boot. No, no, Rhoda was no squaw. She was white, and when it came loving time she was probably like a board.

Mordecai pushed all that aside. They'd been making better time the last few days, but it still wasn't good enough if he figured to overtake the train soon. A good outfit could make up to twenty-five miles a day, and until Mordecai saw for himself what kind of critters Big Nose had he must figure that the train was going full speed.

The woman was slowing him down, she was. Just what Shandy had figured too. *Very important for the Rocky Mountain to take a missionary across the prairies . . .*

Mordecai cursed himself. It was no trouble to be a fool, and when you was stupid drunk, it was even simpler.

They made fair time crossing the empty uplands northwest of the Blue Earth. As the trees began to fall away behind them, the immensity of the plains became apparent. On the second day they saw a furious rainstorm slanting darkly into the earth far away in the south. The knocking balls of thunder rolled around them as they traveled in clear sunshine, and they could see the crackling thrusts of lightning darting like fiery tongues of snakes.

Riding alone in the lead, Mordecai looked back. Ree and the woman were laughing about something.

They struck the wide sprawled Platte. On the south bank were the marks of the Rocky Mountain train. Soon afterward Mordecai came across the remains of a mule. The wolves had cleaned it to the bones, but Mordecai examined a fragment of the hide and figured the animal hadn't been dead a month. That was as close as he wanted to say, although he was sure the mule was from the train.

About two hundred critters, he guessed. It had rained here a few days ago, and he refused to make any close judgment about the age of the tracks. The best he would allow was that he hadn't gained a mile on the train.

Ree thought differently. "About a week old," he said. "We'll catch up, and then what are you going to do?"

"I'll worry about that." The real worry was what the American Company was doing. They had Blas Wimarr's mules, big ground-eating brutes that could walk any pony that ever lived into the ground. If the packers rode mules and set a steady pace, they'd pass the Rocky Mountain train days before it could reach the rendezvous.

"You think the American is coming?" Mordecai asked.

Ree mocked him with a grin. "Bet my rifle on it."

"It pleases you, huh?"

"I don't suffer none for any fur company. I been robbed of beaver by all of them. That's why I don't understand why you're willing to kill yourself for Rocky Mountain."

It wasn't the company. Rocky Mountain was just a name; it was the men who made the outfit who evoked the fierce, unquestioning loyalty in Mordecai. You stuck by the friends who'd stuck by you, else why was beaver made? And maybe, by Old Ephraim, you were some proud of the name too. Ree, who'd been a free trapper more years than he'd stayed with different companies, just couldn't understand how a man felt.

Mordecai increased the pace. It surprised him some that Rhoda stood up to it. Damn' fool thing for a woman who could ride like that to be marrying a missionary.

Three days up the Platte they found two dead horses. This time there were packsaddles, the rawhide eaten away by small varmints. Not much of the horses was left. Mordecai figured the members of the train had eaten them, since there wasn't a sign of game in the whole land.

Weight distributed around from those two dead horses would help break down more pack animals in time. It wasn't too early for a few critters to be dying, or weakening so bad they had to be shot; nevertheless, Mordecai was worried.

Ree read all the signs and didn't say anything, but his look said: What did I tell you?

Mordecai decided to make up some lost time, to travel all night. What could Ree do if he found himself left with Rhoda? Not a thing but bring her along. They'd catch up with the train in time. Meanwhile, Mordecai would be finding out for certain what was wrong with the outfit. If the pack animals were like Ree said, then it was up to Mordecai to ride on ahead of the train and do some trading with whatever Injuns he could find.

When they camped that night, Ree was spreading his robe on the sparse grass when he dropped it suddenly and jammed his rifle butt down on a rattlesnake sliding toward a hole. He crushed the snake's head thoroughly and then kicked it aside.

Rhoda watched in horror when he spread his robes over the burrow. "Aren't there more snakes down that hole?"

"They'd better be," Ree said, "or they ain't going to get in tonight."

Mordecai laughed for the first time in days. Rhoda gave him an angry look as she walked away toward a small stream that ran into the Platte.

"I say she shines, Mordecai. You think so yourself."

Mordecai grunted, watching the woman as she knelt at the stream.

"Too bad she's going all the way to Cass to marry a missionary," Ree said.

"Is it?"

"I might change that."

Mordecai gave Ree a stabbing look. "She'd look good in your lodge somewhere against the Tetons this winter, with the snow belly deep. Be a great help with furs too."

"I ain't going to live like no Indian forever, Mord."

"So? What are you going to do then?"

"I may think of something better." Ree gave his careless, go-to-hell grin, and held some secret behind his eyes.

He was tricky, Ree. Ambitious, too, and that was one reason he was always howling about the small returns for his beaver, where other trappers had their spree and forgot what yesterday had been. Mordecai's suspicions of Ree came to the surface again, and with them a slow-forming jealousy because of what he had said about taking Rhoda away from her missionary.

Maybe he could. Mordecai could do the same thing, he guessed, if he wanted to. It was a treacherous thought. Mordecai watched Rhoda coming back from the stream. She walked straight. Oh, it was nothing against her that she was a white woman, after all. It was just that she wasn't suited to the kind of life Mordecai led. By Old Ephraim, she did have a good walk, and a high, proud look about her. She pitched right in around the camp, too, not a bit afraid of getting her hands dirty. Mordecai couldn't help speculating on how she'd be in bed. In fact, he'd done considerable wondering about it.

He saw Ree watching him with a mocking grin. "She don't shine, huh?"

"Missionary," Mordecai growled.

"I been thinking on something, Mord. We're friends, but was you to try to sneak out of camp some night before we catch that train, thinking to leave me stuck with her, we wouldn't be friends no longer."

"Wouldn't that be turrible?"

"It might. There's something I'm going to tell you when the time comes, but I won't if you try anything sneaky against me."

"Who said I was aiming to sneak out?" Actually, there wasn't much to be gained by striking out for the train ahead of the others. For one thing, if Mordecai rode his Ottoe pony extra hard to overtake the train, it might play out and then he'd be in a worse fix than before. Being afoot on the prairie just didn't shine. Another thing, Ree had already guessed what he had in mind, and that sort of took the polish off the idea.

Mordecai watched Rhoda coming toward camp. He wasn't much given to making up his mind and then changing it, the way he'd just done. He wondered if she was another good reason he didn't want to go rushing on alone, leaving Ree to bring her along.

"See them pony tracks today?" he asked.

"Pawnees, I made it out. Hunting party."

"Yup. Could stand a bait of buffler myself," Mordecai said, still watching Rhoda.

CHAPTER
EIGHT

The lone buffalo that came over the rolling hills the next afternoon was an old bull all ragged and shedding. It went rocking toward the river as if it had been hard run over a great distance.

Mordecai stopped and signaled the others to come up to him quickly.

Rhoda sat her pony between the two men. It was the first buffalo she had ever seen; but, like the two men, she forgot about it and watched the silent land ahead. Even Ree had lost his good nature. His eyes squinted and his lips were grim.

What Ree had told her about the life of Mountain Men had revealed much, but only in words. Now she saw their way of life in their expressions. Silence, a brown, gaunt grimness in the faces. Savageness as they held their stubby rifles against a danger not yet seen. Everything in their attitude was a picture of aggressive survival. A matted, awkward-looking beast had crossed their path, and instantly they were as dangerous as whatever threat lay beyond the hills.

The loneness, the far strangeness of her being here on this desolate plain with two men she really didn't know, came to her strongly. The Cause was something dim and poorly suited for her present mood. Strong declarations by stern men in meetings of the Missionary Society no longer made good armor. She was a scared and lonely woman, but she sat her pony quietly, holding back everything inside her, waiting for what lay ahead.

They were not long in coming, seven or eight wild-haired riders skimming down the hills on ponies. They were after the bull, but they stopped and bunched together when they saw the three motionless riders. And then they shot apart again and came rushing on with high-drawn yells.

"Pawnees, sure enough," Mordecai said.

They came screaming in and then slid their ponies to a walk and made a sedate approach, lithe, dusty men, brown and savage. Even as they changed to their slow approach, Rhoda could not be sure of their intentions. She saw squaws coming over the hill with laden pack horses. A small group of riders veered away from them and went in pursuit of the bull, now floundering across the river in heaving surges.

Ree and Mordecai made signs. Rhoda watched their movements, for these were part of the things she must learn if she would be of great practical help to Elisha Slocum. In the days of riding beside Ree she had learned something of sign talk. Here now was her first test.

She flunked it miserably. She was too busy worrying about the intentions of the Pawnees. Ree and Mordecai got down to smoke and talk. Rhoda noticed that they never relaxed, and that their rifles were always close at hand.

The squaws came up with meat in green hides. Most of them gathered around Rhoda, still on her pony. She had ripped the seams of her oldest skirt to simplify riding, and better to cover what she wore beneath when she was in the saddle. The squaws soon discovered the pantaloons, and tugged at them in astonishment.

With half a mind Mordecai heard the Pawnees' long complaint about the niggardly ways of Big Nose, who by now, they said, was about five camps toward the mountains. He heard also the things the squaws were saying of Rhoda. They doubted that she could scrape a hide or boil a dog to suit her man. Which one was her man? She could never have a baby because of those strange pants she wore beneath her dress. The Pawnee women made much of that point. Some of their gestures were understandable in any language.

Damn their heathen hearts! Mordecai kept a grave face and heard the hunters tell how Big Nose had given them only a little tobacco and small gifts, no powder, no firewater, while all the time he was passing through their country and making the hunting very poor for Pawnees.

Perhaps all this was because Big Nose was so greatly worried about his lack of good horses, Mordecai suggested.

An Indian spokesman said that it was true that Big Nose was carrying much of value in a poor boat. But again: Big Nose was very selfish.

Once more Mordecai dived into Rhoda's trade articles, some of which he had transferred to his possibles sack so that there would be little to display at one time. He gave out everything from the sack, which was not a great deal.

The Pawnees were not satisfied. Did not the white men have more presents in the packs upon the ponies?

No more, Mordecai said, and rose with his rifle in his hands. Ree scrubbed dust from his teeth and spat and shook his head. No more. Though still tormented by the squaws, Rhoda watched the men and saw why two who were trespassers could face down fifteen who were owners of the land: the steel springs of savagery in the two white men were strong and finely set, to be triggered by calculation and not by impulse. Ree and Mordecai were not afraid to die and not afraid to kill. Somewhere in the mountains they had sloughed those basic fears.

The Pawnees saw with straight eyes and became satisfied with what they had received, since it was obvious that they would get no more, unless some of them cared to die.

They gave the white men meat, a liver wrapped in hide, hump ribs dark with dried blood. And then the hunters swept away on their ragged ponies, with the squaws following with the pack horses.

The end of Rhoda's fear came out in a long breath that she kept soundless. "You're free with my possessions."

"No heap of difference whether we spread the Gospel on the plains or at your husband's mission," Mordecai said.

"Elisha Slocum is not my husband — yet, and he doesn't use goods to *bribe* the Indians, Mr. Price."

"What else, then — to rob 'em in trade?"

"Obviously, you're no Christian," Rhoda said.

"Maybe not. Ree is, of course."

They rode on up the lonely river.

Rhoda watched in disgust when Ree and Mordecai cut strips from the liver and ate it raw, chewing as they rode. They offered her some, but she shook her head violently.

They camped that night near where the Pawnees had killed their buffaloes. Ree roasted the hump ribs. Clean shaven, Mordecai and Ree let the juices run down their chins as they ate, wiping their hands wherever it was handy — until they saw Rhoda watching them. Ree was the first to falter. Surreptitiously he began to wipe his chin with his hand, and then with a bunch of grass.

Before he realized it, Mordecai was doing the same. Wagh! It was something, what a woman could do to a man; but he guessed it wouldn't hurt to be some polite, and he remembered some of the long-ago lessons his mother had pounded into him.

She'd been a fine woman, Mordecai's ma, out of Virginia when she was seventeen. Pa had gone back after her from Kentucky, taking along a spare horse for her to ride on in style. But along the way somebody stole one horse from him, and then the other broke its leg, so Pa had to walk his bride all the way back to Kentucky.

Mordecai was their only child. There wasn't any chance for others because the Shawnees got Pa one morning when he was opening the hog shed. After that Ma married a cooper in Maysville. When Mordecai was eight he went to work for his stepfather, who treated Mordecai every bit as good as he did his own children. But there wasn't much to scraping away at barrel staves, not with the Ohio running clear and beautiful just under the limestone banks below the cooper's shop.

It became a little too much for Mordecai to see folks forever going down the Beautiful River. When he was twelve, he told his ma he guessed it was time for him to run away. She wasn't old at thirty, like a lot of women. She was tall and dark and strong. She made Mordecai wait a spell to be sure he still wanted to run away, and when he still wanted to she gave him five Spanish dollars and his pa's flintlock.

Mordecai always figured to go back and see her sometime, but she died of slow fever six years after he left.

Sitting cross-legged by the tiny fire on the Platte, Mordecai kept thinking about his ma. Her early years in Kentucky must have been pretty bad, not like the Rockies now, to be sure, but awful rough just the same; yet she'd never gone sour under adversity.

There were all kinds of women, of course . . . He looked across the fire at Rhoda, and caught her in the act of staring at him; not angry, as she often was because of the things he said to her, or ornery because she knew he was haired up over having her shoved off on him by Jim Shandy, but sort of like she was wondering what he was thinking inside him.

He stared back at her. In some ways she was as fine as Ute buckskin. She didn't remind him none of his ma, except in the way she took things without whining. He wondered what kind of coon this Elisha Slocum was. Right there and then, staring at Rhoda, Mordecai took a dislike to Slocum.

And Ree, he was watching with a little grin; Ree never missed anything.

Suddenly the prairie came alive with wolves, and then the lesser tones of the little wolves set in, until it sounded like a million of them out there where the Pawnees had butchered their kill. It was music to Mordecai's ears, but he saw Rhoda stiffen against the sounds.

"You get used to it," he said gruffly. He put his pipe away, sprinkled dirt on the tiny fire, then took his robes and stalked off into the darkness to sleep close to the picketed ponies.

The wolves snarled and growled all through the night, and the little wolves howled until dawn. At times Mordecai heard Rhoda turning restlessly in her robes.

For breakfast they ate cold meat. Mordecai watched Rhoda scraping congealed grease with a knife. He said: "It's better doin's at a mission, I hear. They got the Indians beat down to do the dirty work of cooking and the like."

Rhoda's eyes flashed. "They're not slaves. They work out of gratitude for what the mission does for them."

"Yeah." No matter what Mordecai said, it always came out wrong. He went to pull the picket pins.

They were riding briskly when the great, bursting sunrise of the plains jumped suddenly in the east. Rhoda went slower and slower to watch it, and then she stopped. Ree was beside her. "It's pretty at that," Ree said. "Like the biggest painted lodge you'll ever see."

Mordecai watched them dourly. They seemed much younger than he was, the woman with the strong and eager look, and Ree with his shaggy, sandy hair taking on a reddish look from the sunrise. The two of them loitered there, watching the explosion of colors on fluffy clouds. It was like they were seeing a future, like they were holding agreed, secret thoughts that Mordecai didn't know about. "It comes up every day!" he said. "Let's git!"

Mordecai set a hard pace. Because of the looks of the sunrise he was willing to bet Old Belcher against a Northwest fusee that it would rain before noon. Rain it did. The big wind came first, driving sand, flattening the sparse grass, jerking bushes near the river. Behind it was a mountain of rain, a leaden world of it.

The three of them were tightly grouped, with the pack animals close hauled behind them. They passed the bodies of three or four horses. That made about fifteen in all that Mordecai had seen. Big Nose Yenzer was making a run of it with the Rocky Mountain train, but he must be near at a standstill now, and the worst part of the trip was still ahead.

104

Ree had given Rhoda a blanket capote. "There just ain't no cover in this country," he said.

"So I see," she answered. "Our skins are waterproof."

The rain struck with an icy fury. In minutes the dusty, shedding hides of the ponies became wet and steaming. The pack ponies wanted to stop. Mordecai swung in behind them to keep them going. He pulled his wolfskin hat tight down around his ears, smelling the strong animal odor of it as soon as it was wet through.

He saw Rhoda's skirts, voluminous as they were, beginning to sag against her body where she had them hitched high about her lap. Her hair began to come down as the rain soaked it during gusts when the hood of her capote was driven back.

The force of the wind died away after a time, but the rain continued, ice-laden and steady. With water running down their fetlocks, the ponies slopped on, plodding through a dismal, gloomy world.

Rhoda's lips were blue, and she kept licking the water from them. "Does it rain like this in Oregon?"

"Hah!" Ree said. "I never was there when it wasn't doing twice as good as this. What do you think made the Pacific Ocean if it wasn't rain washing out of them Oregon woods?"

At intervals they got down to lead the ponies. Rhoda's long skirts dragged in the mud even while she tried to hold them up with one hand. Mordecai saw that her shoes were becoming shapeless and soggy. Stopping at noon would have made their misery worse by inaction. They went on steadily until it was time to camp for the night. It was still raining. Mordecai would have continued, but he saw that Rhoda was almost exhausted.

Mordecai had spent many a worse night, without even a poorly tanned buffalo robe to grow heavy and soggy around him; but he was glad when the rain wore out near dawn the next morning. The others rose when he did.

He saw the prospect of a clear sunrise, and all around the land was sparkling with water beads, a clean-washed land moving gently toward the mighty Rockies, yet unseen by days to travel, but clear in Mordecai's mind.

"We'll cook later in the morning," he said, "when the buffler chips dry out some."

The far distance grew misty with vapor when the sun struck with full force. A wind from the west was chill at first, but warmed gradually as they rode. Hours later, when they stopped for breakfast, the ground was almost dry.

Rhoda took one of her bags and disappeared over a small rise. When she returned, she had changed her clothes. Her hair was in two braids. She was defiant of Mordecai's keen stare.

"We still got them Indian clothes," he said, thinking to be helpful.

"Keep them for one of your women at rendezvous!"

"I ain't got no woman at rendezvous."

"Maybe not this year," Ree said. "But what happened to —" He shut up when Mordecai bore an angry look on him.

106

All that day Mordecai kept looking behind. It was far too early for the American train to be catching up, but the thought kept worrying him. No matter what a man thought of the American Fur Company, he had to respect their ruthless way of getting results; and Mordecai had tremendous respect for those tireless mules he'd help drive from Santa Fe.

He still didn't understand Ree's fix in this business. Ree said he wasn't working for nobody, and Ree generally told the truth, though often in a left-hand way that kept you guessing.

Mordecai signaled for Ree to come up beside him. Busily engaged in teaching Rhoda sign language, Ree took his time before jogging ahead to Mordecai. "What now?"

"I'm thinking you might be figuring to invite Hudson's Bay to the rendezvous."

"The hell!" Ree said genially.

"Just that." Hudson's Bay with their superior goods and master traders who could get along with Indians better than any outfit in the mountains. Mordecai guessed the British could bring a heap of whisky, too, if it was needful in the trading. Which it would be, certain.

"All I'm wondering is why would they need any inviting," Mordecai said. "Second thing, you ain't got time to get to Fort Boise and bring 'em back."

"Sure ain't." Ree glanced around to see how Rhoda was doing. Ornery devil lights were sparkling in his eyes. That had always been a giveaway with him, no matter how solemn he kept the rest of his face.

"Supposing Hudson's Bay was holding a pack train just over the mountains, on the Green, say. What for would they have to wait for word from you or anyone else?"

"Supposing they was doing just that," Ree said. "Maybe they was some leery about starting a fur war, less'n they was plumb sure us Americans was already starting it big amongst ourselves. The British don't *have* to stay west of the mountains."

Mordecai studied Ree hard and long. "The British ain't going to hold no pack train all the way from Vancouver somewheres in the mountains most of the spring just to make sure us Americans are trying to cut each other's throats."

"They might — if they knowed far enough in advance what could happen. How come you went clean to Santy Fee last robe season, Mord? Looking for beaver country, you bet. She ain't what she was, even when I first come out. 'Stead of fighting Injuns now to make your raises, it's fighting each other to grab up what plews there is at rendezvous.

"Damn' right the British would hang off and then come boiling in if they was real sure American and Rocky Mountain was trying to rob each other! She ain't going to last, Mord. They're all going to try to get it while they can. So am I."

"How?"

"I'll tell you when it's time." Ree grinned.

Mordecai tested him again. "Why'n't you take care of Rhoda, while I go on to catch the train?"

Ree shook his head. "You don't want to go that bad. You're scared to leave her alone with me. We'll all catch up, won't we? Then that no-good outfit Shandy sent out will get to rendezvous — in time. Likely won't be anybody left there by then, so you can take Rhoda on to Cass and turn her over to the missionary. Likely she won't even kiss you goodbye, the way you been treating —"

"You run on worse nor a crazy Piute squaw!"

Rhoda came riding up to them.

"We was just arguing about whisky," Ree said, in high humor. "Now Mord here, he claims it ain't good for a man. Beduddles his brains, he says, but I —"

"Mr. Price ought to know," Rhoda said. The wind lifted one of her split skirts and exposed the lower part of her pantaloons, badly discolored from rubbing against the wet hair of the pony.

"What are you going to do when them sculp-decorated leggin's wear plumb out?" Mordecai asked.

CHAPTER
NINE

Fat Cow Creek came down from nowhere into the North Fork. Usually there was only a trickle in it, but now it had flooded from rains, and although the water was going down, sand and silt on the far bank looked some troublesome to Mordecai.

The train had crossed here, and not more than two days back, judging from the looks of the mule that had either died or been shot on the near side. They'd butchered that one for meat, Mordecai observed.

He drove the pack ponies across, swimming his horse behind them. It didn't amount to nothing. He turned to watch Rhoda. She was all right until she let her pony laze off and drift down-stream. She got ashore in bad mud a few rods below Mordecai. The deep silt made the pony frantic. It tried to lunge out. It got in a hole and fell so suddenly that in spite of the high horn Rhoda sailed clean over the saddle and plopped in the mud.

Mordecai waited a little. When she didn't get up, he went slopping over to her and picked her up. Her mouth was shut tight. "You hurt?" he asked. He was holding her in his arms as he stood knee deep in mud.

Ree came splashing across the stream and plunged off his pony.

"You all right?" Mordecai would have sworn that the woman was cussing to herself, but maybe she was just working some of the mud off her lips.

"Of course I'm all right!" she said suddenly. "Put me down!"

Mordecai didn't put her down at once. He kept looking at her, wondering why he had thought her a helpless white woman. She wasn't no fat squaw, and she wasn't puny either. You didn't pick up any woman and not learn something about her. The outer parts of her eyes were startling white as she stared at him, as if she was wondering what kind of hoss he was.

Then she said again, "Put me down!"

Mordecai dropped her feet first into the mud and walked away. Ree came plowing over to help her. "She's all right," Mordecai said. "Long as her tongue's working, she's all right."

He pushed on hard immediately, not giving Rhoda a chance to rest or wash. The mud dried on her face and she brushed it away.

Late in the day Ree killed an antelope. Not far ahead a group of cottonwoods stood near the river. When Mordecai stopped for a few moments to watch Ree hog butchering the animal, Rhoda took one of the pack horses and went on ahead to the cottonwoods, calling back, "I'm camping here."

Mordecai looked at the sky. They could still make five miles before dusk. Ree wiped his bloody hands on his shirt and put his knife away. He slung the antelope up on his pony. "She's camping, Mord. Make your mind up to that." Sudden anger rose in him. "She ain't no damn' squaw to be run till she drops."

"Don't be telling me how to travel, Ree."

"Just leave her be in that grove," Ree said quietly. "She wants to clean up a little. You been treating her worse than any squaw."

Where tawny bluestem grew near the water seep at the far edge of the cottonwood grove, Rhoda's pony stopped suddenly. She tried to urge it on, to go toward the water, but the pony twisted sidewise and stopped again.

It didn't matter; she was close enough. She dismounted wearily and untied one of her bags on the pack horse. The clothes that Mordecai had got from the squaw — oh, God, how many days and miles back was that? — were lashed in a bundle on the horse. She took the bundle and let it drop at her feet.

The horses moved away from her. She knew the responsibility of taking care of them, but now it roused a dull anger in her. Let them go. Let the two savages out there on the prairie worry about them.

She sat down suddenly, weighted with utter weariness, and all the terrors and worries of the trip became a cumulative force that settled on her. The dirt upon her hands, the mud crusted in her braids, and the filthy condition of her clothes were abominations. She felt that she was sinking to the level of a beast because she had borne in calmness rigors that would have

112

appalled her had she known of them before she was actually exposed to them.

The swim from the *Rosebud* was still a nightmare. She could smell the odor of the Ottoe camp, and she could remember her fear at her first sight of the limitless plains. The icy rain and the exhaustion of stumbling through it, mile after mile, were things still fresh in her mind.

There was no return now. She must go on and on, eating bloody meat when it was available, or chewing the blue, chip-like jerky that Ree laughingly had said was made from drowned buffalo. Those great bloated carcasses that she had seen floating down the Missouri rose in her vision to nauseate her.

She had been so tired when she was thrown from her pony into the mud that all she could do was lie and grind her teeth in helpless fury. Then Mordecai had picked her up with an easy strength that gave her a feeling of being protected, but just for an instant, because when he could have shown concern, when he could have said something kind, he had merely asked if she was all right.

And then her spirit and her anger had flared at the gruffness of him. He was a brute who resented her being along, who was determined to make her miserable. She had vowed to show him that his rudeness meant nothing, that she could take any hardship that was offered, but now she felt worn down to the point of collapse.

And it was her time of the month.

She felt too tired and bitter and depleted to move a finger. She sat on the ground, nursing her apathy and tiredness. How many endless miles lay ahead, and what was at the end of them?

Elisha Slocum was someone she had known back home, a tall, fair youth with a fine tenor voice. What was he now? Out of her depression came the thought that she had been hurried and harried spiritually by the Missionary Society, rather than by some driving dedication within her.

But that was doubt, that was faltering. She could not admit how much she had been shaken by the coarse, offhand opinion of Ree Semple when he had said that the Nez Percés were merely seeking mystic powers and not the word of God, as white men knew it, when they came to St. Louis.

She looked back at the two men on the prairie. They were eating raw some part of the antelope Ree had killed. It was revolting. It had been bad enough when, almost at the point of physical collapse, and with her stomach all a-churn from her sickness, she had seen Ree's efficient knife slicing the white underbelly of the antelope, and had seen him roll the steaming stomach and insides of the animal out upon the grass.

I'm not a squeamish woman. I'm not a weakling, she told herself. But, O Lord, how far is it to Fort Cass?

She had her long full minutes of blackness and despair.

After that she rose, refusing to let depression grip her any longer. All her clothes must be washed, even though the stream put more silt into them than it removed.

She walked into the bluestem, going toward the river. The dry, singing rattles came from both sides of her. Terror compressed her whole being during the instant when she was stopping. The snake that struck did not rattle. It lay in a bare spot about two feet ahead of her, its powerfully muscled body thrown in a striking loop. Rhoda saw the grayish scales near its mouth, the pale segments of its underside, the pinched spots of its eyes, and then the down-striking flash of its wide-open mouth. And then the head of it was stuck in her heavy skirts, with its strong body writhing as the snake tried to draw free to strike again.

She leaped back and the fangs tore free. Its mouth adrip with venom, the reptile struck again, but she was clear of it then. She clung to the rough bark of a cottonwood tree as the snake slid away into the tall bluestem. One by one the rattling sounds stopped.

It didn't get me; I didn't feel it. She stared down at her outer skirt, then raised it slowly. Caught in the tight weave was a curved white needle, one of the fangs. She worked it out with a stick. A drop of amber fluid fell away from the broken end.

Mordecai called: "We want to get some wood from there. Don't be all day."

Anger against him, and reaction from the incident that had just happened, threw energy into Rhoda's bloodstream. At the moment the prairie and Mordecai Price had nothing that could make her afraid. "Shut your mouth!" she shouted.

She skirted the bluestem and went on to the stream.

When she came from the grove she had washed her clothes and hung them on limbs to dry. She had brushed the mud from her hair and braided it again. She was wearing the sack-like buckskin dress, caught around the middle with a belt, and moccasins.

Mordecai had given up going to the grove and had built a fire of buffalo chips. He stared at Rhoda as she came walking toward him, and for once had nothing unkind to say.

Ree smiled. "Fits, I'd say."

With a calmness she didn't feel, Rhoda kept her thoughts to herself. The dress, she knew, exposed her ankles and part of her legs when she walked. The freedom of her body underneath the garment made her feel indecent. A few weeks ago even the thought of wearing such a dress would have been dismissed instantly; but conditions were a little different now. Just until her own things dried, that was all.

Mordecai's critical stare seemed endless. "Wasn't for your legs being white, I'd say —"

"That I was a squaw. You think all women ought to be squaws, don't you, Mr. Price?"

"Didn't say it." Mordecai seemed embarrassed. "Didn't say so at all."

Ree walked toward the grove humming to himself. A few moments later they heard him breaking dry branches.

Rhoda stooped down to put a buffalo chip on the fire. Since she looked like a squaw, she guessed she could act like one too. She gave Mordecai a defiant

116

look. Actually, the use of buffalo chips as fuel hadn't bothered her a bit. A person would have to be stubborn and prudish beyond all reason to deny the natural and necessary customs of a strange land.

Revolted before by the sight of Ree gutting the antelope, she was now suddenly ravenously hungry when she looked at the butchered meat lying on the hide.

She owed something to the rattlesnake in the bluestem, terrifying as the encounter had been. It had jarred her completely out of the doldrums and made her so angry that she had forgotten for a time all her troubles. Not that she would voluntarily seek out another snake when she felt bad.

"It's too bad you didn't get a frying pan when you traded my things so freely with those Ottoes," she said.

"The natural way to cook meat is by roasting."

"I see. Did you eat nothing but roasted meat when you were a boy at home?"

"Not always," Mordecai said.

"Many of the *natural* things, then, are what you've learned from Indians since you came out here."

"All right, all right, I guess maybe I can rustle a fry pan when we catch the pack train." Mordecai shook his head. "You're going to be a great help to that missionary, telling him everything to do."

"I hope to be of some help." Rhoda held her head high and gave Mordecai a straight look.

You knew she was white, he thought, even when she looked danged nigh like a Cheyenne. Maybe there was Indian blood in her. He'd heard that there had been

Indians clean back on the Atlantic Coast in the early days. But it wasn't her being one or the other that was unsettling him.

It was just her being a woman that was stirring him up.

He went out to get the two ponies she'd turned loose.

Take a coon settled at a post like this Elisha Slocum was — then it was all right for him to have a white wife, provided she was a woman who could stomach the country. Rhoda could do that, he didn't doubt.

At dusk Mordecai was standing out from the camp, looking at the hills across the river. Even from a distance of ten rods the small fire, set in a depression, did not give much betraying light.

Ree was well back from it, as a man should be when the party was small. Rhoda was sitting on an apishamore smack on top of the flames, with the light in her eyes. What need was there for her to learn any different? She'd live in a cabin at some mission, with a fireplace to warm the place. She'd be surrounded by fat hand-fed Injuns that couldn't hold their own with the plains tribes, and in time her remembrance of coming out would get all mixed up with the things she saw around her day by day.

Mordecai went back to the camp. He raked dirt over the fire with the side of his moccasin. "We ain't no bunch of voyageurs."

He and Ree had been *compañeros* so long that they pretty well knew what was in each other's minds. The way Mordecai had it figured, Ree was about ready to

118

light out. Not knowing yet what he was up to, Mordecai reckoned he couldn't let him go.

Even so, Ree almost made it that night. Silent as smoke he skinned out right under Mordecai's nose and had his horses almost ready to go before Mordecai knew it.

After that it was different. Mordecai moved some quiet himself. It pleased him to get within ten feet of Ree before speaking.

"If you was a Crow horse thief, Ree, you'd be gone beaver right now."

"Danged if that ain't a fact," Ree said calmly.

"Just where you going, old hoss?"

"Free prairie. You always said so yourself."

Mordecai moved in a little closer. "We're getting close on the Rocky Mountain train, and you want to leave all of a sudden."

"Ain't wanting, Mord; I'm going."

Old Belcher was solid as a stone in Mordecai's hands. "Hudson's Bay got a pack train out there, like we talked about?"

"They could have, Mord."

Mordecai heard Rhoda coming up behind him. "I guess I'd better not let you go, Ree."

"There's just one thing you can do then."

"I'll do it. Get away from that pony, Ree."

Rhoda came up beside Mordecai. "What's the matter?"

"Nothing," Mordecai said. "Get back to your robes."

"I'm going," Ree said, "and I'll tell you one thing honest — I'm going to bring that Hudson's Bay pack train to the rendezvous. No hard feelings, Mord, just business."

"Just plain sneaking thievery." Mordecai cocked Old Belcher. "You know me, Ree."

"I won't stand for this!" Rhoda said. "I won't let —"

Mordecai swung his left arm back to brush the woman away. He touched her, but she ducked under his arm and came against him and grabbed Old Belcher. It caught him by surprise. She fought for his rifle with the fury of a Blackfoot squaw. Old Belcher went off. The flash showed Ree leaping in with drawn pistol.

The pistol crashed down on Mordecai's head. The next instant he was sitting on the ground with Rhoda across his lap. She was still clinging to his rifle.

"Now you, by God, listen to me for a while!" Ree said. "Jim Shandy made his sneaky offer to a Hudson's Bay man last winter, about the rendezvous. They didn't take him up, but they figured he'd go to the American Company with the same deal. They figured right, I'm thinking. I was in St. Louie to find out. If there's going to be a pack-train war, Hudson's Bay has got as much right as anybody to be in it. That's all they're waiting to know from me right now."

"So you was working for Hudson's Bay all the time!" Mordecai accused.

"Nope. Just for Ree Semple, like I said. You go ahead, Mord, and be a damn'-fool trapper all your life." Ree swung back to his ponies. He went drumming away in the starlight while Mordecai's head was still fogged from the pistol rap.

120

The proper treatment for Rhoda was a good beating with a stick. Mordecai didn't have the stick, and she wasn't his squaw, so he fell back on the white man's way.

He cursed. "What the devil was you trying to do, woman!"

"To keep you from killing him. He's your friend."

"A friend like that needs killing." Mordecai began to reload Old Belcher.

"He was honest. He told you what he was going to do. For a few dollars you'd take a man's life?"

"There's some I'd kill for nothing," Mordecai growled. He went trotting through the night to see if Ree had cut the picket ropes of the other ponies. If he had done that, then there was no question about his need to be killed.

The ponies were still secure.

Mordecai looked at the sky. About half the night was gone. "Get your plunder together," he ordered.

"We're not going on in the middle of the night?"

"I am. You can stay if it suits you."

Rhoda came closer from the darkness. "I'll do just that, Mr. Price. I'll stay here and go on by myself."

"You're crazy!"

"How far are we behind the pack train?"

"Never mind that. You can't go it alone. Get your plunder gathered up."

Rhoda walked on to the camp and got into her robes.

Mordecai considered bluffing, packing up and riding on from the camp a ways. He was afraid to try it, because he knew he couldn't leave her on the prairie

121

alone. She would stay. By Old Ephraim, she'd stay, and then he'd have to come sneaking back. Already she'd made a greenhorn fool out of him by grabbing his rifle, but he'd be a worse fool if he tried a bluff that didn't work.

He walked away from camp. When he caught the pack train, that's where Rhoda would stay. He'd unload her on Big Nose, while he went on ahead to rustle horses from the Indians.

Once more he made a circle of the camp. Where would the British likely hold their pack outfit? Maybe near Bonneville's fort, although some said Bonneville was dead set against the British, and had been sent out by the government to keep them from coming any farther east. You couldn't believe all the talk you heard in the mountains.

It didn't matter much where the British held their outfit; it would be some place close enough to rendezvous where they could move in fast while the Rocky Mountain was still floundering in the rock desert beyond La Bonte Creek, if Big Nose managed to get the outfit that far.

His mules and horses must be bad overloaded now, considering how they had been dying all along the trail. More of them would die.

Then there was the American coming up with a fast train.

And in the midst of all this Rhoda had gone to bed.

Mordecai cursed under his breath as he paced in the night.

Coming in against the cottonwoods from upriver, he dropped into a crouch with Old Belcher cocked when he saw something pale and ghostly moving in the grass near the grove. The wind blew cold against his neck as he watched intently.

It wasn't no white wolf. Too big and spread out for that. It was a strange, long-armed thing that kept moving one of its hands up and down as it crept along.

After a time Mordecai decided that it wasn't making much progress; still it kept up its queer movement. He stalked it silently.

The ghostly, creeping thing proved to be Rhoda's pantaloons.

CHAPTER
TEN

One day short of the Laramie Fork they overtook the pack train at nooning on a windy day. Even from afar Mordecai did not like what he saw. The train was loosely spread in the camp itself, and small groups were moving about dark mounds scattered widely on the wind-roughened land.

The hunters had got into buffalo, but every Mexican packer and French voyageur with the shebang didn't need to be out butchering. Sioux could go through the camp like a whirlwind, wrecking it and running horses off before rifles could be dragged from cases.

Someone in the camp saw the two riders coming, true enough, and for a short time there was a small stir of action as men leaped up. Mordecai saw the glint of a telescope in someone's hands. Then the whole personnel of the pack outfit seemed to collapse again.

Mordecai rode on in, past the *caballada* of mules and horses. Ree had been right. It was the most miserable collection of animals he had ever seen, except in an Indian camp after a long winter. He wondered how Big Nose had got them this far.

Some of the herders were lying down. Camp tenders were sprawled on the lee side of packs. Mordecai saw few faces that he recognized. Seemed like Shandy had picked his men like he'd picked the pack mules and horses — from the bad side of the corral.

With Rhoda close behind him, he went on and found Big Nose Yenzer, who was debating with a packer whether or not to shoot a mule. Yenzer was a small man, swarthy and waspish, known for his wicked fighting sprees when drunk; but he had a reputation, too, for staying sober on the prairie and at rendezvous — until all business was attended to.

"Shoot him," he growled at the packer. He turned to face Mordecai. Yenzer was instantly hostile. "What do you want, food? Like your old *compañero* Semple?"

It had occurred to Mordecai that Big Nose could be working with Jim Shandy. The fact that he'd got the train this far didn't prove otherwise; but a keen study of the clerk, red-eyed, tired, savagely defiant, wiped out Mordecai's suspicions. Like the Pawnees said, Big Nose had been given a poor boat. And a worse crew. He looked plumb frazzled from fighting the odds. He'd have to be handled easy.

Mordecai got down. "How goes it, Big Nose?"

"You can see, can't you!" It was like a fighting challenge.

Mordecai nodded. "When did Ree Semple come along?"

"Day and a half back."

It was going to be hard to break through Big Nose's anger and defiance. He'd better know the whole story, Mordecai guessed. "You and me got to powwow some."

"Ain't having none," Big Nose said. "If Shandy —"

"Shandy didn't send me to catch this train. We're going to powwow, you and me." Mordecai looked around at the indolence, at the lack of organization. Big Nose had fought himself out, but things had got away from him, and that was what was aching him now.

"Your packers got some of their women along?" Mordecai asked, glancing at Rhoda.

"Naw! That's one more thing I don't need, a bunch of squaws in my train." Big Nose glared at Rhoda. "Where'd you get that Cheyenne?"

"She's Ottoe. Dragged her out of the river one night above Chouteau's Landing." Mordecai grinned as he saw the fury on Rhoda's face.

She started to speak, but just then the packer shot the mule. He did a poor job of it. The mule staggered sidewise and almost lurched into Rhoda's pony, and she had her hands full getting her mount out of the way.

Mordecai tilted Old Belcher casually and killed the wounded mule. A fine bunch Shandy had unloaded on Big Nose, herders that lay down with the pack horses, and packers without brains enough to take a crippled beast ten paces from camp before shooting it. "Come on," Mordecai said. He led the clerk away from the camp and told him about Jim Shandy's treachery.

As first, Big Nose cursed violently, and then he lapsed into sullen silence for a time. At last he said, "Done all I could. I'll keep trying, but . . ." A glance around the camp was enough: the outfit was worn into the ground.

"You ain't giving up?" Mordecai said.

126

"It ain't me! I was beat before I started. I can't carry this plunder to rendezvous on my back."

"We'll get horses from the Indians," Mordecai said.

"Where in hell will you? I seen one bunch of miserable Kaws and one Ree hunting party all the way across, and I couldn't trade them out of a single pony."

"We'll run into Injuns before long. I'll go ahead and rustle ponies." Maybe he would, Mordecai thought. It was a poor time of year, with the grass not fully strong yet, and the high plains tribes weren't moving about like they would a month later.

"Yeah. Well, when you do, take that squaw with you. I got troubles enough as it is," Big Nose grumbled.

Mordecai watched a group of voyageurs who had gathered near Rhoda, grinning at each other. One of them said in French: "Ah, Roger, this woman is truly one for the bed. Except for that great trapper who is her man —"

"He is not my man, and you are a greasy dog!" Rhoda said in French.

The voyageurs were delighted, but they still did not realize that she was white until she spoke to them sharply in English. She removed one moccasin and shook it at them; they saw then the whiteness of her foot in hard contrast to her sun-browned leg. They looked guiltily at Mordecai as they walked away.

"I'll get the train there," Big Nose said. "I don't know when." He was like a Crow whose medicine had gone bad. The difference was that he'd keep trying; still, he was beat.

Words wouldn't put fighting spirit back into him, Mordecai knew. "I got an awful dry, Big Nose."

Minutes later Mordecai was sitting on a pack in the middle of the camp, with a stone jug of whisky. Big Nose watched him resentfully.

"Ain't your fault." Mordecai shook his head at the camp.

Big Nose kept looking at the mess that had gradually overcome him. Mordecai kept repeating that it was not Yenzer's fault.

After ten minutes of that, Big Nose grabbed the jug from Mordecai. "This is Fitzpatrick's whisky, damn you, but that ain't my fault either." He took his first drink.

Fifteen minutes later he was on his way to a murderous drunk. His men observed him. They had suffered too, and they were dry. A packer slyly opened one of the curved tins of alcohol in one of the packs. It began to flow, surreptitiously at first, and then more openly as Big Nose got more drunk.

By then Mordecai was tonguing the jug, holding back on his drinks. The hunters came straggling in with meat. He saw only one among them worth his salt, Joe Hassell, a former trapper. The voyageurs who had insulted Rhoda were now trying to make amends. They were rigging a tent for her of buffalo robes, chattering and bowing and scraping before her as they worked.

Rhoda would get along all right, Mordecai guessed.

"You're about the only man, outside of themselves, the Sublettes would ever trust with a train, Big Nose," Mordecai said.

The clerk nodded morosely, but his reddening eyes were sweeping around the camp. One of the hunters was standing in plain sight, drinking alcohol from a tin cup. "Yeah," Big Nose said, "and look at the goddamn' mess Shandy got me into."

Mordecai agreed. "A bunch like this — nobody could handle 'em."

"What do you mean, nobody could handle 'em?" Big Nose challenged.

"Well, you got 'em this far, but they're like the mules and horses, frazzled down to where nobody can do anything with 'em. It ain't your fault, Big Nose."

"You're all-fired set on saying that!"

"Just agreeing, is all."

"I don't need nobody to agree with me!" Big Nose yelled. "And nobody to tell me how to run a pack train. I was with Bill Sublette when we took wagons to the Popo Agie. Wagons, do you hear?"

"This child hears," Mordecai said sadly.

Big Nose lurched up. "Trying to say I don't know how to run a train no longer, huh?"

"Nothing such. Nobody could make this one go."

"The hell you bawl! I brung it here. I can take it any place from here to the Columbia, without mourning from a ragged-ass trapper like you."

Mordecai shrugged. Big Nose dropped the jug at his feet and spun away, taking longer steps with his right leg than with his left. He was grinning with a curiously wicked expression as he went toward the hunter with the tin cup.

The hunter's name was Lajoie, a tough half-breed, Cree and French. He mistook Big Nose's grin for drunkenness alone and saluted him amiably with the tin cup. An instant later the edge of the cup crashed against his face and he was blinded by alcohol. With a howl of rage he whipped out a knife and began to lash away with it as he pawed at his eyes with his left hand.

Big Nose snatched a rifle leaning against a pack. He knocked the knife from Lajoie's hand with it and went on in to club the hunter down. He would have killed Lajoie if Mordecai, coming up from behind, hadn't stopped him.

Big Nose turned on Mordecai in a fury. The hunters were no good, he shouted, none of them. They cut meat cross-grain, they wasted time finding buffalo, they didn't keep the train supplied. A bunch of sick Omaha squaws could do better.

The hunters grasped the idea. Some of them would have disputed, but Mordecai and Old Belcher stood in agreement with Big Nose.

Big Nose turned to find someone else to vent his fury on. He fell over a pack. That was it; the packers were no good either. They unloaded packs where the mules and horses happened to stop, they didn't cover them proper, and they were thieving bastards to boot.

In a crabbing trot Big Nose went for the packer who had opened the first tin of alcohol. The man began to back away. Big Nose butted him in the belly at full tilt, fell on him and tried to choke him to death. After a time Mordecai hauled the clerk off. He was beginning

130

to wonder if he had unloosed a demon that he couldn't control.

The herders were no good either, Big Nose screamed. He went lurching away toward the *caballada*. One herder, comfortably supine, had slept through the uproar. Big Nose tried to tromp the belly off him, leaping up and down like a long-armed, red-eyed demon from some Indian superstition. The herder woke up thinking Blackfeet were swarming over him. He rolled away and leaped to his feet and collided with a mule's rump. He was too close to receive the full power of the mule's feet, but it managed to kick him ten feet away.

The mules were worthless too, Big Nose howled. He tried to grab Mordecai's rifle to kill them all.

For the next half-hour Mordecai had his hands full as Big Nose raged through the camp. The clerk kicked down the sun shelter the voyageurs had made for Rhoda. What was the idea of pampering squaws?

Mordecai had no time to explain. Besides, Rhoda was still tangled up in the robes when he had to move on with Big Nose to the next complaint.

Things were beginning to improve by the time Mordecai was able to lead Big Nose back to the jug. The clerk drank some more and brooded and looked around for the next objective. He selected the packer who had shot the mule.

"Get it out of camp!" Big Nose ordered.

The packer jumped to get a horse to drag away the dead animal.

"Carry it away, you son of a bitch!" Big Nose howled.

The packer actually did try to drag the dead mule by the hind legs, and when he couldn't he stood still holding the legs and looking in helpless terror at a man gone mad.

"Cut it up and carry it away," Mordecai said.

"Chop it up!" Big Nose said, and then he turned to Mordecai. "Don't tell me how to run this train!"

They stood by while the packer chopped up the mule and carried it away piece by piece. Big Nose went back to the jug. His rage and whisky combined to make him sick soon afterward, but he would be drinking again as soon as his belly was empty, Mordecai knew.

Mordecai went to the hunter, Joe Hassell, a stooped and grizzled man with cold gray eyes under bushy brows. Even in his rage, Big Nose had walked past Hassell without a word of abuse.

"I'm thinking a train is coming behind us," Mordecai said.

"Do ye?"

"American. Can you find out?"

"How fur back?" Hassell asked.

"If it's close enough to beat us is all I'm interested in. Go that far."

Hassell spat and looked around disgustedly. "Ute dog travois could beat this outfit right now."

"Maybe. You going?"

"I'm going. You fixin' to make it all right with Big Nose?"

Mordecai nodded.

132

"Getting him drunk helped some, but it ain't going to make you hosses, old coon, and how do you git him undrunk?"

"You look down the trail. I'll take care of Big Nose."

Hassell slouched away. Later, standing beside Big Nose, who was sitting on a pack in a murderous frame of mind and trying to haul himself together to hit the jug again, Mordecai saw Hassell ride away.

The packers were stacking the train goods properly. The herders were on their feet, and the hunters were taking care of the meat they had brought in. Big Nose's authority was working again, but it wasn't going to replace worn-out horses and mules.

Mordecai couldn't leave right now, like he wanted to; he had started something that he had to see under control before it was safe to move on. He went over to Rhoda.

She looked at him with fine disgust.

"We'll have to stay here tonight," he said.

"To give Mr. Yenzer more whisky?"

"I had to." Oh, hell, Mordecai thought, he couldn't explain to her.

"Now that you've got him started, you won't have to force more whisky on him," Rhoda said. She was looking across the camp at Big Nose.

The clerk was drinking again. "Fix yourself some kind of camp." Mordecai hurried away.

It was a hard go to stay with Big Nose that night. He drank steadily. He prowled the camp to find some carelessness, and when he couldn't find it he tried to start trouble anyway. Once again he tore down Rhoda's shelter. She had put it up herself this time. She stood her ground before him. Mordecai had to drag Big Nose away when the man found out who Rhoda was and became foully abusive of all missionary effort among the Indians.

Late that night Mordecai was considering putting the quietus on Big Nose with a club, when the clerk became sick from drinking melted belly fat. After that, Big Nose couldn't keep his whisky down. He fell into his robes and went to sleep.

Just to make sure that the guards didn't relax, Mordecai made the rounds for two hours afterwards.

Evil-tempered and more red-eyed than ever, Big Nose got up early. He stared around savagely to catch a guard asleep. He was on the point of an outburst when he saw that Rhoda's shelter was up again, and then he gave it up as unimportant.

It was no use to try to hide whisky from him. The train was loaded with it in some form. The jug that Big Nose had worked on last was near his bed. He looked at it for a long time, and then he saw Mordecai watching him. "First time I ever been drunk when I had something to do." He didn't say it but he was accusing Mordecai.

Mordecai didn't answer. He watched Big Nose go over to a fire where camp tenders were roasting meat. The clerk came back gnawing a bloody hump rib. "Where do you think you're going to find horses?" he growled.

"Wherever they are."

134

"It'd better be soon." Big Nose gnawed on the rib. "This shebang ain't going to make it to Deer Creek." He looked toward Rhoda's lodge. "Take that missionary with you. I got bad luck enough."

"I sent Hassell back to look out for the American train."

Big Nose cursed. "He was the only hunter I had! Who told you to send him away?" He was riled, but not like yesterday.

"You want to know where they are, don't you?" Mordecai asked.

"What good's it going to do, unless I got fresh horses?" Big Nose flung the rib away. He belched. For a moment it appeared that he was going to puke. "Get the ponies if you think you can. I'll go as far as this outfit can stand, and that ain't going to be very damn' far."

Mordecai went over to wake Rhoda. She protested when he told her he was going to leave her baggage with the train. "We'll be back," he said.

"I think I'll stay with the train."

"You'll be walking. From the look of Big Nose, I know what he's going to do. Every saddle horse is going to be a pack horse from now on. Besides, he don't want you around. Bad luck. Grab something to eat and let's go."

"That drunken little maniac," Rhoda said.

They rode away before sunrise, gnawing meat in the saddle. The voyageurs stood in a group, waving to Rhoda, until Big Nose charged into them and scattered them off to their work.

"Why are you so contemptuous of voyageurs?" Rhoda asked. "I found them very courteous and agreeable, after they knew I was white."

"Being courteous gets you killed dead." Mordecai squinted ahead. Some of it would have to be blind luck. When you didn't want Injuns, they came swarming. Now when he desperately wanted to find a heap of them with a heap of ponies, no telling how far he might have to go.

"Another beautiful sunrise," Rhoda said.

Mordecai gave it scant attention. He was thinking that any dirty trick went in the fur trade these days. Take Ree, though; he'd been half honest, telling exactly what he aimed to do.

They crossed fresh pony tracks before they were two miles from the train. The way they were headed, Mordecai figured it must be a small bunch of hellers out on a scalp spree, hanging close to the train. He hoped that's where they'd stay.

CHAPTER
ELEVEN

Jim Shandy and his two plug-uglies lost their horses to the Pawnee Loups at dawn one morning a few miles above Brady's Island. Parson Bill Kerr swore he hadn't been dozing at his guard turn, and the fact that he got off two shots before the Indians were clean away supported him.

Still, it was his fault. Shandy put a rifle on him.

A long face and a down-drooped mouth gave Parson Bill his name. Shandy came within a hair of giving him his finish, as the three of them stood with the light breaking around them, listening to the triumphant yelps of the Pawnees glimmering away to the south.

"Ain't the first horses ever been stole," Mike Nesmith said. He spoke as one who had been on both ends of such situations.

"We'll see how that fat gut of yours likes walking." Shandy lowered his rifle. Three men on the prairie were better than two. Also, Nesmith was standing behind Shandy, and for some strange reason Nesmith set great store by Parson Bill.

Nesmith grinned. The ride, the sun, and the lean rations had sweated the whisky out of him but he wasn't gaunted any. It wasn't fat that made him look round and burly, but solid bulk that refused to melt away under exertion. His face looked like laughter, straight lips over good teeth and lively, quick eyes. All that was deceiving too, like the apparent fatness of him, for a second look at him showed the cruelty in the mouth and the cunning in the eyes. If he lacked intelligence, he got along well enough on animal shrewdness and quick reactions.

As a matter of fact, Shandy didn't intend to walk a foot. The American train was somewhere behind them. It was unlikely that Emil Frederick, clerk of the train, would know any more about Shandy's position in American affairs than Nesmith and Parson Bill knew — they thought Shandy was on his way to hurrying along the Rocky Mountain train.

But Frederick would have to hold to the courtesy of the trail and help them out. White men had to stick together in Indian country. They could rob and kill each other between emergencies.

"There's a pack train coming," Shandy said. "We'll wait for it."

"Whose train?" Parson Bill asked.

"American!"

Nesmith laughed. "Ain't that some!" And then the sharp cunning in his face came down to a point as he thought about the American Company train.

He would figure things out, Shandy knew, but he still wouldn't know how Shandy was standing in affairs. Shandy allowed that he could handle any problems caused by Nesmith, or anyone else out here on the prairie.

They were running low on food when the American train came up several days later. It had made better time than Shandy thought it would. Two hundred big, strong mules, horses for the hunters, more than fifty men in all, a tightly organized outfit with big red-faced Emil Frederick in charge.

In that caravan, strung out more than half a mile, Shandy saw the shape of things to come. Randall had put the outfit together in two days. Rocky Mountain could never have done that. Lacking money, and sometimes lacking strong direction, Rocky Mountain was making a strong fight to stay in the fur business, but it was a losing fight. Shandy remembered what Bogard had said about American's determination to wipe out rivals.

Any guilt he had felt about double-dealing vanished: Rocky Mountain was going to be crushed anyway by the power and money of American. What he had done would only hasten things a little.

Frederick looked down from his mule, greatly enjoying Shandy's predicament. "Ever been around thieving Indians afore, Shandy? First time on the prairie, huh?" He grinned around his stubby clay pipe. "Which way you want to go now?"

Shandy took it as best he could. At least he had the satisfaction of knowing that Frederick was ignorant of what was really going on. "Looks like we'll trail with you."

"That's sociable, I swear," Frederick said. The train kept passing. Packers and other engagees grinned.

"Ain't much you can do to boost Rocky Mountain's train along when we go by, is there?"

Shandy didn't like the way he said it, as if he knew that Shandy had betrayed his own company. There seemed to be more contempt than gloating in Frederick's tone.

Frederick left them standing in the dust and rode back along the train. When the loose critters came by, the drivers gave Shandy and his men mules to ride. They were the worst of the lot. Shandy's mount had a sore back and was a vicious biter. The other two were evil, cantankerous brutes to handle.

Under Frederick's expert tyranny the American train ate up the miles. They passed dead animals from the Rocky Mountain train, day after day. It began to amaze Shandy that Big Nose had done as well as he had, hampered as he was by poor beasts and shiftless men.

Nevertheless, American was fast overhauling the Rocky Mountain train, Shandy knew. If he stayed with Frederick and never raised a finger, American was going to get to the rendezvous first.

Except for one thing he was tempted to stay with the American train and let nature take its course; but he worried about the overlay of tracks on the passage of the Rocky Mountain outfit: three people, one of them a woman. It had to be Mordecai Price and Rhoda Marsh. The third must be Ree Semple.

Nobody worked miracles on the Platte Trail, but Price and Ree might come close to it. For his own good Shandy was obliged to see that they did not.

He could have got horses from Frederick then simply by asking for them. All along the way the evidence that the Rocky Mountain train was about done had been increasing: shorter stops between camps, more dead beasts. Emil Frederick was confident that he would overtake and pass a worn-out outfit within ten days, so there was no reason to deny Shandy and his men horses to take them on ahead, and no further reason to watch them closely.

It did not occur to Shandy to ask for horses. He and his two men stole them one night and left the American train. Parson Bill overdid it. He took Frederick's favorite buffalo horse, a nimble-footed bay with white stockings.

Well ahead of the caravan by morning, Shandy's party saw the far movement in the hills ahead — just once. It looked like a scouting Indian, or it could have been a lone bull on its way to water.

They kept their eyes peeled and went ahead.

The next time they saw the object, there was no question about it, for Joe Hassell, having laid low until he was sure the three riders were white men, rode boldly to the top of a hill and waited for them.

Hassell had hardly got anywhere since he left the Rocky Mountain train. Nothing unusual, his adventures still had been frustrating. Before he'd been two hours away from the train, he encountered a small group of Sioux straggling up the trail in hopes of easy pickings. Hassell wasn't it, but they ran him north until he got away from them at dark. They were a persistent bunch, Oglalas, forerunner of the Sioux bands that, with their friends the Cheyennes, would take over the plains clear to the mountains by the time the beaver trade was dead. This group hunted industriously for Joe Hassell. They kept him cached out for five days, and they might have stayed longer than that if a herd of buffalo hadn't come by to divert them.

So Hassell was only getting started on his scout when he met Shandy's group. He was damned glad to see them. They all got down to rest and smoke, and Shandy passed out good American Company jerky.

"'Pears that this child won't have to go a foot farther down the trail," Hassell said. "Mordecai, he had an idea American was sending a pack train. Guess you'd've seen it."

Shandy had to step on Parson Bill's foot to keep him from blabbing. A glance at Nesmith was enough.

"Where is Mordecai?" Shandy asked.

"Rid up ahead to trade Injuns out of hosses," Hassell answered between bites. "Him and Big Nose got drunk and pried up hell and put a chunk under it."

Shandy found out everything he wanted to know. He lumped Ree Semple into the horse-trading deal too. Hudson's Bay, hell! Mordecai and Ree were thicker than Crow horse thieves. Hassell didn't ask about an American train, assuming naturally enough that Shandy certainly would have mentioned it, if there had been one coming.

Still chewing, Hassell got up from his cross-legged position on the ground. "If you ask me, Shandy, somebody better git on to rendezvous and have the boys there come out to git your train. Else it ain't" —

he frowned, staring at Parson Bill's horse — "going to make it before robe time."

By the time they mounted up, Hassell was sure about Frederick's buffalo horse. So far, he was only greatly puzzled, Shandy decided. "You boys come up the Platte?" he asked.

"Sure," Shandy said.

Hassell couldn't help staring at the white-stockinged bay. His suspicions began to harden. That was when Shandy swung his Hawken around and shot Hassell through the heart. The shock knocked the hunter back in the saddle, and then he rocked forward over the horn. Nesmith shot him again.

Parson Bill stared with his mouth open. He was still far behind events when Shandy cursed him for taking Frederick's horse. Parson Bill was completely lost, but Nesmith wasn't. "We better take him *and* Frederick's horse off the trail and leave 'em both," Nesmith said. The killing hadn't upset him a bit.

He was catching on too fast, Shandy thought. His price would be sure to go up.

After a half-hour detour they were riding once more in a direct line to overtake the Rocky Mountain train. Hassell and Frederick's horse were dead in a gully far off the trail. Parson Bill was now riding Hassell's pony, which, according to Shandy's instructions, they would say they had found running loose on the prairie.

They crossed Sioux sign where the Indians had been running buffalo. With a little luck the Sioux would have got Hassell anyway, Shandy thought.

Nesmith kept watching him as they rode.

"Big Nose tried to drink all the whisky in camp," Shandy said. "For all I know, he's been drunk all the way from St. Louis." He looked hard at Nesmith. "Maybe you can boss the train the rest of the way."

Nesmith spat. "Far as it gits, I can."

They understood each other.

"Parson Bill and me, that is," Nesmith said, and his words and his look were a warning that he was going to look out for Parson Bill, stupid and worthless as he had proved.

Let it be so, Shandy thought.

"You don't aim to stay with the train, huh?" Nesmith asked.

"Just long enough to fire Big Nose. Then I'll go on ahead to help Mordecai get horses." Shandy and Nesmith gave each other a long look.

"Semple too?" Nesmith asked.

"I figure he's gone on to rendezvous."

"Maybe he'll have a story to tell."

Let Semple talk. Shandy was going to make it appear that he was doing everything possible to get the Rocky Mountain train through ahead of American. At best, Ree and Mordecai were only guessing. Still, a good guess out here was enough to cost a man his life.

In this case it had better be Mordecai's life.

Ree Semple rode through the wide sage saddle of South Pass and went on down toward the Siskadee. He was doing precisely what Sherman Randall had been afraid he would do, but even Randall could not reach

144

out from St. Louis, immediately, to make him pay for the sin of being ambitious.

It occurred to Ree that if Hudson's Bay actually proved honorable and paid him, according to the somewhat loose agreement he had made last winter with officials at Fort Boise, he had best at once remove himself and his further operations in the fur trade to Bayou Salade and other southern Rockies locations.

Bonneville's fort was still inhabited, but not flourishing, from what Ree observed from a distance. He avoided it and went downstream to a cottonwood grove, and there he ran head-on into a small band of Nez Percés under Great Horse, a minor chief.

They were friendly, as Nez Percés generally were toward white men, but their hearts were bad toward the Sioux and Bannocks. They were made up for war and they desired to know if Ree had seen any of either enemy tribe recently, particularly a small outfit with good horses stolen from the Nez Percés.

Somewhat uneasy because he was so badly outnumbered, even among friendly Indians, Ree said truthfully that he had cut the sign of five or six Bannocks on the Sweetwater.

In return he asked if Great Horse had seen Red Man — James McIlvane — the Hudson's Bay brigade leader, who was even now supposed to be on the Siskadee.

"Far away. Many days far away," Great Horse said. True, he had heard that Red Man was coming with many horses loaded with goods, but he was coming slowly, hunting as he traveled, and with him were many cursed Bannocks. Why did white men always have about them enemies of the Nez Percés?

It was a rhetorical question. Ree suggested that the Bannocks on the Sweetwater might have camped there, waiting for their brothers to come with Red Man. The Nez Percés left soon after to find out, and Ree tried to settle down to wait patiently for the Hudson's Bay brigade.

It was hard waiting. He kept figuring distance and time. Patience was hard to sustain.

Hudson's Bay arrived four days later, a Union Jack at the head of the train, strong British discipline along the length of it. Traveling with Red Man were 150 Bannocks, fifteen Delawares hired away from some luckless American independent, and about thirty free trappers still holding their plews for trading at rendezvous only.

He was in no hurry, Jim McIlvane, or Red Man. He began to set up camp while Ree was urging him to go on toward rendezvous. "There's always time," Red Man said.

The Bannocks, already sour by virtue of being born, were greatly displeased to find fresh sign of Nez Percé around Ree's camp. They were in favor of lifting his hair. His steadiness, his rifle, and Red Man's intervention saved him. Some of the Bannocks at once painted up and took out on the trail of the Nez Percés.

As usual, the no-man's land out there across the pass would be criss-crossed with the pony tracks of warring bands from a half-dozen tribes. A good part of them would then go on to rendezvous and try to get along for a few days. It would be a whingding, certain, Ree knew.

Although a Scot, McIlvane held to ceremony and dressed up a bit before he received Ree in his tent for formal powwow over a bottle of fine brandy. Ree had a dry, all right, though he wasn't much for brandy.

"We've had conflicting reports about the location of the rendezvous," McIlvane said. He was a rawboned, gaunt man who somehow didn't look ludicrous in his red-trimmed uniform. Hudson's Bay was hell for passing out splashy coats like that to the Injuns up north, Ree thought.

"I'll take you there," Ree said, "and we ought to get started by sunup."

"My instructions are clear — up to a point. First, I must be sure that the American Company is actually invading the Rocky Mountain rendezvous, and —"

"They are," Ree said. "Their train left St. Louis a day or two after I did. Then I got news from Indians after it started up the Platte."

McIlvane drank heartily from a tin cup. "But *you* didn't see the train yourself, on the Platte?"

"Only from a long distance," Ree lied cheerfully. About as long as those imaginary Indian scouts who hadn't seen it either. But it was coming, he was sure.

"Where's the Rocky Mountain train?"

"Going like hell through the red desert when I saw it last," Ree said. Anything to hurry Red Man up.

Red Man drank some more brandy, after refilling Ree's cup. He stared hard from under reddish brows. "To the Sweetwater?"

"Wherever the rendezvous is. I'll take you there."

"I could find the place, no doubt, but I might lose a little time."

"That's a fact," Ree said. "Got plenty of whisky?"

"I think so." McIlvane adjusted himself against a Cree back-rest. "Second, you're to receive three thousand dollars if Hudson's Bay succeeds in getting the best of the furs at rendezvous."

Ree nodded. "If you're aiming to do some trading, you'd better get started."

"There's no great hurry at this point." Shady these Americans were, McIlvane thought, as bad as some of the old North-westers had been. He knew where rendezvous was. He'd known for two weeks from the reports of some of his Iroquois scouts, three of whom, curse them, had deserted and stayed at the rendezvous site. So Semple's guidance to the mouth of the Popo Agie was worth exactly nothing. His information about the actual approach of the American Company train was another matter for Hudson's Bay action had hung upon that point. Now that McIlvane had the information, the value of it had depreciated to nothing also. It certainly was not worth three thousand dollars, except on paper. To pay this shady, grasping American rogue his price would be sheer business stupidity, and that was why Hudson's Bay did not plan to pay him.

"Have another drink," McIlvane said. "It's very good brandy."

Thinking about the whole affair, Ree decided he was in it more for the hell of things than for the money, which didn't mean that he wasn't going to grab his

148

three thousand and light out for Santa Fe in a hurry. It was going to be something to see the look of the American Company men when they found out they'd been took.

Rocky Mountain . . . well, that was bad in a way. Ree had *compañeros* in that bunch. Not that it made any difference at trading time. Rocky Mountain would hook you ten dollars a pound for vermilion like any other robbing outfit. No matter who you dealt with, you wound up with a headache big as the sky and a debt about the same size when you dragged your tail back to the beaver streams after rendezvous.

Rocky Mountain was beat anyway, and that wasn't none of Ree's doin's. What he was fixing now was to have the British beat the American Company.

Ree had another slug of Hudson's Bay brandy.

CHAPTER
TWELVE

Spurred on when he had been at the point of quitting, and with good cause, Big Nose Yenzer's eruption of furious energy carried the train for five days. He discovered that the hair of the dog, hitherto scrupulously avoided in times of responsibility, was good medicine after all.

He stayed medium drunk. Mean. It worked.

Thirty dead beasts behind him now. Give him worthless brutes and men to do a job with, would they? He'd show 'em just how really no-good they was! Walk! Every whore's son of you walk. The packs go on the horses.

Lajoie was riled, was he? Lajoie was making big talk because his miserable hunting horses were carrying packs? I'll show that son of a bitch! Big Nose showed him. He fought the half-breed with knives. He cut up Lajoie's arms and shoulders so bad that the hunter could no longer lift a rifle. Big Nose didn't need hunters anyway. There were dead horses and mules to eat every day.

This train is going to rendezvous, you river scum!

Big Nose was the only man who didn't walk. He rode with a jug tied to the horn, with his rifle held just above the jug.

The train had been licked at Laramie Fork. Big Nose had admitted it then. He wouldn't admit it any longer. Dying animals were overloaded. Big Nose hadn't picked them. That was Jim Shandy's doin's. Beat them on.

Did they go down, get them up again. Beat them on. They couldn't get up, could they? Divide the packs onto animals that weren't staggering their last. And do it quick, goddamn you! Butcher up that skeleton and carry it along, if you want to chaw something tonight.

Nooning? To hell with it! They're dying anyway, and it takes too much time to unload and load packs. This train is going to rendezvous, you worthless bastards!

He was a man gone mad, this Big Nose. He rode up and down the line of faltering beasts and sweating, hating men, a red-eyed demon. They figured ways to kill him, talked about doing it, but no one tried. Lajoie stumbled along with his slashed coat stained with blood, with the flapping openings showing the marks of Big Nose's knife. Lajoie hated as only a half-breed can.

He'd kill Big Nose, of course. No one doubted it.

They were done at Deer Creek, but Big Nose didn't say so. They ate more dried-out mule and horse meat, and went on.

And now the greenhorns and the loafers that Shandy had placed in the train knew what going west of the Big Muddy was. It was dust and exhaustion. It was death if they left the train, and where was there to go? It was a crazy man who glared at them with burning eyes, a man who rode with a jug bouncing against the shoulder of a dying horse. It was madness and fear and a curse for the day they were born. Keep going, you pork eaters!

Only a few of the voyageurs could remember worse times. They had worked for American. Now they suffered with the rest and yet they sometimes sang.

Dying mules brayed from sheer misery. Horses died with the same beast patience with which they had lived. Chop them up and take the bloody pieces along. No buffalo in sight and not a horse fit to run a hunter to buffalo if they had been sighted.

Sweat. Groan at night when lifting the packs from trembling beasts. Munch tough, stringy meat that had died with the blood heat high in it. Fall over and sleep. Drag out at dawn to eat sour bacon and weevily hardtack. Put the packs on pitiful critters that flinched at the very sight of burdens. A wild and filthy little man who breathed whisky fumes said the train was going to rendezvous. Some of them almost believed him, and hated him worse because they did.

Sometimes they saw a few Indians, the Oglalas who had chased Joe Hassell. After their buffalo hunt they had found him. He wasn't much good to them then, but they took his scalp and equipment and chopped him up a little out of habit. Now they watched the train. They even considered going down to it to receive presents.

But one of them had Hassell's rifle.

And so the Sioux merely went along. They ranged out when they needed meat. They rode clear around the train as fancy dictated. Some of the white men stumbling along were going to quit and fall behind the

152

train. Always there were some fools among the white-faces.

But the white-faces had seen the Oglala children too. No man deserted or fell behind, largely because a fiend on a horse kept driving them on. The train should have died before Deer Creek. It was dead when it staggered down to the crossing of the Platte beyond Red Buttes. The best of the surviving mules barely had strength to stumble toward the water.

In five days Big Nose had covered a distance that a sound outfit could have made in four. He knew how well he had done, considering. With a week's rest, even overloaded as they were, the brutes could go on by slow stages.

If American was anywhere close, they had him beat. Even if Mordecai and his woman came back with ponies, Rocky Mountain likely would get beat anyway. It wasn't necessarily a good sign that Joe Hassell hadn't returned yet. Hell, he might have found the American train and joined it. The way Big Nose felt at the moment, he wouldn't blame Hassell.

Out of the whole pork-eating bunch, the voyageurs had proved the best men. Three of them were about as good as they came, Roger Letourneau and two more of the French that had gone into such a fret over Mordecai's squaw.

A missionary, by God! That's what this country needed. The thought struck Big Nose with the kind of humor that often rushes up from the hollowness of exhaustion. He began to laugh, standing in the camp with the butt of his rifle resting on a pack.

The little demon had cracked. His men gave him strange, frightened looks. Two Oglalas who had sneaked close in the trees also thought he was touched by the queer spirit. See him with his hairy face turned to the sky, roaring laughter at something no one else could see or understand!

At last Big Nose sank down on a pack, with the tears of his laughing smudged through the caked dust on his cheeks. "Roger!" he croaked. "Come here and bring your two singing *compañeros*!"

The three voyageurs approached him carefully. All he wanted was for them to stand guard over him while he rested. This was natural enough, they thought, eyeing Lajoie.

Forthwith Big Nose got as drunk as a mortal worn-out man could sink. At first he yelled about going on by night, and then he was going to put packs on every lazy bastard in the train, all of them. But he never got up after the first few drinks.

The voyageurs were guarding him and he was lying in a stupor when Jim Shandy and his men rode into camp. It couldn't have been better, Shandy thought. Every man in camp was a witness.

Shandy motioned for Nesmith and Parson Bill to get Big Nose on his feet. They kicked him awake and dragged him upright. The clerk was not so far gone that he didn't recognize Shandy. He began to curse Shandy like a maniac.

"Let him have his rifle and his plunder and throw him out of camp," Shandy ordered.

They did that to Big Nose. He staggered away, shouting curses, weaving. The handful of Sioux that had been hanging around would pick him up soon enough, Shandy knew. Things were working out fine as frog hair. "Kill him if he tries to come back to camp," he told Nesmith. He raised his voice to the gawking packers and greenhorns, pointing to Nesmith. "This hoss is in charge here now. Don't forget it."

After what Big Nose had put them through, most of them didn't care. A few of the voyageurs looked downcast, knowing what was going to happen to Big Nose, but they didn't count.

"Where's Mordecai Price?" Shandy asked Letourneau.

The Frenchman knew no more than Shandy had found out already from Hassell. Both Mordecai and Ree were on ahead scouting for horses, the way it looked to Shandy. "Bring the train on as soon as you can," he told Nesmith.

Nesmith's eyes lighted with wicked understanding. "Just as soon as me and Parson Bill can move her."

"See you at rendezvous." Shandy got on his horse.

"Keerful of them Sioux out there," Parson Bill said.

No five, six prowling Sioux were going to raise hair on Jim Shandy. He swung back downriver before he crossed over into the dry hills. Big Nose would keep the Sioux busy for a spell, he reckoned. Turning west, Shandy made a wide sweep to get around them.

So Mordecai was figuring to bring horses, was he . . . Him and Ree.

★　★　★

155

From the trees Mordecai and Rhoda watched the migration coming up from the south. Three hundred of them, anyway.

"They're Indians," Rhoda said. "I can tell that much, even this far away."

"Yup." A good many greenhorns couldn't have told them from buffler, Mordecai thought. His eyes were narrowed and hard as he watched. Was they Blackfeet, him and Rhoda had just as well sneak away, come dark, and forget all about ponies.

They made a powerful dust coming out of the sage down to the river. There were enough of them, sure, enough not to be afraid in this country that didn't rightly belong to any tribe. It was a sort of dark and bloody ground with no defined ownership closer than the mountains. This bunch could be most anything, Badhearts, Araps, Bloods, or Cheyennes. The one thing they likely wasn't was Sioux. Not that many of them this far west.

"How do you tell about them from so far off?" Rhoda asked.

"Just don't." They'd likely camp on the water, Mordecai knew. He had to have a closer look at them. "You stay here with the ponies. I'll have me a look, I'm thinking."

Rhoda shook her head. "I'll go with you. They're Snakes, so there's nothing to be afraid of."

She plumb stopped Mordecai. For a minute he thought she actually could see better than him.

"They're Snakes," she said, and then he knew she was guessing, and hoping too.

156

She went along with him. Ree had shown her how to toe in her moccasins so her feet wouldn't bother her. She didn't make much noise, at that. Mordecai got a glimpse of the first lodges the squaws were setting up. Snakes, by Old Caleb! He didn't say so though. "You can get the ponies now," he said.

Rhoda went back without hesitation. While he was waiting Mordecai had time to realize that he had ordered her around like a squaw. He didn't apologize. It still bothered him some about her calling the turn on the Indians, even if she had been guessing.

"Well?" Rhoda said when she brought the ponies up.

Mordecai kept looking at her. She was a heap of woman. The closer he got to delivering her to Slocum, the more he was realizing it.

"Snakes," he said.

Old Three Horns was gray, but his eyes were still clear. He knew Mordecai from a distance and he yelled out his glad surprise. "Big Buffalo!"

During the smoking Mordecai kept his eye on Rhoda. She wandered around the camp some, talking to the women with signs, and then she went back to take care of the ponies.

"Big Buffalo's woman is white," Three Horns said.

Mordecai nodded.

"Red Man is bringing much goods." He too was going to the rendezvous. The Snakes were on their way there now, after their successful hunt, Three Horns said. Red Man had many Bannocks with him. This was bad. Though the Snakes and Bannocks were brothers, there had been some trouble between them lately.

Mordecai said it was good to trade with those who were true friends of the Snakes, above all others. Once more he named the leading Rocky Mountain men.

"They are friends," Three Horns agreed. He was not sure where Red Man's train was. Ten sleeps ago Snake scouts had seen it. Red Man was not hurrying greatly, since the Bannocks, those mountain robbers, were hunting as they came.

Above all others it was good to trade with the men of Rocky Mountain, Mordecai said.

Three Horns agreed. Of course it was possible to trade with enemies too. Did not the Blackfeet and Sioux trade with the Crows for fine garments? Did not everyone trade with the Nez Percés for good horses? Did not the No Bow Sioux get their weapons from mountain tribes?

Trading was trading, Three Horns implied. His people were friends of all white men.

"Do your people have many beaver?"

Three Horns shook his head. They had robes to trade and a few beaver, along with other skins.

Buffler robes. American was already starting a big trade in them. Come the time when robes started beating out plews, Mordecai was turning farmer or something.

"Where are the people with the goods?" Three Horns asked.

"On the Platte, near Deer Creek." Mordecai hoped so. "Some of our horses are growing weak."

Three Horns gave him a keen look. "The ponies of Red Man are not weak. Some of the people have seen them." Many Bannocks with Red Man, too. This was bad.

Mordecai explained that he had come a much greater distance than Red Man to trade with his friends the Snakes. That was why the horses had grown weak. Now he needed many ponies in trade from the Snakes. With fresh ponies he would be able to get the train goods to rendezvous so that the Snakes could trade for anything they needed.

One winter many ponies of the Snakes had died from a strange disease, Three Horns said. It was not from carrying great packs, of course, but a strange thing that made them cough and die. He told all about it. Mordecai listened politely, although his eyes kept straying to where Rhoda was making camp. Squaws had given her meat. She was shying sticks at dogs that crept close to test her vigilance.

How many ponies did Big Buffalo need?

"Many," Mordecai said. It was a bad thing that he had nothing but promises to trade. Talk of goods at the pack train was not like having the stuff laid out here where the Snakes could see it.

"The people have many ponies," Three Horns said. The young men had stolen some from the Crows, some from the Blackfeet, who had bad hearts, and a few others here and there. Tomorrow was soon enough to talk of trading. Now it was time to eat and talk. Was Big Buffalo tired of his white squaw? Did he wish a Snake maiden tonight?

Big Buffalo made haste to say that his squaw was good, and that it was not possible to have others while

159

she was with him. He saw Rhoda talking to a group of women. She was some, at that, making out in sign language.

When, in politeness, he could leave Three Horns, he went back to Rhoda.

"Did you get the ponies?" she asked.

"Not so fast. You don't get nothing done with Indians by trying to rush things."

"Is it so important that the Rocky Mountain Company beats everyone to the rendezvous? What is so important about it?"

"My God!" Something like she asked didn't need no explaining, it seemed to Mordecai.

"I know your company will lose a great deal of money," Rhoda said, "but in the long run will it make any great difference to the Indians?"

"Ain't interested in the long run. It's my friends that'll be ruint next week, if I don't get that pack train in first. It ain't just American, either. Hudson's Bay is coming. That's Ree's doin's." Mordecai started to plunge into the whole story.

"I know," Rhoda said quietly. "Ree told me. The day he left he told me exactly what he was going to do."

Mordecai was outraged. "You didn't say nothing!"

"Why should I? You're all a bunch of thieves and bullies. You debauch the Indians with whisky; you steal your own trappers' furs with more whisky. What's the difference who gets to rendezvous first? It will be the same result, as far as the men who do the actual trapping are concerned."

160

"Wagh!" Mordecai growled. "You been talking too much to Ree." He went stomping back to Three Horns' lodge. He ate there. Afterward he sat in the circle with the chief and lesser chiefs and smoked. It was a beautiful, clear evening. An old crier went around the camp, calling out in a high voice that Big Buffalo, friend of the Blanket Chief, who was a friend of the Snakes, wished to trade for many ponies tomorrow.

The crossed lodgepoles raked the sky. Spring colts frisked through the pony herd across the river. Somewhere a woman who had lost a son to the Blackfeet wailed. Smoke rose straight from the cooking fires. Young men and girls, dressed in finery, strolled around the camp, eyeing each other.

Mordecai smoked. His belly was full. Beaver Tails was telling of a fight with Blackfeet on Godin Creek that spring. Young Snake women stood beyond the circle of listeners, watching Mordecai. His white squaw had eaten alone and was staying alone by her fire. Perhaps he was ready to send her back to her people. He had been married to a Snake before, until the Blackfeet killed her on Henry's Fork. There was nothing wrong with hoping.

It was good. All of it was good, and so Mordecai kept wondering why there was a snag inside him that kept going against the smooth flow of things. Maybe it was the ponies. He didn't have them yet, and he wasn't going to get them just by saying the Rocky Mountain pack train was dead without them.

He saw a young man parading in front of Rhoda, showing his scalps, showing his fine buckskins and

161

strong body. She was paying him no mind. Maybe it was her that was troubling Mordecai. She had no call to look at him so hot and accuse every man that was in the mountains of being a thief. That Ree, he sure had filled her ears with a heap of nonsense.

Beaver Tails told how he had struck coup on Little Crow. His listeners grunted their admiration, Mordecai along with the rest.

Maybe the Rocky Mountain did rob trappers a little, but not near so bad as American did, and with none of the pious, non-whisky dealing of the British. It was the way of things. Who was going to change it? Who among the trappers, except a few like Ree, ever complained more than normal?

By Old Ephraim, Rhoda ought to know how things were before she said everybody was a robber.

Beaver Tails killed all the Blackfeet he had a rightful claim to. An old warrior began a story about what the grasshopper said to the bear. Mordecai got up and went over to Rhoda.

She was sitting on an apishamore by her fire. The flush of the flames gave a soft brownness to her face, a clear liquidity to her eyes. Mordecai looked down at the long center part in her braided hair. Danged if he didn't forget some of the angry arguments he'd come to throw at her.

"About this here robbing —" he began.

"I know it isn't all as simple as I stated it. There's one thing that does impress me in the middle of all the double-dealing and trickery."

"Yeah?" Mordecai asked suspiciously. "What's that?"

"Your loyalty to your company, Mordecai. Ree told me that you'd make no money out of all your exertions."

Mordecai was taken aback. "Well, it ain't the company; it's the men."

The woman watched him thoughtfully. "If Mr. Shandy *is* guilty of what you think, what will you do about it when you go back to St. Louis?"

"I'll put him under, if someone else don't beat me." Mordecai could see how set she was against killing.

"Ree?" she asked.

"That's some different. He never claimed to be no company man. Ree is honest dirty."

"Will you get the ponies, Mordecai?"

"I got to."

"You seem worried that you won't."

"The Snakes ain't busting to skyugle clean over to the Platte. They're heading to rendezvous, and they know they can trade there. They ain't worried about who they trade with."

"I don't blame them," Rhoda said. She stirred with a stick in the dirt near the fire. "Didn't you say you thought it was Sioux sign we saw soon after we left the train?"

That would help! Should have thought of it himself. Besides offering the Snakes that wanted to trade a deal at the train, he could promise the chance of picking up a Sioux or two. "You're larning fast, Rhoda."

"They won't really catch the Sioux, will they? I mean, out there in all that bigness and everything. We can't change their thinking quickly, I know, but I don't like to encourage them to kill each other."

"Naw! Nobody's going to catch up with them Sioux." Maybe not, Mordecai thought. He deemed it best not to add that Injuns skulping Injuns was their own business. As he started to leave, he said, "We're supposed to sleep in Three Horns' lodge tonight." Cool and steady, Rhoda kept looking at him until he said: "It ain't like it sounded! I mean, he thinks we're married."

"I suppose he would."

"I'll fix it up. You sleep right here." Mordecai decided he'd tell old Three Horns that he'd kicked Rhoda out for sassing him and was going to make her sleep alone for a while.

He hurried back to the chief's lodge. Trading always took a heap of jawing. He'd better dangle those Sioux before the Snakes, and at the same time get in a few more licks for Rocky Mountain.

The old man was still going strong on the grasshopper-bear story.

CHAPTER
THIRTEEN

They sat. They smoked. Sometimes they rose to go across the river to look at ponies. Beaver Tails, scarred, nimble, lighter in color even than the average Snake, was rich in ponies. He could spare twenty-five. Some of his close friends might trade forty more altogether.

That would do it, Mordecai figured, but he didn't have the ponies yet. Trouble was, the Snakes were on their way to rendezvous, and it was no skin off their rumps that the Rocky Mountain train was busted down.

They stood looking at ponies. Beaver Tails bragged on them. Mordecai increased his offer of goods at the pack train a little.

Thinking more of alcohol than of the Sioux scalps which Mordecai had said might be available, Iron Hawk said, "I will go with Big Buffalo to trade ponies." Hell of it, he had only five.

They waded the Sweetwater and sat down to smoke it over some more. Rhoda had been overhopeful: she had saddled Mordecai's ponies. She watched and waited. It sort of put a weight on Mordecai, like if she was saying he didn't know his business.

It was up to Beaver Tails. His friends would go along with him, either way he decided. Once more Mordecai spoke of the great friendship of the Snakes and the men of the Rocky Mountain Company. He went back to Lewis and Clark and made them Rocky Mountain men too.

"All that Big Buffalo says is true," Beaver Tails agreed. He looked toward the Wind River Mountains, stark and clear in the early light. He was sure that a small bunch of Blackfeet the Snakes had flushed out of the buffalo country had hidden there. He thought he knew about where. He was not against killing Sioux, but he preferred Blackfeet. If he went to trade ponies, the Blackfeet would escape.

It was a half-true argument, Mordecai knew. Something else was sticking him. Then he saw Beaver Tails look at Rhoda. So that was where the wind was blowing!

"Big Buffalo is tired of his squaw. They sleep in different lodges. She is ugly but Beaver Tails will take her in the trade," the Snake said.

Damp powder and no fire to dry it, for certain. Beaver Tails knew she was white, but it would make him a big man to have a white squaw along with his two others. He was damn' good and set on the point, Mordecai could tell. Blank refusal would insult him, likely ruin the whole trade.

Mordecai never changed expression. Wasn't things at a hell of a pass when the year's profits of the Rocky Mountain depended on the vanity of one Injun. Wouldn't do any good to threaten to go trade with the

Bannocks that was coming with McIlvane. There wasn't time, and Beaver Tails knew it.

Any time the spirit moved, the Snakes would start tearing down to go on toward rendezvous. When that started, Beaver Tails might forget the whole deal and light out with them.

The Wind Mountains were hazing some as the sun got higher. From the corner of his eye Mordecai saw squaws and boys bringing in ponies to lodges at the outer edge of camp. Mordecai looked at the sky and spoke.

"Talking Woman is lazy. I have to beat her much. She is ugly. Her tongue is a pointed stick tearing the peace of my lodge." He shook his head.

"You will be glad then to be without her," Beaver Tails said. "My squaws will beat her and she will not be lazy." He glanced toward the edge of camp where the first lodge was coming down.

"I would not have a friend suffer from her tongue," Mordecai said. He called to Rhoda to come over. As she came toward him he felt guilty about calling her ugly. She'd never know, of course.

"Are you ready to leave?" she asked.

"Beaver Tails wants you as part of the trade. That's him with the scars."

"What kind of savage are you, Mordecai Price?" Rhoda said coldly. "I actually believe you'd try to sell me to that ugly monster."

Mordecai gave the Indian grunt of agreement. He spoke to Beaver Tails. "Talking Woman says she has

167

heard you are a brave warrior with many coups. Seeing you, she knows the stories are true."

Beaver Tails grunted his approval of that.

"What did you say to him?" Rhoda asked.

"That I can't trade you to a friend because your tongue is too sharp." He translated to Beaver Tails: "She says it would be good to be the squaw of a brave fighter like Beaver Tails."

Beaver Tails was pleased. He almost lost his dignity by starting to rise quickly, but then he settled back and frowned a little to show that the praise of a squaw meant nothing.

"What are you trying to do?" Rhoda demanded, spacing her words with hard emphasis.

"You'd better cut loose talking mad about something, or else we're both in a kettle of stew." By Old Caleb, Mordecai thought, he might have been better off trying to steal the ponies.

"You'd do anything for the Rocky Mountain Company, wouldn't you?" Rhoda said. "Why you —"

"Be still!" Mordecai said in Shoshoni.

He had to allow she could catch on to things. She ripped into him for getting them both in such a fix, and when that ran out she dived into an angry speech about a knife fighter named Spartacus who was jawing a bunch of coons about to be et by lions. She even acted like she was Spartacus hisself, the way she yelled and flung her arms around and pointed at Mordecai in an accusing way, as if he ought to be run out of camp for not showing more interest in being chawed by the painters.

168

It was some of a tale. Mordecai was sort of took with it. Now and then he said in Injun for her to shut up, which was the signal for her to go a little stronger.

Iron Hawk sneaked off. Beaver Tails looked like he wanted to put his hands over his ears, and finally he did. Quite a crowd gathered. If it was going to work, it had gone far enough. Mordecai got up like he was madder than a sore-nosed bear. He clapped his hand over Rhoda's mouth.

She bit him hard. He let out a startled yell. Hell in a handbasket! He hadn't aimed for her to get that het up over the performance.

"Talking Woman. Wagh!" Beaver Tails rose. "Big Buffalo can keep her. Let us go pick the ponies."

"You did real fine," Mordecai muttered to Rhoda, like he was giving her the devil. Then he beat it across the river to join Beaver Tails and the others.

They were a tough breed, in good shape, the Snake ponies. The bargain Beaver Tails drove was a little tough too, but Mordecai figured the ponies could be traded back to the Snakes or someone else at rendezvous, once the whisky got to flowing strong.

Mordecai and Rhoda left the camp with Beaver Tails and five of his friends, driving seventy ponies. Through Three Horns, Mordecai had arranged for a Snake courier to scoot on to rendezvous and tell Bridger and the rest what had happened to the train. Old Gabe wouldn't sit on his haunches when he knew the fix it was in.

Rhoda stayed beside Mordecai at the tail end of the herd. "I swear you've been trying to get rid of me, one way or another, since we left St. Louis. Marrying me to an Indian . . ." She shook her head. Danged if her eyes wasn't laughing though.

Mordecai wondered how it would be trailing alone with her when he didn't have no worrisome problems. He couldn't give it too much thought. He kept looking behind at the Snakes moving toward rendezvous. Far beyond the strung-out Indians he fancied he could see a Hudson's Bay outfit in the foothills below the Wind Mountains, headed toward the Popo Agie.

Maybe by now American had overtaken Big Nose. If Big Nose had got past Deer Creek, Mordecai was going to be surprised.

The herd was raising dust in the sage. In one way it was good. Any small bunch of prowling Indians could mistake it from afar for mounted men. In another way it was bad. Any Crow or Sioux or any other Indian worth scalping would get in close enough to find out it was a pony herd with only seven men and one squaw along.

The bad outweighed the good, and then the good slipped a mite more when the Snakes discovered where five Sioux had camped recently. Mordecai wished to hell those Sioux hadn't been so wandering restless. Trailing him and Rhoda, that's what they'd been doing most likely.

In spite of Three Horns' counsel — he had twenty-seven ponies in the herd — three of the Snakes began to paint up.

"Can't you make them stay?" Rhoda asked.

"Make 'em, my foot!" Mordecai watched the three eager ones ride off to find themselves some Sioux. He'd promised them hair. It was out there if they could get it.

Three Snakes left now. Seventy ponies. Wear 'em down to the hocks and it would still be three days to Deer Creek. Four to get back this far. Two more, crowding things, to make rendezvous where the Popo met the Wind. Nine days.

Hudson's Bay might be come and gone by then.

Two night camps. That would be the time. If somebody cut in and run off a batch of the ponies, Mordecai knew just what the Snakes would say: Your ponies, Big Buffalo. You didn't pay for them but they were yours from the time we left the camp of Three Horns. That was why they weren't overconcerned about helping him get the herd to the train, but no matter what happened they'd want to be paid.

Mordecai knew how high the odds against him were. He didn't know for sure where either Hudson's Bay or the American train was. He'd know about American as soon as he got to the Rocky Mountain train and talked to Joe Hassell — if he didn't meet the American train before them.

"How far do you think Mr. Yenzer has come since we left the train?" Rhoda asked.

"I'm thinking he made it to Deer Creek."

"Where we saw the elk?"

"Yup."

"That's a long way from here."

It was for a fact. Mordecai watched the three coup-happy Snakes disappear into the hills. He said to Rhoda, "You wouldn't eat so much dust up ahead there."

"I'll stay with you."

Mordecai sort of liked the way she said it, though he guessed it didn't mean much. He watched Beaver Tails and the others. They were driving the ponies real loose, in the Indian fashion, and they were keeping a sharp eye out all around them. This wasn't their country, there were few of them, and they weren't feeling easy about things.

They stopped that night close to the Devil's Gate, where the Sweetwater swept down between tight rock walls. The Snakes, who had et about as much grizzly hair as any tribe, wanted to huddle up instead of spreading wide around the herd. Mordecai had to keep talking to them to keep them widened out some.

Late that afternoon they'd seen a single rider, far off. Sioux scout, of course, who by now had rounded up help. Mordecai was inclined to believe the Snakes were right. Beaver Tails remembered a bad thing he had seen during the day, sage-hen feathers caught in brush and crossed in an evil manner.

Mordecai made one slow prowl around the camp after dark. It was as good a place as he could have selected. One side was against a steep rock bluff. The other side was grassy land sloping to the solid blackness of the trees along the river. If the Snakes kept strung out, nobody would have much chance to creep in

172

across the open ground between the herd and the stream.

Beaver Tails came to where Mordecai was sitting. "Let us go on by night, Big Buffalo."

"The hills are rough. We would lose many ponies."

"This is an evil place." Beaver Tails repeated the story about the sage-hen feathers. He remembered, too, that he had had a bad dream the night before.

"It is a good place," Mordecai said. "Any camp is good when Big Buffalo has brave fighters with him." He built it up as much as he could. Beaver Tails listened but he didn't show any sign of becoming less uneasy. He went away disgruntled when Mordecai refused a second time to move on. They would bunch up solid and mutter about bad medicine, Mordecai knew.

Pony-stealing time was any time Injuns of any tribe could get at 'em, so Mordecai couldn't set himself for any critical period of the night. Though he dozed some, a part of him was alert. Having established the lay of the land by night, he no longer moved in any kind of patrol pattern. Mainly he sat still at the edge of the herd, facing the river with Old Belcher across his knees.

Rhoda was lying over by the bluff. She hadn't been asleep the last time Mordecai passed, for she had recognized his footstep and asked if she could help guard the ponies. "Everything's all right," Mordecai said, and went on.

Each dark hour that passed was an hour won. Coyotes mourned on the hills. Nary a red one in the bunch, Mordecai was sure. With the night more than half gone, Beaver Tails came silently to where Mordecai sat. It had been wise, the Indian said, not to go on in the night. His companions, he added, had been uncertain for a time, but now they were strong in the spirit again. They were no longer all together.

A few minutes after he left, the ponies began to stir. It wasn't much at first, no more than if a wolf was prowling the edge of the herd and the animals were bunching inward to defend themselves. They were still quiet near Mordecai, and there seemed to be no disturbance anywhere along the side that faced the river.

Mordecai heard more of them bumping against each other, more hoofs thumping as the ponies veered away from something. The excitement began to spread to the side of the herd where he was standing. Whatever it was, the source was about in the middle of the herd, and over toward the bluff, over there where Rhoda was sleeping.

The ponies broke as Mordecai was working his way around the bulge that had started toward the river. In a moment the chill night was bitter with dust and rocketing hoofs. Dark bodies flashed past him. He stood still, trusting the nimbleness of the ponies, rather than his own motion, to avoid being knocked down.

One of the Snakes fired his trade musket. Mordecai didn't see the flash. The roar served to scare the herd even more. The ponies were crashing among the trees and bushes at the river in no time. Dust hung thick and bitter.

Mordecai had never seen the beat of it. No Indian yells, no snorting from the herd, no cries of any kind.

174

Just the pounding of hoofs when the ponies broke, and that one shot. He ran toward the bluff to find Rhoda. She had run back into the rocks. Mordecai was casting around her sleeping place when she called to him.

"Did you see 'em?" he asked.

"I heard someone come out of the rocks. I'm sure he came down from the rocks. At first I thought it was you."

The Snakes were signaling to each other. Down by the river there were still sounds of ponies, and from the stony hills beyond Mordecai heard others scattering in the rocks.

"One man? You sure you heard just one man?" he asked.

"I'm sure I heard only one man."

Mordecai trotted to where he had left his and Rhoda's ponies. They were still picketed. He mounted up bareback and went to find the Snakes. Their ponies had been picketed too, although Iron Hawk's had broken loose. He had already gone to the river to catch another mount.

"I fired the shot," Beaver Tails said. "One man."

Some of the herd had stopped in the trees. Mordecai and the Snakes gathered up about twenty of them and brought them back to the grass.

"Not Sioux," Beaver Tails said. "No shouts." Later on, he decided that an evil spirit had run the ponies away.

Mordecai knew there was no use to argue about it until daylight. By then the matter settled itself, for one of the Snakes found a buffalo robe trampled in the

175

dust. The Indians handled it excitedly. It had been tanned by Blackfeet, Beaver Tails said. Yes, a cowardly Blackfoot had waved it at the ponies. A fluttering, ghostly trick that would scare horses even in daylight.

None of the Snakes wanted to stay with the recovered ponies. They had Blackfeet on the brain now, even though Mordecai doubted that they, or anyone else, could say where the robe had come from originally.

"I'll watch the ponies," Rhoda said.

Mordecai didn't want to leave her alone but he had to. Before he rode away with the Snakes, he gave her his pistol. He thought of a lot of advice to give her, but all he said was, "Forget everything and ride after us if trouble comes."

When he was a mile away he wondered if she knew how to use the pistol.

CHAPTER
FOURTEEN

By sunrise Mordecai and the Snakes had found eighteen more ponies along the river. It required a council to determine who would drive them back to camp. None of the Snakes wanted to return, but after Mordecai promised extra goods from the pack train Wounded Crow took the job.

Shortly afterward Beaver Tails began to trail a pony that had veered purposefully from the herd. He determined that it was carrying a rider. "Blackfoot." Beaver Tails' mind was set on the point.

"White man," Mordecai said. One with everything it took, too. He'd left his horse somewhere, come down the bluff on foot, put the herd on the run and got away on a stolen pony. All that took a little doin'. No Indian had done it, or else he would have picked out some of the best ponies and taken them with him.

This man was circling back now to pick up the horse he'd left. An American Company son of a bitch, sure as shooting. They'd got word of what Mordecai was up to and had sent him out to briggle up the detail.

Beaver Tails was unconvinced. "Blackfoot," he said.

Beaver Tails took off on the horseman's trail, into rough gullied land that lifted toward small mountains dark with cedar. Mordecai had to promise away more goods to keep the last Snake from going with Beaver Tails.

Here and there Mordecai and Little Foolish Bear picked up eight more ponies. Mordecai balanced time against need and decided he didn't even have hours to spare. He'd have to do with what he had.

When he got back to camp, Rhoda was cooking antelope meat that Wounded Crow had brought in. There wasn't time to wait on it. Once more Rhoda was forced to eat in the saddle, this time half-done meat.

Beaver Tails caught up late in the morning. He rode along silent for a while. Then he said, "White man." After another spell of brooding he explained that he had trailed the man back to where a pony had been left beyond the bluffs, and there he had read the sign and changed his mind about the man being a Blackfoot.

"Which way did he go?" Mordecai asked.

Beaver Tails pointed west.

Sure it was someone sent by the American. That meant their train was close, maybe even ahead of the Rocky Mountain outfit. That wouldn't make 'em ease off one bit. They turned the Crows against Rocky Mountain's trappers, tried to work on the Blackfeet, did anything they could to make it miserable for Rocky Mountain. Now they were down to running off ponies.

Shandy had a spare horse now as he rode on west from where he had picketed his mount before going down the bluff to bust up the pony herd. Slick, that had been.

178

Only poor luck of the whole thing was not getting a crack at Mordecai.

Before dark Shandy had wolfed in close enough to study the camp. He was surprised, and some worried, not to see Ree there. Just Mordecai and the Snakes and a squaw. Maybe Ree had gone on with the missionary woman, but there was a big chance he was also looking for ponies. If he'd gone on to rendezvous for help, that was bad medicine.

As she stood now, Rocky Mountain was in a fix. Mordecai wasn't going to have time enough to round up all the ponies he needed, but if Ree and a bunch came boiling in from rendezvous with a herd Rocky Mountain could still make a tight race of it.

Shandy aimed to see that no more ponies got to that crippled train. He'd run off one herd; he guessed he could handle another. If Semple wasn't after ponies at all — that was good enough. Shandy wouldn't have another lick to do; but he had to be sure.

Later on, Shandy knew he would have to settle with Mordecai. He guessed he could handle that too, when the time came. It could work out awful easy for Shandy, at that. Nesmith and Parson Bill were both back there with the train. If they didn't get overhasty and try to meet Mordecai head-on, the two of them could put him under.

Shandy rode west to take care of Ree Semple.

The Sweetwater divide was behind them now and the Platte was off to the right. A hot, gritty wind was flaying the back of Mordecai's neck. Rump hair on the scrubby ponies was lifting to it. Mordecai kept searching ahead for the dust of a pack train, knowing that if he saw dust it would be from American's big mules.

Beaver Tails spotted the man on foot. He didn't yell Blackfoot, but the way him and the other Snakes took out you could figure they was thinking they had at last an unhorsed Blood or Piegan.

Rhoda watched in horror as the Snakes rode a wide circle around their victim. "Is that all they think of — scalps?"

"About all. They're Injuns."

The Snakes didn't get a scalp. They came back to the herd with the man riding behind Little Foolish Bear.

A vision of complete disaster at the Rocky Mountain train came to Mordecai when he recognized Big Nose.

The clerk was coated with dust. His eyes were wild. His moccasins had worn out and his feet were wrapped in part of his shirt. He had a guilty, sullen look.

"Where's the train?" Mordecai asked.

Big Nose wiped dust from his lips. "This side of Red Buttes."

"What's wrong with it?"

"Everything." Big Nose eyed the ponies. "You ain't got enough to do the job."

"It'll have to be enough."

Rhoda gave Big Nose a drink from her water flask. The Snakes gave him pemmican and rigged him a bridle. He ate as he rode, telling his story between bites.

"Shandy!" Mordecai growled.

180

"That's who I said, damn it! You got ears." Big Nose told his story flatly and defiantly. "I'd been drunk since before Laramie Fork. I was dead drunk when he found me. He run me out of camp and that's it."

"You couldn't have been too drunk," Mordecai said, "or you wouldn't've got near as far as you brought the train."

"That's as far as it's going."

"We'll see. Who's carrying the pipe there now?"

"Who the hell would it be — Shandy."

"Nobody from American passed you?" Mordecai asked.

"No!"

"I don't think Shandy's with the train." Likely as sunrise, he was the one who had run off the ponies.

Big Nose stared morosely into the hazy alcoholic past. He shook his head. "If Shandy ain't in charge, I don't know who is. Maybe nobody."

"You are," Mordecai said. "And you're going to make it, too. Did Joe Hassell come back?"

"Nope."

"No word at all on the American train?"

"Nope." Big Nose spat out a hard piece of meat. He kept sizing up the herd. "You got enough horses to help some. Everybody'll still have to walk."

"I sent word to Bridger."

"Long way to rendezvous."

Once more Big Nose was working his way out of a broody spell. He was grumbling, but Mordecai could see that he was figuring too. "Lucky you didn't run into any Injuns."

Big Nose grinned briefly. "Did. Right at the start. Didn't even have my bearings yet. I was rolling along talking to myself and cussing Shandy. I seen half a dozen Sioux watching me, not fifteen rod away. For a minute I was so mad I didn't care. I started cussing them too.

"They didn't make no move, and then I begun to catch on. Thought I was crazy, they did. About that time I got sense enough back to see the fix I was in. More than tight, she was. I waved my arms around and made a speech, looking at the sky, making signs. Then I had me a vision, kneeling down, but I still had my eye on them Injuns. It worked. They left me alone. By then I was stone sober and had the shakes so bad I could hardly get the wiping stick in my rifle. Unloaded, she'd been, all that time."

"Wagh!" Mordecai said. "That'll be something to tell the boys when we roll into rendezvous."

"We can make it," Big Nose said, "but I don't know who we'll beat." After a time, he went on, slowly: "Thinking on it, I seem to recall Shandy had a man with him. Could've been two or three."

Mordecai gave him a dark stare. "I'm glad you're remembering something."

"Another thing — Lajoie, he's one of the hunters — I had a little argument with him."

"I know which one he is. Anything else?"

"If so, I can't remember." Big Nose looked down at his rifle. "Me and you go in alone, huh?"

Mordecai nodded. He looked at Rhoda. She'd heard most of it.

The sun had set when they drove the ponies down to the Platte about a mile above the Rocky Mountain camp, according to Big Nose. Mordecai pointed to himself and the clerk. "We will go to the camp so that all the white men may be prepared to receive our brothers, the Snakes."

This was pleasing to Beaver Tails and his friends.

"Big Buffalo's squaw will stay here with you," Mordecai added.

That was easy to tell the Indians, but it didn't stick with Big Buffalo's squaw when he told her.

"You're going down there to start a fight, Mordecai."

"Could happen. You're better off staying here."

"I don't think so," Rhoda said. "I'll go along."

Mordecai shook his head disgustedly.

"What are you trying to protect me from? If you and Big Nose and a half dozen others all shoot each other full of holes, I've still got to travel as far as rendezvous with the train. I may as well go back to the train now as later."

"Stay out of the way when we get there."

They crossed the Platte and went down the roughest side of the river. They went in the last quarter of a mile on foot. No guards were out. Across the river from the camp, three hunters with meat on mules were yelling for someone to come over and help them get the game across the stream. Nobody was paying much attention to the hunters.

Most of the camp, it seemed, was gathered around a card game being played on the packs.

Mordecai and Big Nose and Rhoda left the trees and walked across grass that had been cropped down to dust by the pack animals. "Stay off to one side," Mordecai said to the woman.

Someone at the card game saw them. After a quick buzz of talk there was silence. One of the players who stood up to look was still holding the pack of cards. "That's Lajoie," Big Nose muttered, "him in the cut-up shirt."

Loafers all around the camp began to rise, craning their necks. Someone said, "Big Nose!" Mainly they were silent, looking on the face of trouble, and with few exceptions having no stake in the matter.

The exceptions were the ones Mordecai wanted. "See your men?" he asked softly of Big Nose.

Big Nose hesitated. "I don't. By God I don't!"

Mordecai stopped about twenty feet from the main body of men. From the corner of his eye he noted that Rhoda had obeyed and moved away. He held Old Belcher waist high. "Who thinks he's running this shebang?" he challenged.

The turning of heads did it. Men looked down toward the packs that had been stacked to make a gaming table. A man was seated there, partly obscured by those around him. But after Mordecai's harsh question, they moved away.

"That's one of the sons of bitches!" Big Nose said.

Nesmith's hands were on the canvas that had been spread over the packs. He was not directly facing Mordecai, so that Mordecai's view was from the side.

184

Nesmith was looking along his shoulder. There seemed to be a merry twinkle in his eyes.

"You're one of Shandy's men?" Mordecai asked.

"Reckon I am."

"You just lost the job."

"So?" Nesmith said pleasantly. He did not reveal any help he had by glancing toward it. "Who're you?"

"Git!" Mordecai said.

The hunters across the river yelled angrily for help. Aside from that, the muttering of the river was the only sound.

Big Nose searched frantically for a strange face other than Nesmith's. He seemed to remember there had been only two men with Shandy, but he wasn't sure. He couldn't locate any strangers. Then in haste he settled on a man. A moment later he realized with disgust that the fellow was a packer who had been with him all the way. God damn them! If they'd spread out a little . . . But they were massed up like sheep.

Watching Nesmith, Mordecai saw the man spread his hands like a Frenchman. At the outer edge of vision, the cards fell from Lajoie's hands, not fluttering down, but in slaps like an old buffler cow letting go.

"Ain't no use to get haired up," Nesmith said. "I don't even know you." He put his left hand palm up on the packs. The other fell naturally at his side, as if he were shrugging off the whole thing. That attitude was still with him when he flipped a short rifle up from beside his leg. The forestock slapped down into his left hand in a smooth motion.

Mordecai heard the click of the big hammer as he was swinging his own weapon. He aimed and fired without time to raise Old Belcher.

Mordecai saw the smoke from Nesmith's shot, but he didn't hear the explosion of his own. He saw Nesmith's big body turn, as if the man were looking at something on his right. He was gone beaver, Mordecai was sure, but it wasn't a fact until Nesmith rolled down between the packs. Mordecai dropped Old Belcher. He drew his knife and went leaping toward Lajoie.

Lajoie had a pistol. He put his hand on it, and then he saw how Mordecai was holding the knife, poised for a throw. It ran out of Lajoie. For one uncertain moment he stood his ground, and then joined the packers and engagees who were scattering away from Mordecai's charge. Lajoie tripped over a pack. He fell and rolled on his back, putting his hands up defensively.

Mordecai spun toward the scatterment of men. He heard the voyageur Letourneau let out a high-pitched yell, "Behind! Behind!"

It was too late when Mordecai turned. He saw the rifle bearing on him, a heavy eight-sider held by a man who was kneeling behind the packs. Off balance, he hurled his knife at the sour, whiskered face behind the rifle, but he was still too late.

Big Nose's rifle boomed. He had located his man at last. Parson Bill tipped forward. His rifle barrel came down on the packs as Big Nose's bullet struck him. The ball from Parson Bill's rifle punctured one of the curved tins of alcohol in the packs.

186

The doin's was over, though Mordecai and Big Nose didn't know it for a while. Mordecai dragged out his pistol to meet further threats. Still killing mad, Big Nose was busy with his wiping stick. All the while Letourneau was saying that there were no other evil ones in camp, but his words didn't stick until the blood heat began to run out of Mordecai and Big Nose.

Mordecai saw Rhoda, stock still, staring at him as if he'd just scalped a half-dozen innocents. He turned away from her angrily. What did she think the fur trade was, a picnic on a slow Massachusetts river!

He wasn't apologizing to no one or explaining nothing.

"This here train is going on tomorrow!" he yelled.

They were building packsaddles around big fires to replace the ones left behind on dead animals. Rhoda stood alone near the river. The violence had stunned her, or so she thought at first. Now she was wondering if it had been the quickness of it all that had astonished her, and she was wrestling with the thought that it had been unavoidable.

Thou shalt not kill.

She could see Mordecai racing toward Lajoie with his knife raised. His face was ferocity itself. He was grunting like an angry bear. She was caught again with a terrible fear that Lajoie would shoot him. Something primitive in her cried out for Mordecai to win.

Then Lajoie was rolling on his back, throwing up his hands in submission and in pleading. She cried out

187

then for mercy for the helpless, although no sound came from her.

What she had seen was part of the life of "the depraved Mountain Men, more vicious than the savages with whom they consort in heathen practice," in the words of a speaker who had been as far west as St. Louis. She walked along the river slowly, still watching the camp.

The Snakes who had forsaken the pony drive to hunt Sioux were returned. Before dusk they had howled from across the river, waving a scalp. Now, apart from all the camp, they were having a victory dance, pumping their knees high, chanting, "Hey-ya! Hey-ya! Hey-i-a-a-a!"

Centuries of that.

The best of all the men of the Missionary Society, the gentle Reverend Shandy, had left a vast unmapped area between the glowing picture of salvation for the Indians and the Stone Age culture wherein they lived. Gentle words about a gentle God, hymns in a foreign tongue, and hoes thrust into brown hands trained to bear weapons were not going to roll away centuries of darkness. Or was it darkness?

"Hey-ya! Hey-ya! Hey-i-a-a-a!" The Snakes had set a pole up, with the small dark patch of the scalp suspended at the top. Terrible, yes. But they were happy too.

She was faltering and she knew it, but she knew, also, that her doubts came not from some selfish weakness within her but from a hard logic born into her. Simple prayer could not change her brain any more than a

188

blessing could change the established ways of those leaping Indians.

There was a strangeness in the whole scene from her view beyond the cast of firelight. It was like looking from some safe point in civilization upon the advance of white man into the realm of heathens. What served in dress and custom the white men had taken from their brown brothers, rejecting what did not serve them well.

But one of the Snakes in the scalp dance was staggering from drunkenness. Therein lay the whole history of the white man's encroachment from east to west: He had nothing that the Indian needed, not even religion. There could be no such thing as a quick and painless substitution of Deity.

"But I am here. I must go on."

Slowly, Rhoda went back toward the fires, knowing now beyond doubt that it wasn't she who had made the plans that had brought her here. But she had pledged herself, and now it was too late to turn aside.

The night was suddenly chill. She was aware of the great unknown country all around her. Somewhere out there a Sioux was dead, a sparrow fallen on the prairie. Someone would wail and mourn for him. Revenge. Blood. But the Snakes who had killed him were celebrating. All this was an oldness beyond time, with a familiar pattern, the strangeness lying only on the surface.

She stepped up to a fire. The men around became silent as they adjusted their minds to speaking without profanity while she was there. Mordecai had just passed on to where a group was cutting parfleche in strips to bind together the parts of the packsaddles they were making. Rhoda saw Lajoie raise his head and stare, all animal still, at Mordecai's back.

The yelling of the Snakes, suddenly more frenzied than ever, was a wail going up to the cold stars. Their noise no longer greatly bothered Rhoda, not while she was here at the fire, watching Mordecai going from one group of workers to another. Lajoie looked at her with a sneer, but she did not notice.

Across the flames she kept watching Mordecai.

CHAPTER
FIFTEEN

Late at night Mordecai and Big Nose conferred by one of the dying fires. The camp was quiet then, with even the celebrating Snakes asleep. All Big Nose's angry energy had revived while there was work to be done, but now he was weary and unusually silent.

"I'll send the Injuns down the river tomorrow," Mordecai said.

Big Nose shrugged, implying that it would be of little value to know where the American train was.

"You're against caching any goods?" Mordecai asked.

"Firewater's the heaviest thing we got." Big Nose then expressed a basic practice of the fur trade when he said, "No use to get to rendezvous without a heap of whisky."

Mordecai turned his back to the fire. "We got about forty-five Injun ponies to make up for the sixty critters that died." Tough, scrubby little beasts, but they couldn't carry like the bigger horses of white men.

"Killed the others getting this far. I'll kill some more getting on. We'll see what happens."

Twice tired enough to go to bed, they stayed by the fire with the perversity of men who know there is nothing to be wrung from fate by denying the body rest.

"What do we get out of it all?" Mordecai asked.

Big Nose looked at him as if Mordecai was crazy. "Nobody beats us, that's what. We do the job for the people that hired us."

That was about all there was to it, Mordecai allowed. It wasn't like Ree, having himself a hell of a time and thinking to get rich in the bargain.

"Don't give Shandy no chance when you rub him out," Big Nose said. "You palavered too long with Nesmith."

"Did I? You looked too long for Parson Bill, I'm thinking."

"Didn't know him, to start. That made it bad." Big Nose stretched wearily. "Guess your missionary will have to stay with us to rendezvous, after all. Bad luck, Mord."

"She ain't no missionary. Told you what she was."

"You taking her on to Cass?"

"If I don't find somebody else to do it."

Big Nose snorted. "Huh! Way you two was watching each other tonight, you ain't going to find nobody else." He stumped off to bed suddenly.

Fool thing for a woman like Rhoda to bury herself in a damp Oregon woods with a white medicine man. She'd get old and bent just as quick as if she was living in a lodge. It wouldn't do the Injuns one damn' bit of good, either. About the time everybody figured they was tamed from gobbling white man's food, which wasn't good for 'em in the first place, and grunting out

192

a few hymns, they'd get up one of their dark spites over something that didn't seem important to a white man, and then they'd go bloody, like a bunch of Blackfeet.

Mordecai had tried a time or two to explain a few things about Injun thinking to Rhoda, but he guessed she just didn't have ears for something said by a man like him. He knocked out his pipe and went to bed.

The Snake wolves came skimming back to the train in the afternoon, signaling that they'd spotted a heap of white men. Little Foolish Bear made the signs for three hundred horses. "Much dust. One sleep away."

He had overestimated the size of the train, Mordecai knew, but it couldn't be anybody but American Company. Big Nose and Mordecai looked at each other. They couldn't go one step faster than they were going at the moment. In fact, they both knew they couldn't even hope to keep up their present speed.

They watched the train moving past. The rest had benefited some of the original animals, but it hadn't been enough rest. Mules with backs rubbed raw when they were badly overloaded on the Platte trail were trying to hold back now. Some of the lame ones weren't going to last two days more. Some of the packers slogging by, a few of them nigh barefooted, looked resentfully at the mounted Snakes. Mordecai saw Rhoda riding near Lajoie, talking to him as if she found him agreeable.

"Go back," Mordecai told Beaver Tails and the other Snakes. "Watch. See if they come faster."

The Snakes had nothing better to do. It was interesting work, without risk, and they were getting paid for it. They went away happy enough.

"Know any shortcuts?" Big Nose asked.

Mordecai shook his head.

Big Nose looked back down the trail. "They're tired too. They frazzled them mules some by hurrying." But it was only wishful thinking, and they both knew it.

They were raising camp when the Snakes came in to report three men coming on from the American train. Emil Frederick himself was one of them. Grim as an insulted Crow, he was, with dust thickly overlaying the burned redness of his features. He came riding in like he meant business, instead of just coming on a pretend visit to gloat over the condition of Rocky Mountain's outfit. He always rode with a tomahawk tied at his saddle horn, and it was said he could throw it better nor he could shoot a rifle at close range. "Where's Shandy?" he demanded.

"He ain't with us," Big Nose said. "What d'you want?"

Frederick looked around the camp. He took an insulting long time in answering. "Three horses. Shandy stole 'em."

"He ain't with us," Mordecai said. "His two men ain't with us any longer, either. Have we got any of Frederick's horses, Big Nose?"

"Maybe one. You can have it back at rendezvous, Frederick."

194

"I see that one," Frederick said. "It ain't the one I'm most interested in. My buffalo horse . . . You say that's the one Shandy's got?"

"Nope." Big Nose shook his head. "I know that buffler horse of yours. He ain't been near this train."

"Best damn buffler horse there ever was," Frederick said. "Shandy stole him. I'd've give him horses if he'd asked." He looked hard at Mordecai and Big Nose, as if he had more to say about Shandy. But he didn't say it.

"I guess you'll stay with us tonight," Big Nose said. "Not that there's anything you ain't seen already."

"Thanks kindly." Frederick grinned. "Sure we'll stay." Now that the matter of the stolen horses was fairly settled in his mind, he was friendly enough.

He sat around a fire and yarned away that night with Mordecai and Big Nose. Now and then Frederick got in a careless question that was a bid for information, and a few times, caught off guard, Mordecai answered carelessly. No doubt at all, Frederick knew that Shandy had made a deal with American, and now he was fairly certain that Mordecai and Big Nose had discovered Shandy's treachery.

Where the firelight spilled but dimly against the packs some distance away, Rhoda was talking to young Etienne Beauregard, one of Frederick's aides. By Old Ephraim, she was flirting with him, Mordecai thought. First that bastard Lajoie, who would have to be killed sooner or later, and now this handsome young rooster of a Frenchman. Letourneau and the other voyageurs, who had treated her like a queen, sat at their fire and stared darkly at Beauregard.

Big Nose grumbled: "There you are, Mord. Right there's why I said no women with my train."

Frederick had a drink of Jim Bridger's good whisky. "What happened to the missionary you was taking out, Mord?"

"That's her."

Frederick stared at Rhoda. "My God!" He started to get up.

"Set still," Big Nose said. "We got trouble enough."

Under the rap of anger in Big Nose's voice, Frederick grinned and resumed his seat. "Any particular place you want me to pass you?"

"Wherever you can make it," Mordecai said. "If you think you can. Your mules pretty tired?"

Frederick motioned into the darkness where the Rocky Mountain's animals were. "Not like them. Not like them. Hear anything about Hudson's Bay coming east this year?"

"Not a thing," Mordecai said. "I guess they got a right, if they want to try it."

Frederick gave him a searching look. "Sure they do."

It was all friendly enough on the surface, as it had to be when white men met on the trail or in camp, no matter how deadly and bitter the rivalry was between the companies they represented.

In spite of his loyalty to Rocky Mountain, Mordecai had a premonition of evil days ahead. In other years when they left their forts and went into the mountains to compete for furs, American had bungled, lost men, come out a bad second — but they had learned.

It was proof of their power and learning that Frederick had come so boldly into this camp, demanding the return of stolen horses. He knew the strength that lay behind him. He was confident that nothing would happen to him, and he was sure that American would win this race and, in the end, the struggle for complete domination of the fur trade.

"Where *is* Shandy?" Frederick asked.

"Up ahead somewhere," Mordecai said curtly.

"Keep that horse he stole?"

"Nope," Big Nose said. "We ain't that bad off."

"Not that it's going to do you any good." Frederick lit his pipe. "You two could go to work for American."

"I worked for 'em once," Big Nose said. "Keep your damn' company, Frederick."

"I figure to."

Mordecai watched Rhoda going toward her shelter. Etienne Beauregard was looking after her like a moonstruck calf. Young, hell! He just had the appearance; he'd been with American anyway six years, Mordecai knew.

Frederick went to bed, yawning mightily, well pleased with himself, and as secure as if he'd been with his own train.

Big Nose said, "You'd better sleep near her lodge tonight, Mord."

Mordecai gave him a long, hard look.

"Missionary or not, she's still a woman, and a heap better looking than most."

"I ain't fretting over her," Mordecai growled.

"Yeah." Big Nose went to bed.

After he was sure Big Nose was asleep, Mordecai did go over and put his robes down near Rhoda's lodge. Wasn't no need of it, of course, but just in case Beauregard did get to stumbling around in the night Mordecai would take pleasure in breaking his head.

One of the horse guards got excited during the night and fired his musket at a white wolf. The whole camp roused up for a while, and then, cursing, went back to bed.

In the morning Lajoie and two other hunters were gone. They'd taken ponies, and the tracks led back toward the American train. Two of the ponies belonged to Lajoie, his hunting horses.

Ordinarily, Big Nose would have led a party back to overtake the deserters and deal them harsh punishment. There was no time for that now. He did accuse Frederick of luring the men away.

Frederick shook his head disgustedly. "Your men are walking. Why wouldn't they desert? I never even talked to those three."

"You'll hire 'em though, won't you!" Big Nose raged.

"Of course. The more men hired away from Rocky Mountain, the sooner you'll be wiped out." Frederick watched the packers loading scarecrow animals. More and more of the bulk of goods was being shifted to the Indian ponies. Frederick was very plainly thinking that he would pass this train soon. He was right. Both Big Nose and Mordecai knew it.

The American men didn't bother to hurry back toward their own train. They were still loafing at the campsite when the last mule groaned away under its

198

heavy burden. The Snakes who circled back later to scout reported in the afternoon that Frederick met his people halfway between the two camping places of the night before.

"Come fast," Wounded Crow said. He made the rapid passing sign with his hands. "Maybe tomorrow." He grinned, as if it all were a very fine game.

"If Bridger sends us some more ponies when he gets my message . . ." Mordecai said. Big Nose nodded glumly.

Mordecai was at the head of the train when Rhoda came up beside him. He tried to ignore her, thinking of the way she had played up to Lajoie, and then to Beauregard. She wasn't no fly-up-the-crick but sure as hell was a flirt.

After a time she said, "I suggested desertion to Lajoie."

"What for?"

"So you wouldn't kill him, or he might have killed you. Isn't it simpler just to have him out of the way?"

Mordecai was startled. She was not only looking like an Injun; she was thinking like one too.

"You or Big Nose would have killed him," Rhoda said.

"Yup. So he takes two packers with him and three ponies."

"You said the packers were no good. Two of the ponies belonged to Lajoie. You're even on the third one because you've still got one that was stolen by Shandy."

"You've got everything figured out, ain't you?" In spite of himself, Mordecai had to grin.

"What happened to Joe Hassell?" Rhoda asked.

"Shandy rubbed him out, I'm thinking. Frederick never seen him. Letourneau says Parson Bill rode his horse back to camp, claiming he found it loose. Could be them Oglalas got him, but that's a long chance."

"You think it was Shandy, though?"

"Yup."

"So you'll kill him?"

"Yup."

Rhoda kept studying him.

"What else is there to do?" Mordecai asked.

"You don't have to carry all the woes of the Rocky Mountain Company, Mordecai. Shandy has disgraced himself. Everybody will know it, and he'll be shunned and hated as a traitor. I don't see why you must kill him."

"Mainly because it'll do him good," Mordecai said.

"There was some excuse for what you had to do back there on the Platte. I don't know how it could have been settled otherwise," Rhoda said, "but you don't *have* to kill Shandy."

"On account his brother is a preacher, you mean?"

"Perhaps I thought of that, yes, but mostly I'm trying to determine whether you're a savage at heart or by necessity."

"Some of both," Mordecai said. Not kill Jim Shandy? What kind of thinking was that? If he didn't do it, somebody else sure would when they heard the story. Of course, that wasn't looking square at the thing Rhoda was talking about.

200

Take it when you wiped out a bunch of troublesome Injuns: sometimes you let one or two go so's they'd could scoot back to the main band and tell what hard doin's it was to tangle with trappers. Or you take an Injun that showed himself a big coward fighting other Injuns; like as not they'd whack him some with their bows and let him live, so's he could remember all the rest of his life what a coward he was.

Neither one of them things fitted what Rhoda was after, though. What she wanted was for Mordecai not to kill Shandy as a matter of principle, like being merciful. There was a point there, Mordecai allowed, but it didn't shine much. Get all tangled up with being merciful, and a man might end up crying over the beavers that lost toes and feet in traps, instead of cussin' them for cheating you out of prime plews.

Yup, killing would do Jim Shandy good, and Mordecai wasn't changing his ways because a woman snapped her fingers; but dang it all, she still had him trying to think over the good and bad of the thing! The next thing, if he wasn't careful, he'd be setting on a hill waiting to have himself a vision that would straighten everything out.

"You've seen an Injun or two since we started," Mordecai said. "Do you figure a little preaching and singing is going to fix 'em up with a spanking-new religion?"

"I am not the judge of that," Rhoda answered quickly.

"You'd better start being one. Ten days or so you'll be meeting this missionary coon of yours at Cass."

"That soon?"

"Yup. Then if you hurry you can make it to the mission just in time for the rain."

"You make it sound very unpleasant. You act like you don't want me to fulfill my promise."

"I don't." It came out of Mordecai without any conscious prompting from his brain.

They looked at each other steadily, until Rhoda's gaze faltered. "How far to the next camp?" she asked.

"Quite a piece." Mordecai turned back to confer with Big Nose about something. When he got to the clerk he couldn't remember what the problem was.

They camped on the Sweetwater that night. It had been a long day against a gritty wind. In spite of Big Nose's constant urging, the train had made no more than twenty miles. Mordecai doubted that they would do as well tomorrow.

He watched two packers unloading a mule. It stood with its feet wide-braced, trembling. When the packers dragged the packsaddle off and stripped the apishamore, bloody running sores showed in the steaming, flattened hair of its back. There were many more like that one, horses and mules that had done their share on the first long stretches of the Platte trail, and twice their share during the five killing days from below Laramie Fork to Red Buttes.

Shots came from near the river where packers were killing four animals that had reached the camp only because their packs had been redistributed on other beasts at nooning that day. Hard doin's and tough meat.

202

The Snakes came in with the choice parts of a buffalo cow. They said that Sun-in-the-Face, as they called Frederick, was now only a short ride away. With simple French practicality Roger Letourneau suggested to Big Nose and Mordecai, "We go back thees night, weez small party. Blankets, ze shooting . . ." He spread his hands to illustrate the American mule herd in explosive flight.

Such doin's had occurred to Mordecai already, but two or three things were immediately against the idea. Dealing in such practices themselves, the American Company would be on guard. Also, they double-hobbled their pack mules at night. And if Rocky Mountain did cause them some trouble, Rocky Mountain sure as hell couldn't stand the return visit that would be sure to come.

Big Nose mulled over another idea. "We can leave the worst of the pack horses here and make a run for it with just the Injun ponies." Then he shook his head. "Even so, Frederick could beat us, and it wouldn't do much good to get to rendezvous with just part of the packs."

"Ready to get drunk, Big Nose?"

"Nope, but I'd just as well."

Any way you laid your sights, Rocky Mountain was done, beat by Shandy's treachery. Unless Bridger showed up quick with plenty of horses, there was no hope left.

Hudson's Bay might be at rendezvous already. If they were, then there was some satisfaction in knowing that American wasn't going to make a killing. Thing of it

203

was, though, American could stand the loss. They could take their unsold goods on to Cass, their own post. Rocky Mountain had no place to go, and without any great fortune backing them they'd be ruined.

"We'll go on," Mordecai said.

"Hell yes!" Big Nose said angrily. "What else is there?"

Wolves howled all night. A great herd of buffalo rumbled by somewhere to the west during the dark hours. At breakfast Mordecai saw a packer, cutting mule meat to roast on a stick, point with his bloody knife at a wolf watching from a hill. In Injun thinking that was about as bad as you could do, point at a wolf with a knife. It was a heap worse than the white man's superstition about busting a looking glass.

Well, things couldn't be much worse anyway.

It turned out they were.

The crippled Rocky Mountain train was moving sullenly two miles from their last camp when Beaver Tails, scouting ahead, signaled excitedly that he had sighted a large body of enemies.

"Blackfeet, that's what we need about now," Big Nose growled.

Mordecai went on ahead, conscious of how his pony was failing more every day. He joined Beaver Tails to look over the enemy.

Mordecai wasn't surprised when he saw the American Company train a mile ahead. With each puff of dust from the hoofs of the big mules, the lead was increasing.

"Go in night," Beaver Tails said.

Mordecai got off his tired pony. He watched the rival train marching strongly toward the distant Mountains of the Wind.

CHAPTER
SIXTEEN

In desperation and in anger Big Nose and Mordecai
kept the train going. If Frederick traveled even part of
the night from now on, he would, Mordecai figured, be
two days up on them at rendezvous. Two days would do
it; there wouldn't be anything left but grubby furs that
nobody wanted.

As if the omen Mordecai had seen at breakfast really
had evil power, the weather changed. The sky turned a
dirty brownish color. There was a stillness in the air not
usual on the high plains. Dust clung worse than ever to
sweating bodies. The pack beasts plodded along,
chuffing dust from their nostrils, following each other
with drooping heads.

Word that American was now ahead spread through
the train. A deeper sullenness and resentment against
walking settled on the packers. There was constant
muttering each time Big Nose passed, snarling his
orders.

Only the Snakes were unaffected. They were
mounted. They had nothing to lose. Quite wisely they
had deferred taking full payment for their ponies until
the train was at rendezvous. Why should they carry all

the articles that had been promised, when the white men could carry the goods for them?

Rhoda commented on this point when she said, "I think I almost envy the freedom of Indians."

Mordecai had reason later to be thankful for the weather shrewdness of the Snakes. He was riding ahead with them when Wounded Crow pointed at the sky and said, "Great wind."

"Nothing strange in that," Mordecai said.

"Great wind. Heap great wind," the Snake insisted.

It *was* the dangedest clabbered-up sky Mordecai had ever seen so close to the mountains.

"Like Union Pass," Wounded Crow said. "Only more."

If they got wind any worse than the ones that rifled through Union Pass, it would be a dinger. Mordecai decided it would be best to camp out from the cottonwoods and close hobble every critter in the train that evening.

And then he saw the lone horseman bearing in from the trail ahead. The closer the rider came, the more familiar his way of sitting his pony was. By Old Caleb, it was too!

Ree.

Ree came in like he'd just left an hour or so before on some errand, with no argument or bad feelings possible. He took the rag off the bush for guts, that was certain.

"What's up, hoss?" he asked Mordecai.

"You tell me, you lowdown, sneaking —"

"Don't say it, Mord. I allow to everything you're thinking."

"What d'you want, Ree?"

"Nothing. Just come back to die with Rocky Mountain, is all."

Mordecai studied him with dark suspicion. "What changed your mind?"

"Just recollecting how you and me always got along so good, and all about *compañeros* in the Rocky Mountain." Ree looked over his shoulder toward the train, as if searching for someone.

"She's there," Mordecai growled. "Soft-headed enough to be glad to see you, I'm thinking. I ain't."

Ree grinned.

You had to like him, even knowing he was tricky; but you had to remember he was dirty honest. What Mordecai didn't like about him was the way he kept looking to see where Rhoda was.

"We ain't gone under yet," Mordecai said. "Why'd you come back, Ree?"

"Thought I could help. Looking at that there train, I see I can't. Warned you about American, didn't I?"

They started on ahead.

"Just once, tell the truth," Mordecai said. "Where's Hudson's Bay?"

"Just about coming up the pass now, I'd guess. The whole shebang is figuring mighty close, them, old Frederick up there, and Rocky Mountain."

"Just scouting things out, huh?"

"Done with the British, Mord."

Mordecai grunted his disbelief.

"They tried to get around me."

"That would be the day I'd like to see!"

"Swear it on my mother's grave," Ree said.

"Let's hear the rest of the lie."

"Told you what I was going to do with Hudson's Bay, didn't I? I started to do it and then —"

"You got religion."

"Shut up and let me say it! They're coming, Mord. I ain't saying that some of it ain't my fault either, but maybe they'd've come anyway. McIlvane, it is, with a whole bunch of Bannocks." Ree hesitated like he didn't want to go on.

"You look like a dog with a mouthful of bad meat," Mordecai said. "Spit it out and tell your big lie."

"Damn it, it ain't no lie! They was going to pay me, and that was fine. Then I found out the pay was an order on a bank in London. London, by Old Ephraim! Why, hell, that's clean around the world! All I had was a piece of paper with fancy writing."

Mordecai grinned. "Maybe you could've got money for it closer than London."

"Hell I could! McIlvane said I'd have to take it all the way to London."

"And you get so scared of water you dump over canoes on a piddling river like the Yellowstone."

"I'll fight you about that later," Ree said.

Mordecai looked at the sky. "So you was going to make a big raise and you pulled up nothing but chawed-off toes and mushrats. Now you come sneaking back with your troubles."

"I ain't sneaking. Thought I'd see if I could help you. You can go to hell if you say I'm sneaking back."

Ree could have stopped with the American train, no doubt.

"You're too late to help us any," Mordecai said, "but hang around and eat mule meat if you want to."

"Guess I will." Ree turned his pony and went trotting back toward the train, straight back to Rhoda.

"Big wind soon," Wounded Crow called.

"Just had one," Mordecai said.

Mordecai wasn't one to overlook an Injun's warning about nothing. He took it in dead earnest when the Snakes veered off into a rocky gulch and began to unsaddle their ponies. The air was deadly still then, with an oppressive feeling of heaviness and tension.

Mordecai went racing back to the train. Down near the Sweetwater were heavy willow thickets reaching out a piece from flooded ground near small beaver ponds. A few cottonwoods and box elders grew near the higher ground at the head of the thicket.

Big Nose had been worrying about the weather too. He began to turn the train as soon as Mordecai shouted. Ree left Rhoda and rode back down the line, urging the packers on toward the willow thicket. Tired as the men were, the urgency spurred them on, although few understood it and most of them yelled questions about an Indian attack.

The lead mules crashed into the thicket. Mordecai turned them back and yelled for the packers to unload on dry ground. The willows were flooded worse than he'd thought, but when he rode through them he

210

discovered that it was recent flooding from the dams and that there was strong sod still underfoot.

They heard it coming from the west then, a distant humming sound, and then a roaring that made the still air around them vibrate.

Some of the packers left the animals and dived into the willows. Ree and Mordecai and Big Nose drove them out, nearly trampling two of them with their horses. Mordecai caught a glimpse of Rhoda and Letourneau turning mules that were trying to run away. Others with their packs still on stumbled into the willows, and some of them went too far and bogged down. Yelling as they rode, Ree and Mordecai and Big Nose at last beat some system into the confusion.

Run the pack animals to the cottonwoods in three lines. Pile the packs. Freeze into it, you pork eaters! Move! Hell with the packsaddles; leave 'em on! Get them horses into the willows!

The flooded bottom began to fill with splashing animals. A horse snorted when its forefeet dropped into a beaver run. It snapped a leg and threshed desperately to rise, and then other horses, crowded from behind and lashed by frantic packers, trampled over the struggling pony and drowned it.

Letourneau and another voyageur were roping the packs together as fast as they fell upon the ground. There was no longer any order in the stacking. The two Frenchmen ran ropes through the loops of the panniers, dragged the packs into the pile, and secured the ropes to the base of the cottonwoods.

The booming noise was coming closer. Mordecai saw the vague form of it, a gigantic whirlpool dark with dust. It seemed that it would come twisting in directly where the pack train was. The packers near the end of the line thought so too. Mordecai had to threaten them with Old Belcher to keep them from leaving the frightened animals. Even so, two of them scurried under the bellies of the horses and plunged away into the willows, wading out until they were chest deep.

There wasn't time to unload all the pack horses. Mordecai ran to where Ree was lifting packs. "Take some men and watch the lower end of the willows to keep the horses from running away!"

"They ain't got the strength to run!" Ree shouted, but he spun away and grabbed Letourneau by the shoulder, yelling at him. Letourneau charged into a group of voyageurs who were pawing aimlessly at ropes while their eyes looked wildly at the oncoming tornado. Letourneau drove them before him toward the downstream end of the thicket. A moment later Mordecai saw Ree grab Rhoda by the arm and hustle her along with him as he ran to take charge of the voyageurs.

Big Nose was hauling men away from lifting the packs, shouting at them to go to the other end of the willows to keep the horses from running. The wind itself would hold one side and the beaver ponds would block the other.

With the help of the few packers that were left, Big Nose and Mordecai drove the last of the still-burdened pack animals into the willows. One of the mules turned stubbornly away and went bucking directly into the path of the whirlwind. It stopped suddenly when the saddle slipped and the packs swung under its belly.

Big Nose took two steps toward it, and then turned and ran into the thicket, crying something over his shoulder at Mordecai. The grass was lifting and bits of sage were spinning through the air.

As Mordecai leaped into ankle-deep water at the edge of the thicket he saw a tarpaulin rise and wrap itself around a cottonwood like a living thing. He saw the stubborn mule turn its rump to the wind. It lifted its head and brayed, but the sound was lost in the awesome roaring.

The worst on Union Pass was a gentle breeze compared to the force that struck an instant later. Mordecai dropped flat in the shallow water, with Old Belcher under him. He grabbed the base of a willow clump. He felt himself bounced up and down. He struck soggy turf. The water under him had been sucked away. An instant later it came sweeping over him two feet deep, and then once more he was lying on soaked ground and the willow clump was vibrating under the terrible force of the wind.

It was he who should have watched after Rhoda, he thought, and then he wondered if the packs would be torn apart and scattered.

Dust to choke a prairie dog. The wind hammered with monstrous eagle wings. Mordecai was aware of the odor of bruised sage. He heard but dimly the noise of the cottonwoods being splintered. The terror-stricken braying of mules was a thin wail in the violence.

And then the whirlwind was gone, belting away with terrible force through a heavy growth of cottonwoods a short distance up the river. Where the river turned to the south, the twisting power slammed straight on into a rocky hill, leaving in its wake a swath of uprooted sagebrush.

All along the edge of the willows where Mordecai had clung the leaves had been stripped from the growth. For a moment longer he held hard to the toughly rooted clump of willows. Then he stood up. Shredded leaves and bits of sage were settling on the dripping mules and horses. Wide-eyed men were popping up from behind the willows. Some of them had stood deep in the water. Thin against the receding booming of the wind came Big Nose's shout, "Get them mules out of there!"

Mordecai went over to the packs. From the height of his head the cottonwoods had been torn away, with the whole top masses down to the last twig borne away by the wind, so that the ground around the packs was bare. Most of the ropes the voyageurs had tied to the trees had held, though some of the panniers were ripped. One of the tins of alcohol had been smashed against a tree. It was making a slow thumping sound as the liquid drained out in spasmodic surges.

Mordecai was going toward the lower end of the thicket when he saw Ree and Rhoda coming toward him. He turned away then and went to find Big Nose. The packers were talking excitedly now, telling of their individual escapes from death as they drove the pack animals from the thicket.

214

"It don't look so bad," Big Nose said. "How about the packs?"

"They're not hurt much," Mordecai said.

"I hope it scattered American from here to the Yellowstone," Big Nose said savagely. "It might've too, unless they got into the rocks awful fast up there ahead."

When the Snakes came riding back a short time later, Mordecai sent them out to see what damage Frederick's outfit had sustained. Rocky Mountain was straightening out and counting losses then. Two horses and a mule dead from drowning. No sign at all of the loaded mule that had broken away from going into the thicket. Some damaged packs but only a light loss in goods, mostly sugar and flour from sacks broken by the hasty dropping of packs.

By no means had the outfit caught the full force of the whirlwind. Mordecai knew that when he walked up toward a hill a few hundred yards away. There the sage had been ripped off at ground level, and where bunch grass grew it stood in clumps several inches high above the earth, with the soil around it scoured away.

The dismal brown overcast still hung in the west, but off in the south there was a sign of clearing.

Mordecai was walking back to where Big Nose was having camp set up, when a rider with a led horse appeared on the downriver trail as if he had been spawned from the whirlwind. Mordecai walked out a ways to meet him.

It was Tom Fitzpatrick, grizzled, red-eyed from dust, with a gauntness in his face more marked than usual.

He got off his pony stiffly. "This child has seen some wind."

"We was in it," Mordecai said. "Where's the ponies?"

"What ponies?"

"I sent word by a Snake to rendezvous, about the fix we was in."

"Spotted Dog, yeah. It warn't clear what he was trying to say, outside of you was taking back all the ponies you needed, and wanted somebody to meet you."

"Ain't got the ponies now," Mordecai said.

Fitzpatrick frowned at the herd of pack animals. "Seemed like twice that many where I first struck the sign."

"It was. Our tracks are on top of the sign of two hundred mules. Emil Frederick is ahead of us now."

Fitzpatrick turned white. "American? You're fooling!"

"Half a day ahead, at least."

They sat down cross-legged on the ground. Mordecai told the whole story.

"Don't hardly want to believe Shandy would do it," Fitzpatrick said, "or nobody else Campbell and Sublette would trust. If Big Nose was drunk, like you say —"

"I ain't arguing about Shandy. Believe anything you damn please about him! What did Spotted Dog say about the Hudson's Bay train? He hadn't even mentioned American's train."

"He said it was coming toward the Siskadee."

Injun messengers! Mordecai cursed them all. "McIlvane is on his way to rendezvous, damn it!"

"Wagh! From what Spotted Dog said, we figured the British was going to set up on the Siskadee and try to draw some of the trade away."

Mordecai glanced toward camp. Ree was striding out toward them. "I'm thinking the British are remembering when Ashley lifted their fur cache, and that time you out-likkered plews away from Ogden."

"Maybe so." Fitzpatrick looked at Ree. "Semple working for Campbell and Sublette?"

"Nope. He sort of come along, is all."

"He'll do, that Ree," Fitzpatrick said, "providing he ain't up to something, like usual."

"He ain't." Mordecai knew his voice was carrying to Ree. "He rode clean over the pass to the Siskadee to see where the British was."

"Find 'em, Ree?" Fitzpatrick asked.

"I seen 'em. I didn't get along." Ree gave Mordecai a brief, apologetic look, as if thanking him for the lie.

"Thing is," Fitzpatrick said, staring at the miserable collection of animals, "what're we going to do?"

"Go on as best we can," Mordecai said. "There's a chance Frederick got busted up by the whirlwind. The Snakes just went ahead to have a look."

Fitzpatrick got up and mounted his pony. "I'll see for myself." He went bumping past the camp with his faded blanket leggins aswing against the sides of the pony. He twisted to gawk as he passed Rhoda, and then twisted even further to look back at Ree and Mordecai.

"So you wouldn't have me skulped by my own people?" Ree mused.

"I lied. Don't know why. You ain't scarcely worth it."

"Make it up to you, I will, comes a chance." Ree went back to where Rhoda was sorting out her plunder from a wind-ripped pack. Mordecai saw her hastily shoving the Mandan-dancer pantaloons into a bag as Ree approached.

Fitzpatrick and the Snakes returned at dusk.

"The wind got at 'em, sartin," Fitzpatrick said. "They're some scattered up, but they're riding like hell to get things pulled together."

"How bad they hurt, you figure?" Big Nose asked.

"Wouldn't bet on more'n a day, knowing Frederick."

"That's something," Mordecai said.

Big Nose shook his head. "Not near enough."

Three voyageurs, intrigued by the disappearance of the mule that had shied away from the willows, had gone down the whirlwind's path looking for it. They returned as Fitzpatrick was talking, lugging items from the pack. They were staggering drunk, also. One of them explained that they had found a tin of alcohol smashed shapeless against the rocks, with a little of the contents still remaining, though not enough to warrant carrying the tin back to camp.

"They must've had stronger medicine than that with 'em," Fitzpatrick commented. "They's a handful of Blackfeet down that way. Chased me, they did, almost from the time I left rendezvous."

Beaver Tails perked up at once. Blackfeet, huh? In the morning the Snakes would see about that.

218

That night the Snakes jarred the weary camp when they fired twice at shadowy figures close to the ponies. They didn't bring down anything but neither did they lose any ponies. Little Foolish Bear swore that the intruders were Crows, saying that he had caught a glimpse of their hair as they raced away.

Beaver Tails would settle for nothing but Blackfeet, and Fitzpatrick supported him. "The Crows plumb disappeared this spring when they heerd the spotted death was killing off plains Injuns," Fitzpatrick said. "They been cached out somewheres for months."

When the train moved on in the morning the Snakes stayed behind to do some purifying and praying before going on the trail of Blackfeet.

Ree and Rhoda stayed along close together, talking something over real earnest. Now and then they laughed.

It sort of soured Mordecai to see them laughing like that, considering the fix Rocky Mountain was in.

CHAPTER
SEVENTEEN

They passed the American train in camp that day. Packers and voyageurs who had grumbled about Big Nose's tyranny and talked secretly of killing him quickened their pace, although some of them were walking now without boots, with parfleche crudely bound around their feet; but they went a little faster and let out a ragged cheer when they saw the opposition camped against the river.

Mordecai and Fitzpatrick rode down to have a look.

Frederick was gone, away with the men who were looking for mules that had stampeded when the whirlwind struck. Mordecai saw one of the men who had deserted with Lajoie, although the fellow tried to hide behind a mule. The Rocky Mountain men sized things up and started back to their own train, passing slowly through the hills south of the river.

Fitzpatrick shook his head. "It's mules that run off with packs they're after. They could move right now with what they got."

"Yup." Frederick would be moving soon, Mordecai was willing to bet. He had men enough to leave a party behind to chase after those valuable packs. That was

American for you: more men, more money, more size to take losses than any outfit in the mountains.

They passed two sore-footed ponies that Big Nose had left behind.

The Sweetwater was becoming smaller. Off to the north lay the Rattlesnake Hills. Soon it would be time to turn that way, around the western flank of the hills and up the small divide above the Popo Agie. Frederick could make it to rendezvous in two days; less time than that if he cared to.

They caught up with the Rocky Mountain train. It was stopped while Big Nose was cutting out more dying animals and redistributing their packs. Mordecai wondered if the outfit would last to the next steep hill.

He rode on past to go out in front as a scout. About an hour later he saw Fitzpatrick angling off toward the northern hills at a fast trot, with his spare pony streaming along behind him. He waved when Mordecai signaled, but he didn't slow up or change direction. It was too late to do any good by bringing ponies back from rendezvous, but that must be what Fitz had in mind.

Big Nose didn't know much about it when Mordecai talked to him in camp that night. "He said to keep going. Said he'd be back, and that's all I know. Better ask your missionary and Ree. Fitz had a big powwow with them afore he streaked off."

Ree was no more helpful than Big Nose. "Said he was going to rendezvous to bring back the Snakes."

"It's too late for that!"

"That's what he said." Ree shrugged. The tricky lights were in his eyes again. By Old Caleb, he never changed. He was always up to something.

Mordecai eyed him hard and turned away, not even asking Rhoda what she knew about Fitzpatrick's going. Whatever was tickling Ree, it wasn't nothing that could hurt Rocky Mountain now.

They watered on the narrowing Sweetwater for the last time. In the morning, when they were loading up for one more try, the American train went by. Once more they'd traveled part of the night.

Mordecai saw a packer drop a saddle in the middle of its swing to the back of a pony. The man just let the saddle drop and stood beaten and disgusted, watching the powerful mules stride past.

"Swing those packs, you pork eaters!" Big Nose yelled. "Load 'em up and move!" He ignored three mules that had lain down the night before and now were too far gone to get on their feet.

Busy with helping get the dispirited outfit on its way, a last futile effort, it seemed, Mordecai didn't know until the American train was out of sight that Ree had gone with it and taken Rhoda along. It was a crowning blow. Ree — hell, he'd do anything, but Mordecai had sort of figured that Rhoda would stick it out.

Letourneau said: "She say she must get quick to ze rendezvous to meet her hosband to marry. Zis is too slow. She ask Ree to take her now."

Maybe that was it, but Slocum wasn't at rendezvous; he was supposed to be waiting at Cass. All right, let Ree take her all the way now. He had more tricks than an

222

Arapahoe medicine chief, damn his soul. He always came out with something good while others were getting their heads cracked.

I ought to go put him under, Mordecai thought.

But he didn't go. Whatever happened to Rhoda now was her own choosing. In spite of all that, Mordecai every now and then glanced back along the line of broken horses and beaten men, and had to remember that she wasn't with the train any more.

Only the Injun ponies were making it at all now. Tonight's camp would likely be the end of moving for a while.

Late in the day Mordecai found out that Rhoda had taken none of her baggage with her, except, according to Letourneau, the small bag she always carried on her pony.

Emil Frederick got even more red in the face as he welcomed Rhoda Marsh to the American train. He had met her before, of course, when he spent the night in camp with Rocky Mountain. She explained honestly enough that Rocky Mountain's train was in poor condition and might have to rest before it could reach the rendezvous, and that she was somewhat anxious to get on as fast as possible.

"You come to the right place," Frederick said. It pleased him that a good-looking white woman, though clothed in Indian garb, chose to put herself under the protection of his command. Further, it would humiliate Rocky Mountain even a little more. Even a missionary woman had got disgusted with them.

223

"The American Company has always been interested in helping out missionaries and such," Frederick bragged in a careless moment, and then blinked in a bewildered way when he considered the enormity of that lie.

To return to more familiar, safer ground, Frederick looked at Ree. There was nothing bewildered about the American Company clerk then. "I don't want you around, Semple."

"Mr. Semple is to accompany me to Fort Cass," Rhoda said. "He's been very kind and helpful."

"So?" Frederick glowered at Mr. Semple. "Wouldn't want no wimmin of mine 'companied nowhere by the likes of him." He added hastily, "No disrespect to you, ma'am." He considered, thoroughly in command of things. "We'll be at rendezvous day after tomorrow. Happens I'm sending some reliable men to Fort Cass — that's an American Company post, you know. I'll fix it so —"

"That's very kind of you, Mr. Frederick," Rhoda said, "but I wish it understood that I have the utmost confidence in Mr. Semple."

Frederick's glare at Ree implied that there was something too unholy to mention involved when a man like him could gain the confidence of a woman like Rhoda. "Well, he can stay with my train, I guess."

The American Company had a heavy score against Ree Semple, and Frederick was well aware of the tab. Not least was the loss of twenty trappers and their furs on the Madison two years before when Ree had talked the whole kit and caboodle into defecting to become free trappers.

The King of Missouri, Kenneth MacKenzie, down at Fort Union, would have grown purple talking about the crimes of Ree Semple against the American Company. "The man is a trouble-maker. He has no loyalty anywhere."

Far from pleased at having Ree with his train, Frederick let him stay. He watched him, though, and warned his head men to do likewise. Ree went along as happily as a stuffed Indian, doing nothing more dangerous than entertaining American Company engagees with stories around the fire at night.

So absorbed was Frederick in watching him that he worried not a bit about Rhoda's friendly conversations with the Rocky Mountain deserter, Lajoie.

Tom Fitzpatrick broke down one pony and abandoned it soon after he crossed the Little Beaver. The second one was near dead when it carried him into rendezvous at the mouth of the Popo Agie that evening. He'd ridden sixty-some miles.

On a grassy place against the two rivers, the Wind and the Popo Agie, the rendezvous site was one of the prettiest places in the mountains. Old Fitz had no time for beauty tonight.

He left his heaving, near done pony near the lodges of Three Horns' Snakes and ran on toward the hill where Bridger was camped with his squaw and a passel of her Ute kin. He saw that another big bunch of Injuns had come in since he left. Bannocks. Their lodges were near the upper end of the camping place.

Bannocks! They was supposed to be coming with the Hudson's Bay train. Maybe he was too late. But he didn't see no signs of a train, and the trapper camps spread all over the place were no noisier than usual, which was a good sign no whisky drinking and trading was under way.

Fitzpatrick busted in on Bridger as he was eating. Only his wife and little daughter were in the lodge with him. "Bad doin's, Jim. American's almost here with a train."

Bridger got up. He tossed the bone he was gnawing on outside to the dogs. He was a hard man to shake, but right now he was some jarred. "McIlvane is coming too, we found out. Campbell took a bunch and went to palaver with him to see if he could slow him down." Bridger stepped outside and yelled toward the company lodges near his, "Sublette! Hey, Sublette!"

Fitzpatrick picked up a boss rib and began to eat ravenously.

The three of them conferred, Milt Sublette, with short pipe in his long, quiet, scarred face; slow-spoken Bridger; and quick-minded Fitzpatrick, the shrewdest and most enterprising of them all. It was in an Indian lodge against a forested hill, but it was no less desperate and sharp than any business conference anywhere among men facing financial extinction.

They gave the facts ruthless consideration: They didn't have much chance. Then Fitzpatrick stated his wild plan. It sounded so bad at first that Sublette and Bridger looked away from him, as if they couldn't

226

witness the shame of an old *compañero* losing his mind.

"Ree Semple," Sublette said. "Anybody mixes with him and his ideas and somebody winds up getting his ass scorched."

"It's still an idea," Fitzpatrick said. "You got one?"

"Take some doin's to get the Bannocks and Snakes together right now," Bridger said. He explained that they'd had a fierce family quarrel over some pony thieving early in the summer. Three Horns had been angry as all get-out when the Bannocks paraded into rendezvous this afternoon, after leaving the Hudson's Bay train three sleeps back. "Kept 'em from fighting, I did. They give each other gifts." Bridger was dubious about getting the two groups together for something like Fitzpatrick wanted.

"Got to make it work," Sublette said. "What else is there?"

"You got the best savvy with Injuns, Gabe," Fitzpatrick said. "Let's get some chiefs together and get the powwow started."

They held the council in Bridger's lodge, with the door flaps tied back so that the ranks of Indians outside, with their heads and shoulders standing against the dark skyline, could hear what was going on.

The lodge was full: Three Horns and five lesser Snake chiefs; Bell Rock, Catch-a-Fish, and other ranking men of the Bannocks, brothers of the Snakes, but brothers who often had bad hearts against everyone but themselves.

Nothing could be hurried. Bridger smoked and spoke of the long friendship of the Snakes and Bannocks — he was stretching things considerable on the last — with the trappers of the Rocky Mountain Company. Did not the Rocky Mountain — he had to name the men, for the company meant nothing to the Indians — always come into the country of their friends with goods to trade, unlike the men of Red Coat MacKenzie, who stayed in forts and asked the Indians to come to them?

He made much of friendship, valor, and the strong spirit of Rocky Mountain and its Indian friends.

The Snakes knew straight words when they heard them. The Bannocks sat with their mouths down-turned. Silent stood a great crowd of fighting men of both tribes outside, and in silence the squaws behind them listened.

Bridger established friendship. Now, Rocky Mountain, always naming the white men present and others that the Indians knew, was again coming with much trade goods to the rendezvous. They were having trouble with weak mules and horses, having come such a great distance to trade with their friends. Others were ahead of them.

The Bannocks' dark eyes glittered with malicious humor.

This would hurt Rocky Mountain greatly, but that was not the bad thing about it. There was much worse, and that was why the council had been called to warn the people of the Snakes and Bannocks.

228

In the trains of Hudson's Bay and American Company was the spotted death.

Some of the lesser chiefs covered their mouths. From the crowd outside there came a grunt of rage and fear.

"The spotted death is in the firewater that Sun-on-the-Face and Red Man bring," Bridger said solemnly. "It is also in their food, and it crawls like little lice in all their trade goods, waiting to bite those who receive them."

Terror and anger leaped in the eyes of the Indians. The spotted death that rotted the faces of strong warriors, of children, of squaws. Once it started, flight did not help. The spotted death followed like the wind.

"Why have no Crows been seen this summer?" Bridger asked. They knew about the spotted death. Red Coat at Fort Union had sent word to warn them to stay deep in the mountains, but he was sending his train to the Snakes and Bannocks, a train that crawled with the lice of the rotten-faced sickness. Rocky Mountain would not do this.

The rage increased. The council almost got away from Bridger. Some of the lesser chiefs who should have waited for their elders to speak forgot themselves and suggested that it might be well to kill all the white men in the mountains.

Others were for running away at once, like the Crows.

Three Horns began to speak. "We have known that the Crows have been afraid of the spotted death, but we have seen none. Why is it that the trains of Red Man and the American Company chief bring the death, but the other train, which is behind, brings nothing but good?"

"It is in the firewater. It escapes and goes everywhere when the firewater is released," Bridger said.

Three Horns, very grave, wanted to know if it was not so that firewater was all made the same way, in great kettles stirred by white men with red masks, with burning rocks making the flames underneath.

That was so, Bridger allowed.

Then why did the firewater of one train contain the spotted death while the firewater of another did not?

"It's a difference in the way of cookin'," Bridger said. He made mystical signs and stirred with his hands as he tried to explain.

"Boiled white beaver, Gabe," Fitzpatrick said quickly.

"Should've thought of it." Bridger had his head again. He asked the Indians why it was that white-meated beaver, such as were found on a few streams, poisoned anyone who ate it as boiled meat, while causing no harm at all if eaten roasted.

The Snakes grunted. This was a fact well known to them. The Bannocks could not deny it either.

It was the same thing with firewater, Bridger said. It had to be cooked properly; but this time, being in a great hurry, the American Company and the British had got their firewater from people who didn't know any better than to boil a white-meated beaver.

Fitzpatrick and Joe Meek and Sublette gave solid grunts of affirmation.

230

"Nobody has to get the spotted death," Bridger told the Indians. Were the Snakes and Bannocks who had come a great distance to trade with their friends to be scared away into the mountains before they did any trading? All they had to do was to ride in force and warn the two bad trains not to come any farther, but to return to their homes at once.

They were brave people, the Snakes and Bannocks, and there were many of them. Some of the Blanket Chief's men would ride with them to parley with the white men of the bad trains and to advise them strongly that the Indians would not have them come any closer to rendezvous.

"Jesus, Gabe," Joe Meek muttered, "you'll have 'em rubbing out the whole shebang."

There would be no fighting, Bridger said, but the two bad trains with their deadly sickness must be made to stop.

Once more old Three Horns, who knew well that the Crows considered Jim Bridger a greater liar than even a Crow, interposed a shrewd question: "Who has seen the spotted death coming?" The Bannocks had traveled far with Red Man. They had seen no sickness among his men.

Fitzpatrick said, "I have seen the sickness on the face of a Frenchman with the train of Sun-on-the-Face."

"Little Thief, the Nez Percé, saw the sickness last night on the face of a man with Red Man's train," Sublette said. "That was why Little Thief left so hastily for his own country in the mountains." As a matter of fact, Little Thief had left hastily because of a quarrel with his relatives. Sublette hoped he would stay mad a long time.

The truth was easy to find out, Bridger said. Let all the Snakes and Bannocks go to meet the train. Then let a few of the chiefs ride close enough to see for themselves if the spotted death was there.

Catch-a-Fish glowered. This would take council, he said. He himself favored striking out for the mountains at once, without going near the white men who had the spotted death. Why was it that white men always brought bad things to the Indians?

Not the men of Rocky Mountain, Bridger said. They were bringing many good things. It was the others who were of such bad hearts that they didn't care if the Bannocks died like leaves falling in the autumn. Let them be warned not to come farther. That was all that was needed, except some ponies to help the Rocky Mountain train reach rendezvous.

Bell Rock of the Bannocks said his people had much to trade. They would not like to carry everything back to their homes. Neither did they wish to die of the spotted death. Yes, this would require a council.

Three Horns said that his people were friends of all the white men. He was afraid that if the Indians went to warn the trains not to come closer, the white men would not stop. All white men were very anxious to get beaver furs, and there were many packs of furs at this place. If the two trains were carrying spotted death and refused to stop, then some of Three Horns' young men might lose their heads and begin shooting.

This would be bad.

232

Yes, there should be a council, with no one but the Snakes and Bannocks present.

Let it not last too long, Fitzpatrick said. The spotted death cared nothing for councils.

The Indians went away to make preparations for the council. The Mountain Men stepped out of Bridger's lodge for fresh air.

"She don't look good, I'm thinking," Meek said.

"Wal, I've lost everything before," Bridger said. "All of us have."

"Hell to be depending on Injuns." Meek shook his head.

They all knew what he was thinking: They could take some of their most loyal trappers and make a fight of it to keep the rival trains from coming in.

They looked at the scene before them, fires bright against the night at the camps of various groups, free trappers, Rocky Mountain trappers, and the two great encampments of the Indians. On the slope behind Bridger's lodge, in the edge of the trees, was the fire of the Slocum fellow and another missionary who had arrived two days before, guided by Flatheads.

The missionaries had chosen to stay apart from the general welter of rendezvous, while the Flatheads, like the small group of Nez Percés, hung close to the lodges of the white chiefs for protection.

"Heap of beaver packs around here," Fitzpatrick said.

"Campbell ain't going to do no good stopping Hudson's Bay with words," Meek said.

They heard the distant voices of the criers announcing the council.

"*Got* to depend on the Injuns," Sublette said.

It was the final word and they knew it. Even in the fur trade some things wouldn't go. Robbery was allowable. Ashley had handed the British a dose of that long ago. MacKenzie, the American Company king, regularly employed the Crows and Blackfeet to steal from rivals with the Blackfeet mixing killing into the process.

Cheating was all right. Backing out of contracts was not considered unfair, except by those who lost because of it. Individuals of different companies could kill one another, and sometimes did. That was their business. But massed, bloody war by one group of white men against another just didn't shine.

Hudson's Bay and the Northwesters had driven each other to the verge of ruin by years of wholesale murder — until they had had to give up and get together.

"Was a heap of plews here," Meek said, as if they were already in the hands of American or the British. " 'Pears we'll be working for Hudson's Bay or old MacKenzie this robe season."

"I'll starve first," Bridger said.

From the massed Indians listening to the council came deep grunts of approval, "Hagh! Hagh!" as some speaker made his point.

"Hell to have to have it resting on Injuns," Joe Meek said.

"How else was it ever?" Bridger said. "Wasn't no Injuns, greenhorns would be dabbing traps in every crick in the mountains, and most of the buffler wallers too."

The council was still in full swing when a courier from Campbell arrived. He reported that a powwow with McIlvane and threats to invade the British country west of the mountains hadn't slowed "the damn' stubborn Scotsman one little bit." McIlvane would camp tonight — which meant he was already camped — on Squaw Fork near the head of Little Beaver.

That meant he would be into rendezvous day after tomorrow.

Campbell was still trying words, but things looked hopeless. His last suggestion was to move the rendezvous.

Two weeks ago, even maybe a week, that might have been possible, since everyone at rendezvous thought only one train was coming, Rocky Mountain's, but now they knew from the Bannocks and Snakes that there were others close at hand. Nobody was going to move now.

"Sure was a nice bunch of plews," Meek said.

Elisha Slocum, one of the missionaries, had seen the courier arrive. He came down the slope to ask Bridger if there was any fresh news about a white woman traveling with either of the Yankee trains. He was a fair-looking man, Slocum, tall and square-faced, polite as anything.

Fitzpatrick said he reckoned the woman Slocum was asking about was with the American Company train.

"Oh? And when will it arrive?" Slocum asked.

"Too damn' quick, I'm thinking," Meek said.

"It might be held up some," Bridger said.

Meek laughed with quick humor that puzzled Slocum, who said, "My Flatheads have it from the Shoshones that the lady was originally with your train. Can you tell me why the change?"

"Everything out this way changes except the mountains," Sublette said.

"I see." Slocum didn't see anything except that these savages disliked him and resented his presence and would give him nothing but evasive answers. He went back to his camp.

"Enough of *them* out here, and even the mountains are going to change," Meek grunted. "My Flatheads!"

"When you hear some greenhorn say 'my Blackfeet,' then, by God, you'll sure enough know things are going to hell!" Sublette said. "I'm going down to that council and —"

"Won't do no good," Bridger said. "Stay away."

Meek went to his lodge and returned with a piece of hump meat. He looked toward the council and chewed, his chin shining with grease. "Them Hudson's Bay blankets do shine considerable. You got to allow that, boys. How many plews do you figure they'll want this year for a couple?"

"You find out, Joe," Old Gabe said. "They'll be handy to hold all the different parts of your carcass when we're burying you."

Meek liked to choke on his meat as he laughed. Nothing tickled him more than to rile Old Gabe and make him growl.

Down at the council there was a deep silence except for a thin old voice speaking slowly. From one of the winking campfires of the free trappers came a sudden outburst of laughter as someone finished a story. At the edge of the trees behind the lodges of the company men Slocum was trying to lead the Flatheads in a hymn. He had a fine tenor voice.

CHAPTER
EIGHTEEN

Baptiste Lajoie squatted beside Rhoda's campfire, not yet quite sure enough of himself to sit down, as Ree did when he was there. Ree was farther up the slope, with the hunters who were butchering elk that had been brought in that afternoon. It was not yet dusk.

"Good medicine, yes?" Lajoie pointed at the little rawhide bag which hung in a buckskin netting above the swell of Rhoda's breasts.

Rhoda smiled briefly. She nodded.

He was suspicious by nature, Lajoie, hating darkly from both the Cree and French sides of his heritage. He hated this woman because she was white, and at the same time there was a boiling lust in him to have her because she was white.

If she had been too friendly, he would have withdrawn to figure out why it was so. No woman like her wanted a half-breed, he was sure. She was polite to him, but no more polite than to other members of the American Company train.

And yet sometimes Lajoie thought there was a hint of something else in her dark eyes, something for him alone. This, also, made him suspicious. He could not trust anyone. He could not trust himself.

But still he kept coming to her fire when he could. Tomorrow the train would be at rendezvous, and then what would Baptiste Lajoie be among the swaggering, dangerous trappers? Nothing. Someone to guard the furs bought by Frederick. Someone to take a giggling squaw out in the tall grass for a piece of strouding or other bauble given to her husband.

Hating but fascinated, Lajoie squatted by the fire. The wide piece of buckskin that was tied to the net of the medicine bag ran around Rhoda's neck on the outside of her braids, bending the shining hair where it touched. She dressed like a squaw; she should be like a squaw.

But Lajoie knew better. He had seen her eyes change when he was stumbling to say things that would be easy to say to a squaw. She was no squaw whore. By damn, then why was she friendly to Lajoie?

One of the guards on a small hill above the camp yelled, "Hoss!" He held his rifle high and pointed north. It was not enough to throw alarm into the seasoned men of the train, although they picked up their rifles, and some of them walked in the opposite direction from the warning to have a look around.

A dozen riders came over a hill to the north. Most of them were Indians, with two or three white men among them. They stopped and made the signs of peace and asked for a talk.

Emil Frederick went out to meet them.

Standing close to Lajoie, Rhoda touched his arm and then withdrew her hand quickly. "It is nothing?"

"*Les sauvages?*" Lajoie's tone implied that he killed a few of them every day. "Poof! Nossing!"

Rhoda saw Ree wipe his knife in the grass. He rose and lifted his shapeless wool hat and scratched his head, looking toward her as he did so. A moment later he started walking slowly toward the Indians.

Rhoda turned toward the brush and trees behind Frederick's small lodge. Lajoie picked up his rifle. He was about to walk away when Rhoda stopped and looked at him. For a moment he didn't believe what he saw.

But he had seen. She was no different. She was a whore squaw after all. In the tilt of her head, in the flashing invitation of her eyes, Lajoie had seen.

He put his rifle down. He glanced around him. They were all watching the Indians. Lajoie strolled after Rhoda as she disappeared. That Ree, who frowned when Lajoie came near the woman's fire . . . That Frederick, son of a sick dog, who looked with cold eyes upon Lajoie because his blood was mixed — would they not roar in rage if they knew what was going to happen under their noses?

She was standing in a small opening, toying with the medicine bag which she had unslung from around her neck.

Baptiste Lajoie, with his various emotions never far submerged, was not one for small talk or small motions which were a waste of time when a willing woman stood before him.

He would be quick and full of great force.

There was a quickness, but not as Lajoie had thought. A fear raised sharply in the woman's eyes as Lajoie stepped in to take her. She was looking past his shoulder and she raised one hand to her mouth.

Lajoie spun around with his hand on his knife to see who was intruding.

Rhoda held the medicine bag by the thong. She swung it short and hard. The lethal weight of bullets in the bag took Lajoie above the right ear. It was indeed strong medicine. Baptiste Lajoie fell like a dead man.

From under her dress she took the oilskin packet with the mixture of vermilion and bacon grease that Ree had stirred together two days before. She snatched a twig and knelt beside Lajoie.

The mixture was warm from her body. It stood in heavy globules as she touched it to Lajoie's face and hands with the stick. Some of the vermilion had darkened from the grease, so that black streaks showed in the hideous pustules she created on Lajoie's face and hands.

He didn't move. She began to fear she had killed him, and then she saw a slow heaving of his chest and heard the faint guttering of his breathing.

"If he starts to show life, hit him again," Ree had told her.

How much life? She was afraid to hit him again. What if he rolled over suddenly and smeared away the marks on his face?

She heard Frederick's voice raised angrily: "It's one of your dirty tricks, Fitzpatrick! You've lied to them!"

"Then it won't hurt none if they look, will it?"

241

She heard the sounds of ponies somewhere close to Frederick's lodge.

"I ain't seen nobody sick since I been along," Ree said.

Rhoda burst from the trees then. She worked her mouth soundlessly and pointed back to where Lajoie lay. Fitzpatrick crowded his pony hard into the brush. "Wagh!" he cried and wheeled away.

Three Horns and Catch-a-Fish and some of the other chiefs looked at Lajoie for just an instant. Terror leaped across their faces. "Spotted death!" Catch-a-Fish cried. With shouts of fear and anger the Indians spun their horses and went streaking from the camp. Fitzpatrick and Joe Meek went with them.

Frederick was the last to see Lajoie. For just a moment he too was taken in, and then his cold, hard mind brushed the initial shock away. He smeared his hand across Lajoie's face, cursing wildly when he saw what he suspicioned.

"Hold on!" he yelled at the Indians. He tried to run after them on foot, and then he veered off and grabbed a hunter's pony and went racing up the slope to the north.

The guard who had first spotted the chiefs yelled at Frederick and tried to warn him back. The guard was then running toward the camp, waving his rifle toward the crest of the hill.

"Injuns!" he yelled as he ran past Frederick.

"I know it, goddamn it!" Frederick shouted, but he really didn't know it until a moment later when a three-deep line of mounted Snakes and Bannocks came to the top of the hill and stopped.

Frederick hauled his pony in. He tried to shout his case, but the chiefs had seen what they had seen. They waved him back. He saw how hopeless, and how dangerous it was when the Indians began to dismount. This was no shoot-and-run bunch. They were in unholy earnest any time they got off their ponies for a fight.

By God, they meant to stop the train where it was!

Emil Frederick was no greenhorn fool to think that he could take a train through four to one of roused-up Indians, with maybe twice that number on beyond the hills.

"It's a trick!" he shouted, forgetting all the Indian words he knew. "It's one of Fitzpatrick's lying tricks!"

Old Three Horns waved him away, and then the grizzled chief, who had always been a friend of white men, shook out a Crow war-bonnet from its case and put it on.

It was more than time to go, Frederick knew.

His mind was working cool and hard as he rode back toward camp where his excited men were forting up along the edge of the timber. He kept yelling at them, "Don't shoot, don't shoot!" It would be royal hell with handles on it if a fight got started.

There was some way out of this, some way to quiet the red bastards down and get on to rendezvous. Maybe clean Lajoie off and take him out where the chiefs could see that he was all right . . . No, he'd never get the worthless son of a bitch that close, and he doubted that the chiefs would recognize him anyway.

All they'd seen was the spotted death, not a man.

"Hold your fire! Hold your fire!" Frederick shouted.

The veterans steadied the voyageurs and scared engagees. The veterans knew that if there had been a fight intended, it would have been started by the Indians before now.

Frederick was dismounting when one of his hunters came loping through the camp, yelling Frederick's name.

"Now what the hell?" Frederick growled.

"Hudson's Bay!" The hunter pointed west toward the foothills of the Wind Mountains. "The British got a pack train four miles away!"

Up till then Frederick had been steady enough, with his wits all in place, but now things were piling up too fast. "Who?" he asked.

"Hudson's Bay! They got a pack train pointing for rendezvous."

The British! They were behind the whole foul mess. When it come to being thick with Injuns, the British had everybody beat. But that was wrong. Joe Meek and Tom Fitzpatrick were with the whole damn' Snake nation and Bannock robbers up there on the hill.

"Hudson's Bay?" Frederick said. He couldn't get his thinking straight.

It was then that Lajoie, with one hand against the side of his head, staggered out of the trees.

"Billy Jesus!" a packer exclaimed. "Smallpox!" He began to back away from Lajoie.

244

"Vermilion, you fool!" Frederick yelled. His mind began to recover from the shock of Hudson's Bay. "Where's Ree Semple?"

"Here a minute ago," a packer said, looking around. He was not the first man to telescope time because of excitement and confusion. His minute was fifteen times as long as he thought.

"Bring him here!" Frederick ordered.

By then Ree was at least fourteen minutes away, with an oilskin packet of bacon grease mixed with vermilion, pointing as fast as his pony could stand toward the Hudson's Bay train. It was going to be a mite touch and go, he knew. The devilment in him was soaring high. He was in his glory.

While Frederick raged at him with questions that were nine-tenths accusations, Lajoie sat on the ground, pawing at his crimsoned face. He denied frantically that Rocky Mountain had sent him to the American train. He turned sullen when it came to explaining the vermilion on his face. Seven ways from the middle he lied to keep from revealing that a look and gesture by a white squaw had brought him, Baptiste Lajoie, to this pass.

But Frederick got the truth out of him, which was well for Lajoie; otherwise Frederick would have killed him.

The packers reported that Ree was gone.

"Where's the woman?" Frederick asked.

She was gone too.

A missionary. I should have known, Frederick thought. Missionary, hell! The two of them were Rocky

Mountain spies, and they'd pulled a trick that would make men laugh from this day on whenever they saw Emil Frederick.

Sherman Randall wouldn't laugh. Frederick saw his face across a thousand miles, cold and dead looking. Randall just wouldn't understand how this had happened.

Frederick gave Lajoie one last kick and turned away. He had to figure a way to get through the Indians, and it had to be done without a fight. Only their lookout wolves were showing now, but Frederick knew the main body was there behind the hill.

If he didn't provoke a fight, they'd go away — in time. Time was one thing he didn't have; nevertheless he decided, and quite prudently, to wait until morning before trying to powwow again.

The country lately traveled by the American train was bare and empty now. Riding across it, Rhoda kept looking back, and then she would look ahead at the hollows and the hills that were losing sharp outline as the light failed slowly.

She hoped Lajoie wasn't dead, or even seriously hurt. He hated her. All those times when he had squatted by her fire, trying to talk to her, his face had shown some deep buried roiling that she couldn't understand.

The hollow ahead could have held a dozen riders. She was into it before she realized, riding across it, conscious of the dust her pony was raising. Beyond were other silent hills watching her.

246

She looked behind, and that was silence and waiting too, and nothing looked the same as when she'd passed. "Bear some to the east — a little," Ree had said. "You can't miss running straight into them."

When Lajoie came toward her in the trees — that was when the hating in his eyes had been a monstrous thing, even greater than his lust. Fear had put more power than she had thought to use into her arm when she swung the medicine bag.

But she hoped he wasn't dead.

Death was nothing here. White bones passed on the trail with no more than a casual glance. Talk of scalping, of men gone under, of Indians taught a lesson by galena. Death was a way of life.

Suddenly she realized that she was off the trail. She had chosen to stay on the marks of the train, instead of striking out carelessly, as Ree had advised, but now she had lost the marks.

She stopped her pony. On the right, the massive Mountains of the Wind were watching her. Their streaks of snow looked faintly blue in the early twilight. On her left and ahead of her were hills with an unfamiliar look, although she had studied them in passing that very day.

Everything spoke of oldness, quietness, and she was alone. Not lost. The trail was close, somewhere close. She couldn't find it as she rode slowly to the west. It was west? Of course it was! There were the mountains. But there was no trail of mule hoofs. Bear east then. How far? Had she gone too far east already?

247

All at once she wished desperately that Mordecai were with her.

She turned to the east, and then she saw the thin dust smoke lying on a hill. She watched for several moments before she knew for sure that it was moving, changing shape slowly. She trotted the pony then, taking it behind the shoulder of a bare ridge. With the light rawhide war rope in her hand she was crouching to watch behind the crest when she heard the dry whirr of a rattlesnake, ten or fifteen feet away. She tossed a stone toward the sound. It came again, and then there was silence. The dust was coming at her. She heard the pound of hoofs and a high Indian yell. Except in Three Horns' camp, she had never seen so many Indians in one group. A moment later she knew she had seen wrong; it was a pony herd being driven by three men.

They swept along the hill below her. One of the riders stopped. He looked up the hill to where she crouched. He turned his pony out to where her tracks were, leaning low to stare down at the ground.

Another rider came racing back to the first. " 'Pears she turned off thataway," the first man said, pointing toward the hill.

Only then did Rhoda stand up and wave her arm. She pulled the pony after her as she ran down the hill to join Fitzpatrick and a man she had never seen before.

Fitzpatrick raised his hand as if he were going to clap her mightily upon the back. Grinning, he said: "Worked a charm, it did! That half-breed give me a tolerable fright, seeing him laying there like that."

Moments later Rhoda was going on with the three of them, Fitzpatrick, Meek, and Etienne Paris, who were taking a hundred ponies to the Rocky Mountain train.

Boldness would work about as good as most anything, Ree figured. He was some late hitting the Hudson's Bay camp, but he reckoned he could depend on Bridger and Sublette keeping the powwow going until things was proper fixed.

Old Gabe and Sublette were doing just that when Ree came upon the scene. Bell Rock and some of the Snake chiefs were with them, out from the camp quite a jump. They had McIlvane and three of his men stood off some distance, but it was a powwow just the same.

The camp itself was setting up tight for defense. They didn't come apart easy, these Hudson's Bay outfits. Bold as all hell would do her, Ree figured. He kept dodging along the edge of the pack herd men were bringing in. He kept in the open as much as he could, walking easy as you please through the camp, until he was sure Bridger had seen him.

McIlvane's tent was 'way up front toward the head end of the shebang. Ree put an eye on that, and what came to him then was fairly pleasing. He went along like he had a heap of business, or like he owned a great big share of Hudson's Bay, including this outfit and half of Fort Vancouver.

Men were shifting around, getting things in order in case the war-stripped Snakes and Bannocks out there beyond the powwow got blood in their eyes and cut loose. Plenty of men saw Ree. They'd seen him before, too, when he was well received by McIlvane on the Siskadee; but they didn't observe anything about him with the same full intentness they would have borne on him if there hadn't been two hundred Indians dismounted beyond the chiefs, whose voices and gestures were plainly angry.

Ree came up beside an Iroquois who was lying with his rifle stuck across a pile of firewood, facing toward the powwow. Without looking directly at him, Ree stopped and said, "No fight. Talk. Talk till night."

The Iroquois grunted.

"Medicine water. Heap medicine water in Red Man's lodge. No fight. Much talk." Ree didn't have to look to know it was working. He heard the moist sound of the Indian rolling his lips.

"Get medicine water. Good." Ree went on slowly. He heard the *shush* of the man's moccasins behind him.

When he came to McIlvane's tent, Ree crouched near the entrance, holding his rifle toward the powwow. He took a casual look around him. Here's where she was tickling close. The Iroquois was settled down in the grass near the backside of the tent. Ree saw Old Gabe reach up and mash his hat around some, like it wasn't setting just right.

Good enough so far, but there were too many men watching from the camp. And then three ponies broke out of the herd that the guards were bunching against a hill.

They came running through the camp, dipping their necks and dodging as men here and there leaped up to try to turn them back. Someone shouted, "Let them go!" For an instant men looked toward the man who had yelled.

That was when Ree disappeared into McIlvane's tent. The Iroquois was wriggling under the back wall, his brown eyes darting around the interior as he looked for medicine water. From a double-walled leather pack, with deer hair stuffed between the walls, Ree took two bottles of McIlvane's brandy.

Unconsciously the Iroquois rubbed his belly as he stood up and reached for one of the bottles. "Good!"

He was drinking deep, with his eyes closed and his bronze throat making jerking movements, when Ree hit him about the ear with his rifle barrel. With an eye toward avoiding waste, Ree set the gurgling bottle upright before he drew out his vermilion mixture and went to work.

Take the Iroquois, good hunters though they were, they were always giving the British trouble with their thieving ways. This one had got into some of that poisoned medicine water that caused the spotted death — and look how quick he got sick.

Ree poured some more out of the bottle and set it close to the Indian's hand. He went under the backside of the tent. They were coming from the powwow, riding down to inspect the camp.

Without hurrying, Ree walked away. Two bottles of McIlvane's brandy clinked a little under his shirt. He was getting on his pony in the trees when the excitement broke out at McIlvane's tent.

Go to London to collect, huh?

CHAPTER
NINETEEN

Mordecai didn't feel scarcely no better than when he'd walked into the Beaver Palace after coming from Santa Fe. Good and drunk, that's what he ought to be right now, having himself a spree down there at the horse races by the river, or gambling with one of the bunches of free trappers.

She was sure some, this rendezvous. Mordecai had to admit that, even while he set like a lone old buffler bull kicked out of the herd. From Bridger's lodge he could see the whole shebang, the trading down there at the robe-covered pole counter, the fighting and cavorting here and there, the free trappers strutting around with strouding tied on 'em fit to kill.

She made a plumb big sound, she did, with the yelling and singing and whooping. More and more of the Bannocks and Snakes had been sneaking away from their jobs of holding back Hudson's Bay and the American Company. Like as not in a day or two the whole kit and caboodle of them would be gone, and then the other trains could come in as they pleased.

The Injuns would light out, though, when those trains started moving. The Injuns wasn't having anything to do with smallpox even when it was all talk and vermilion.

Wouldn't do McIlvane or Frederick much good to come in now, though. Rocky Mountain had taken the top off things in a hurry. She started at four pints for a plew, the trading did, which put a tolerable looseness into things right off. Even most of the free trappers and Delawares with McIlvane had sneaked around the Injuns and brought their plews to rendezvous. Down to one or two pints now.

Mordecai knew he ought to feel fine. He didn't.

By turning some he could have looked to where Slocum and the other preacher, Arnwine, were lecturing three Flatheads who had sneaked off and got drunker than fiddler's bitches by trading off their muskets. Mordecai didn't want to look. Rhoda's little lodge was up there too. She'd changed back to white woman's fixin's again.

That Slocum, he hadn't even recognized her when the train came sweeping into rendezvous, with three hundred trappers that had gone out a piece to meet it riding along beside it, screaming and firing rifles and whooping. It was a fair moment, like always when a train hit rendezvous.

Even after the long grind, Mordecai had let loose a few howls himself, all the time keeping close to Rhoda so as one of the trappers wouldn't mistake her for a squaw and swoop her over on his pony, even in fun. He noticed how Rhoda kept looking for Slocum, knowing he was here because Fitz had told her.

She recognized him quick enough.

Mordecai was beside her. He'd waited a long time to see what kind of coon Slocum was. Fair put together, he was, maybe some like Old Gabe, not no bear, but enough of him. Light-colored face, like some Hudson's Bay Scots. What he said and did was going to be more important. Any man could be born with legs and arms and everything fairly well in place.

Rhoda didn't say nothing.

Slocum looked past her, into the boil of work at the counter where trade goods from St. Louis were being unloaded for the last time.

"Mr. Fitzpatrick!" Slocum yelled, but old Fitz was busier than a badger with seventeen Injun dogs yelping around it.

Slocum turned to Mordecai. "Perhaps you can help me, sir. A young lady from the States —" He caught on when Mordecai said nothing, but kept looking sidewise at Rhoda.

Rhoda said, "Hello, Elisha."

Slocum was thrown plumb in his tracks. His mouth opened and he started to say something, and then he got the look of a man who discovers he's traded a good rifle for a pack of poor beaver. He kept looking at Rhoda like he thought she ought to be dressed in white, without a speck of dust on her, and maybe with a prayer book in her paws.

"Rhoda!" he said at last. "You took me by surprise!"

Mordecai just kept staring at the two or them, mostly at Slocum.

254

"Well, you're here safe," Slocum said. "Reverend Arnwine and I have been praying for your safety and good health since I received your letter last summer."

It must have helped a heap, Mordecai thought.

"All the Rocky Mountain men get their winter outfit before any trading starts!" Bridger yelled. Whoops and curses greeted this announcement, the curses from those who had a big dry and were going to have to wait until the clerks did all the figuring with Rocky Mountain's trappers.

"This is hardly the place to talk," Slocum said.

Mordecai started to turn away, but Rhoda said, "Elisha, I want you to meet Mr. Price. He brought me all the way from St. Louis."

Mordecai nodded. When Slocum stuck out his hand, Mordecai hesitated and then took it.

"I certainly want to thank you, Mr. Price," Slocum said. "I assume you've been paid in full?"

"Yup." Mordecai went on over to help throw down packs. He heard Slocum saying, "I suggest you change from those heathen clothes as soon as possible, Rhoda," and then they were walking away, with Rhoda leading her pony.

Mordecai lifted a pack and tossed it down without any regard for contents that might be squashed or busted; and then he realized that everything about the pack train was no longer any of his business.

At his shoulder Ree said, "What do you think of the missionary hoss, Mord?"

"I ain't going on no fall hunt with him, so what's the difference if I think anything about him?"

Ree let that one go. "Well, then here's a hunk of meat that maybe won't swell in your mouth when you chaw on it. Some of Wyeth's men just come in. They run into Jim Shandy several days back. He'd been looking for me, he said. Then he mentioned coming on in to rendezvous."

"Good." Mordecai went over to jaw with Jake Creed and some other free trappers who were cussing because all three trains hadn't come in at once. "Then you'd've seen a price for beaver!" Creed said.

Some of the group talked about taking their plews down to the other trains, but it was all talk and even they knew it. Not a half dozen men would leave rendezvous until their last plew was gone. Mordecai moved around considerable, but somehow things didn't shine the way they should have.

Now she was in full whoop and he was sitting alone, not admitting any more of the truth to himself than was necessary to keep him unhappy.

He heard Rhoda coming around the lodge. Even shoes couldn't change the sound of her tread, nor could the ground-dusting skirts she had on. Her hair was fixed the way it had been when he first saw her in front of the Beaver Palace. "Sublette and Campbell square up with you for all your plunder I used?" Mordecai asked.

Rhoda nodded like it was nothing important.

She stood for a while without speaking. "How long before fall?"

"Month — about. You'll be there afore then."

256

"Elisha says as soon as the Flatheads get well, we'll go on."

Mordecai made marks in the dust between his legs. "Get sober, you mean?"

"Yes. They aren't from his mission, you know."

Oh, hell no! No Injun around *his* mission would get drunk. Mordecai stood up, thinking to tell her what a hopeless thing it was trying to make hymn-singing white people outen any kind of Injuns, but when he was on his feet he didn't say it. If she didn't know from even as little as she'd seen of Injuns, then he was wasting his wind.

The thing of it was, there was no cause to be sore at Elisha Slocum because he had a Brindel rifle and wanted to play come-to-Jesus with the Injuns, any kind, any more than Slocum had a right to look down his nose at trappers.

"Rather boisterous, aren't they?" he'd said to Mordecai last night, while looking at the rendezvous, but from his tightened-up expression, Mordecai knew what he meant was "Holy hell, what a bunch of savages!"

Mordecai saw a band of Snakes ride in at the south end of the rendezvous where their camp was. Pretty big bunch, too. He guessed they'd just about give up on holding the trains off any longer. The truth of the whole trick had been around for some time, coming from the free trappers and the Delawares that had left McIlvane's train. Nobody had got in from the American train, not yet.

It had been a pretty miserable thing to pull on men like old Three Horns, but Mordecai guessed he would have done it himself, if he had been the one to think of it.

"That Lajoie," he said to Rhoda, "it was sort of dangerous for you to be fooling with him."

"It's more the shame of it that's troubled me since."

"Slocum know about it?" Slocum didn't get around the rendezvous enough to find out, but Mordecai thought maybe Rhoda had figured she ought to tell him.

She shook her head.

"No need to be ashamed. You saved our hides."

Rhoda was watching a group of staggering trappers dancing as the Snakes had danced around their scalp pole. One of the trappers with red strouding worked into his plaited hair was dancing with a cup of whisky balanced on his head.

"It would have been the same," Mordecai said, "no matter whose train got here first."

"I suppose."

"I got to tell you something, Rhoda. Was it back in the settlements, or even was I working around a fort somewhere, I'd be real set against you marrying Slocum."

Rhoda met his look honestly, quietly. She didn't ask what did he mean or any trifling talk like that. She knew what he was saying. She looked at him quite a spell before lowering her eyes.

Ree was breaking out of things below, coming fast up the slope.

258

"Where are you going this winter, Mordecai?" Rhoda asked.

"In around Bayou Salade and about there. Likely run into the Taos bunch now and then."

Ree had something on his mind. He always did when he came along trying to look easy and unconcerned. He was dressed in wool now, like any other trapper, when he could get wool clothes.

"Shandy's here," he said.

"So . . ."

"It ain't cut just the way you're figuring, Mord. That Shandy, he's got a story of his own. Came close to killing Big Nose, he did, for trying to say different. Bridger and Fitz done stopped it. Sublette don't believe him a damn, but . . ." Ree shrugged. "That's how she is." He glanced at Rhoda.

"Says he was trying to help the train all the time, huh?"

Ree nodded. "He made Big Nose admit he was drunk when Shandy kicked him out. Then Shandy went on to help you and me get Injun ponies." Ree shook his head. "It don't sound too bad, even when you know."

"What'd you say?"

"Huh-uh. I ain't no Rocky Mountain man, Mord. I just let him lie away."

"What happened when he went for ponies?"

"Sioux got after him. Chased hell out of him. He said."

Just showing up at rendezvous was a powerful help in making Shandy's lies sound better.

Mordecai picked up Old Belcher. He was walking off when he thought to turn and say, "I got to, Rhoda."

"Do you?" She was as cool as a sprung trap just raised.

Ree got in his oar. "How much of Rocky Mountain you own, Mord?"

Mordecai didn't bother to answer. But he hung on a while longer, looking at Rhoda, wondering what her look was saying, beyond she didn't favor him killing Jim Shandy. She'd said before she didn't think he ought to rub Shandy out, but that was when it seemed nobody would doubt what a slippery son of a bitch he was.

Now maybe even Old Gabe and Fitz were wondering if Mordecai hadn't pulled his bow string too tight when he was telling about Shandy.

Mordecai looked at his priming and walked off. Ree didn't say anything; he just came along behind him.

Shandy was there by the robe-covered bales of beaver that had been pressed into tight packs. Fitz was still near him, but the others, Old Gabe and Sublette and Campbell, were watching some of the last furs come in from a few die-hard free trappers.

Shandy shifted his rifle easy and said, "Hello, hoss."

"Hear you been telling a heap of lies," Mordecai said.

The trading stopped right then.

It was hard doin's with rifles, close together as they were, him and Shandy. Likely couldn't get out of it with a whole hide, Mordecai knew, but that wasn't stopping him none. He was ready and so was Shandy.

260

Hanging on a second like it was, there was no reason for Shandy to try to hide what he was feeling. Mordecai guessed he couldn't have if he'd tried. He saw how Shandy hated him and it wasn't no ordinary kind of thing, but such a force as twisted and knotted a man's guts. Shandy was outdoing any half-breed Mordecai had ever seen.

Mordecai flopped his thumb up on the hammer of Old Belcher.

"Don't recollect telling any lies about you," Shandy said. He eased off suddenly and went over to the counter, with his back to Mordecai. Mordecai wouldn't have believed it. They didn't eat dirt that way, not men like Shandy.

Ree spoke up. "Bet a pack of beaver American comes in tonight."

"You ain't got a pack of beaver," Sublette said.

"Bet it just the same." Ree was grinning with his mouth but his eyes were looking hard at Mordecai, telling him there was something that needed talking about.

Mordecai figured it out as they walked off toward the junction of the rivers. Shandy hadn't eat dirt; he'd been so bad beat, he'd backed off for a minute, was all. Mordecai cussed Ree. "Shoved your stick in, didn't you? You had him in your sights!"

"Right across my arm, she was," Ree said, "cocked and looking into his stinking black heart. Did he take a deep breath or bat his eye, he was gone beaver."

"It was none of your business, Ree!"

"Just one time. He's still there if you want him."

Mordecai couldn't understand it. They walked on until they came against the river. The horse herds had just about cleaned up the grass on this side of the Popo Agie. In the back swirling water where the bright flow of the Wind and Popo met, Injun kids were swimming, their wet heads gleaming like prime beaver, their brown bottoms flashing as they bent their bodies in dives from the surface.

A dead-drunk Bannock was sleeping in the shade close to the edge of the stream, his mouth loose and twitching a little as black gnats and mosquitoes worked on him.

"Good way to lose his hair." Ree kicked a buffalo chip at the Indian's legs. Part of the dried splatter stuck to the grass, but a wedge-shaped piece broke free and went sailing over the Bannock's legs to drop into the river and float lightly away.

"He come here just to kill me," Mordecai said.

"That goes. It's a pure fact."

"Why'd you shove your stick in, Ree?"

Ree tried the rest of the buffalo chip. It went all to pieces when his moccasin struck it. He gave Mordecai a sober look. "Just one time is all. Now it's up to you."

"He'll lie his way out of it!"

"Don't think so." Ree watched a stinging fly settle on the Bannock's belly. "I ain't going to be your keeper no longer, Mord."

"You never was!" By Old Caleb, it was like when Fitz and Ree and Rhoda cooked up that smallpox business, not saying nothing to Mordecai about it, as if he was too oak-headed to be in on it or even know. Afterward,

Rhoda said it was because they were afraid it wouldn't work, and didn't want the Rocky Mountain train to get all hopeful.

Now Ree was talking riddles. "I'm going back and finish it," Mordecai said.

"Up to you." Ree shrugged like a Frenchman. Then he grinned and stepped over to the Bannock. One of the Indian's arms had come across his belly in protest against the stinging fly. Ree rolled the Bannock on his stomach. Then he took the hand that was under him and gave a hard tug.

The Bannock rolled loosely and dropped over the sod bank into the river face up. He began to float away with no more struggles than a weak patting of his hands. The current turned him toward the middle of the stream where the water ran slow over a rocky bottom.

With his head downstream and water slapping into his mouth and his hind end bumping over the smooth rocks, the Injun still didn't wake up or make any struggle that amounted to a hill of beans. The grin left Ree's face. He yelled at the swimming boys to haul the Bannock out, but they misunderstood him and went splashing toward shore as if there were some danger.

"Hell!" Ree said. He had to go slipping and stumbling into the stream to drag the Injun ashore. At the bank he had trouble hoisting the man, but at last Ree got him across his shoulder. The Bannock grunted, and then, with no further warning, belched vomit all over Ree's new shirt.

Ree heaved him up on the bank and then knelt in the water to clean himself. "The ongrateful bastard! After me saving his life that way!"

Mordecai laughed until he was weak. He was still laughing and making fun of Ree when they walked back toward the counter. Shandy wasn't in sight nowhere. If Fitz and the others wanted to be fools, Mordecai guessed he could let Shandy go a little longer, but he wasn't forgetting it by no means.

Take a man that wanted to rub you out as bad as Shandy did, only sensible thing was to let him have it.

CHAPTER
TWENTY

In the afternoon the Snakes and Bannocks picked up and skyugled within an hour's time. Where their smoke-dark lodges had made two big camps, there were now cropped-down grass, a few still-smoking fire pits and the bones of their feasting.

Frederick came down the river two hours later, camping upstream and on the opposite side from the rendezvous in order to have grass for his mules. All he could do now was go on down the Bighorn to Fort Cass. Things were aching hard inside him when he came over to call on the Rocky Mountain men, but he held a tight smile as if he was thinking that this was only a temporary defeat.

He even controlled his temper when he heard Ree Semple and Fitzpatrick and Joe Meek laughing.

"All debts are generally paid — in time," Frederick said, and took the cup of whisky Bridger offered him.

Elisha Slocum, stepping long-legged and hard on his heels, came over to inquire about letters for white people at his mission. "No letters for anyone this trip," Frederick said.

Ree laughed. "Nobody was supposed to know he was coming!"

265

"I thought I'd ask," Slocum said, unnecessarily, "since I'm leaving in the morning." He began to dicker with Frederick about rifles to replace the weapons the Flatheads had traded for alcohol.

Mordecai went off to tell Rhoda goodbye. He could see her traps all neat and stacked against the back wall of the lodge. She heard him coming and stepped out, still wearing her settlement clothes.

"I hear you're leaving in the morning," Mordecai said.

"Yes. Elisha says we'll go back by way of South Pass."

Mordecai wiped a smidgin of dust off the muzzle of Old Belcher. "Best way, sure enough."

"Reverend Arnwine is to marry us this evening."

Anger and loudness broke out down at the counter. There was scuffling and shoving around, and then the noise went down to no more than an excited buzz of talking. Mordecai looked off toward the Bighorn. He wasn't casting around for words; he'd already said them, and that ought to be the end of it.

What was the sense of telling this woman he wanted her like he never had wanted any woman, and likely never would again? His way just wasn't fit for no white woman, not that someone like Rhoda couldn't stand the life as far as the body went; but it was the way they thought about things that made it bad.

"I'm glad you didn't kill Shandy, Mordecai."

"Yup." Just a little delay, was all.

"What stopped you a while ago?"

"Ree." Ree wouldn't horn in again, though. He'd promised, along with all that mysterious talk about things being up to Mordecai now.

Rhoda was smiling, and as Mordecai watched her he thought he was beginning to get the hang of what Ree had been talking about. It struck Mordecai so hard and it was such a big idea that he unfolded it carefully, something like fanning out a grasshopper's wing real slow and easy so as not to hurt it or miss any of the colors.

Was Ree hinting that if Mordecai put Shandy under, when it wasn't pure necessary, then Rhoda would be sure he was the hell-sparking savage she'd sometimes called him? But if he didn't do it, then she'd think . . . Just what would she think? That she'd managed to get in a lick of civilizing on a wild man during the trip from St. Louie? Or did it go some farther than that?

Mordecai had to think on it, and it wasn't the kind of thinking he was used to. Rhoda made it tougher for him, the way she was standing there like she might be inviting him to leave some ponies tied in front of her lodge.

Get away from that Injun thinking, damn it, Mordecai told himself.

He was still wrastling things around in his head, and Rhoda was waiting, when Old Gabe spoke from real close, "Mord!"

Ree was with him. Mordecai gave them the Indian sign to go away.

"Got to palaver a little," Old Gabe said. "Frederick just told us private — American hired Shandy, sure enough. The dirty fish-eating, underhand —" he looked at Rhoda and didn't finish.

"Seems I mentioned something about that myself," Mordecai said irritably, as he watched Rhoda go into her lodge and pull the door flap closed.

"We didn't disbelieve you none," Old Gabe said. "We figured you was going to rub him out." The gaunt brown face peered hard at Mordecai.

Mordecai glanced at Ree. Ree was looking off into distance like he was already a thousand miles away.

"He's your Injun now, hoss," Mordecai said to Bridger.

Old Gabe nodded. "We figure to give him a pony and a bow and arrers and turn him loose. Some was for stripping him bare and giving him nothing. I ain't so sure but what that ain't the best way myself."

"Your Injun," Mordecai said.

He watched Ree and Old Gabe go back to the counter, and pretty soon, followed by jeers and curses, Shandy started out of camp on a miserable pony, saddleless. The Rocky Mountain men began to fire over his head. The way Shandy ducked, some of the shots must have been close. He got the pony into a rough lope, the quiver and the unslung bow bouncing on his back. Knowing Old Gabe and the rest, Mordecai was sure the weapons were a child's from some half-Injun kid in one of the trappers' lodges.

Good enough. It was Injun punishment Shandy was getting. You could kill a man without disgracing him, but when you left him alive in scorn, that was something he never could wipe out.

268

Mordecai looked back at Rhoda's lodge. "What are you doing in there?"

"Just a minute!"

It was some more than a minute before she came out. Mordecai didn't have to do any more thinking then. He knew. She was dressed in beautifully decorated white doeskin and her hair was braided once more. Her eyes were soft and shining.

Mordecai put Old Belcher down and went over to her.

After a while they saw Slocum and Arnwine coming up the slope. That Slocum, he wasn't such a bad coon, at that. Mordecai felt sorry for him.

Steve Frazee was born in Salida, Colorado, and for the decade 1926–1936 he worked in heavy construction and mining in his native state. He also managed to pay his way through Western State College in Gunnison, Colorado, from which in 1937 he graduated with a bachelor's degree in journalism. The same year he also married. He began making major contributions to the Western pulp magazines with stories set in the American West as well as a number of North-Western tales published in *Adventure*. Few can match his Western novels which are notable for their evocative, lyrical descriptions of the open range and the awesome power of natural forces and their effects on human efforts. CRY COYOTE (1955) is memorable for its strong female protagonists who actually influence most of the major events and bring about the resolution of the central conflict in this story of wheat growers and expansionist cattlemen. HIGH CAGE (1957) concerns five miners and a woman snowbound at an isolated gold mine on top of Bulmer Peak in which the twin themes of the lust for gold and the struggle against the savagery of both the elements and human nature interplay with increasing, almost tormented intensity. BRAGG'S FANCY WOMAN (1966) concerns a free-spirited woman who is able to tame a family of thieves. RENDEZVOUS (1958) ranks as one of the finest Mountain Man books and THE WAY THROUGH THE MOUNTAINS (1972) is a major historical novel. Not surprisingly, many of Frazee's novels have become major motion pictures. According to the second edition of TWENTIETH CENTURY WESTERN WRITERS, a Frazee story is possessed of "flawless characterization, particularly when it involves the clash of human passions; believable dialogue; and the ability to create and sustain damp-palmed suspense." His latest Western novel is TOWER OF ROCKS (2004) published as a Five Star Western.

ISIS publish a wide range of books in large print, from fiction to biography. Any suggestions for books you would like to see in large print or audio are always welcome. Please send to the Editorial department at:

ISIS Publishing Ltd.
7 Centremead
Osney Mead
Oxford OX2 0ES
(01865) 250 333

A full list of titles is available free of charge from:
Ulverscroft large print books

(UK)
The Green
Bradgate Road, Anstey
Leicester LE7 7FU
Tel: (0116) 236 4325

(Australia)
P.O Box 953
Crows Nest
NSW 1585
Tel: (02) 9436 2622

(USA)
1881 Ridge Road
P.O Box 1230, West Seneca,
N.Y. 14224-1230
Tel: (716) 674 4270

(Canada)
P.O Box 80038
Burlington
Ontario L7L 6B1
Tel: (905) 637 8734

(New Zealand)
P.O Box 456
Feilding
Tel: (06) 323 6828

Details of **ISIS** complete and unabridged audio books are also available from these offices. Alternatively, contact your local library for details of their collection of **ISIS** large print and unabridged audio books.